T0354489

DECIMATION

DECIMATION

DECIMATION

MARISA CANTRELL-RODRIGUEZ

DECIMATION

iUniverse books may be ordered through booksellers or by contacting:

iUniverse
1663 Liberty Drive
Bloomington, IN 47403
www.iuniverse.com
1-800-Authors (1-800-288-4677)

ISBN: 978-1-5320-4713-8 (sc)
ISBN: 978-1-5320-4712-1 (e)

Library of Congress Control Number: 2018906729

Print information available on the last page.

iUniverse rev. date: 06/07/2018

CHAPTER 1

As Mr. Leer lectures on the North America from years past, I think back to the stories Grandpa and Grandma told me of the Great Wars and how Nambitus was created. Mr. Leer could take lecture notes from my grandparents, two soldiers who fought, won, and survived; they could provide key details on the world we live in today.

I knew Mr. Leer would ask for this assignment, so I personally collected souvenirs, interviews, and eye-witness accounts on the subject to correct some of his facts and dates.

Now, I look at my older sister, Tevan, who purses her lips at me disapprovingly as I lay out my artifacts, and at my best friend, Matthew Larkin, as he gives me that competitive stance. Matthew has done his homework as well. He and I are locked in a game of who will surpass whom to get an A+ on this assignment. Matthew's presentation was well detailed; he used Mr. Leer's facts on the strict system in which we live and how it's the "glue that holds our very foundation together," particularly as our world faced uncertainty as the wars ended.

I again ignore Tevan as she gives me a look. I fluff my papers and get ready for my presentation.

"Miss Lewis, you are up," Mr. Leer says, breaking my concentration.

I nod and then quickly turn red because he has called on me

in class; I'm a shy person who holds true to her convictions. I grab my grandpa's uniform and bullets and make my way to the front of the class.

Shaking as I hold my papers, I say, "North America was once broken into borders. The populace between these countries became so vast that fighting broke out, which eventually led to wars. Famine, disease, and economic devastation followed on such a great scale that many called it the Dark Times."

Mr. Leer coughs. "Stick to the facts, Miss Lewis."

I turn another shade of red as he reprimands me in front of the class. I try not to get upset, but I know my facts from my grandpa on the Great Wars; I know what happened. I hold my papers tightly and try my best to stay with facts that I know Mr. Leer has deemed appropriate.

"After so many countries began going to war with one another, other countries began seeing vulnerabilities and they attacked, thus causing the Great Wars. Young men and women were drafted during this time. This is my grandfather's uniform and these are bullets pulled from his body."

Mr. Leer gives me a look as I hold up my items for inspection.

"Many young men and women died in creating the Nambitus we know today. The Great Wars lasted over twenty years. Nuclear rain and bombs devastated the land. Much of the terrain shows the remnants of what occurred during those wars, thus giving us hot, windy days and cold Nambitus nights. This is due to the attempt to destroy civilization. Diseases were released, animals went extinct, and crops were unable to grow." I crumble up some plants, getting into character.

"Miss Lewis, thank you, but wrap it up," Mr. Leer says.

"After so many deaths, in one last attempt to negotiate peace, all borders were broken down. We become one populace within North America, resulting in the continent of Nambitus. Once-great cities such as New York and Los Angeles ceased to exist in the windy barren wasteland." I am speaking very quickly as Mr. Leer looks over his glasses at me, and Matt coughs, trying not to laugh. "Out of the ashes from Nambitus, Lexicon arose, becoming the most powerful city on the planet, led by the business class and those within the government, all with an agenda, which was to rule the world. Soon the smaller cities, Magnis and Sorellis, followed. Each city was walled for protection, thus creating barriers that humankind negotiated to never again create, making us once again come full circle."

Mr. Leer stands up and crosses his arms. "That is enough, Miss Lewis. Thank you."

"But we broke down borders within countries in North America with wars, only to have giant walled cities," I argue.

"Enough!" Mr. Leer snaps at me.

"I would like to continue my presentation on the nomad populace outside the walls of Lexicon, as well as the rigid social structure that dictates with whom we associate and then eventually wed, based on the Nambitus social hierarchy, which was created after the Great Wars by fascists." As I'm speaking, I see Tevan hitting her head on her desk.

"Miss Lewis, have you been speaking to your grandfather again?" Mr. Leer asks.

I nod. "Yes, and we agree that some of your curriculum and opinions are indeed incorrect."

Mr. Leer's face begins to turn red.

"Well, is it not true that the very institution many people fought to disassemble by negotiating peace and creating a unified Nambitus is now being barricaded by thick walls and big business?" I ask.

Mr. Leer takes off his glasses. It is never a good sign when Mr. Leer takes off his glasses and turns a tomato shade of red. "Miss Lewis, you are arguing against one of the very institutions in which you have been raised. You live in a walled community within the walled Lexicon and are—dare I say it—privileged."

"I am a victim of circumstance," I say, trying to control my anger. "I cannot help who I am." The class begins to laugh. "Stop laughing!" I snap. The bell rings, and I ask, "Do I need to stay after?"

Everyone leaves, and Mr. Leer refuses to look at me as he hands me my bullets. "No, just get out."

My name is Kaya Lewis, and this is the world I know.

CHAPTER 2

I slowly walk to my locker and get my lunch. I look down the dark hallways, once full of students, where dust now collects. Mr. Leer called me privileged, and while that was true in times past, my father's once-powerful reputation is fading in the competitive business world of Lexicon. He indeed is the smartest scientist on the planet, but he is failing in the business and political aspects of Lexicon.

John Lewis is dedicated to curing every illness that plagues humankind. His Vitae Corporation is where nature meets science in terms of healing. He has offices worldwide, and when Tevan and I were younger, he was all over the globe, curing diseases and illnesses that potentially could eliminate the human race. Once he was treated like a superstar. I remember his bringing us trinkets and pictures—from primitive villages to high-tech cities, all grateful for the cures and treatments created within his labs.

Privileged, I think as I fumble over my locker combination. Lexicon is a walled city and the Vitae Corporation, and within those walls of my "privileged" existence is Axis, the once-great center of my father's empire.

I think back to the technology that was once within this place. Axis had the capability of worldwide access. It had the technological information to access every human on the planet. I know this because

I stumbled upon it while exploring a dusty old lab a few years earlier. My father had shut down operations on such data because if placed in the wrong hands, it could jeopardize the fate of the entire world.

How dare Mr. Leer call me privileged, and shame on me for allowing it to happen. It was an insult to me as well as to my father. My father has left an imprint on humankind, and all Mr. Leer has done is torment and insult teens within this so-called privileged, walled community.

Why can't I ever stand my ground and finish my debates with him? I think. *I have to confront Mr. Leer.* I shut my locker and make my way back to the classroom.

"Kaya, let it go." I feel a tug on my arm just as I am about to reenter the classroom.

"I can't," I insist as Matt shakes his head at me.

"He shouldn't have called you privileged. I already saw Mr. Leer talking to your mom. At least have lunch first; then attack."

I stare at Matt. "Fine."

Matt steers me toward the cafeteria. "You know, Axis is a bit of a privileged place compared to other parts of Lexicon."

I glare at Matt through narrowed eyes. "How dare you take Mr. Leer's side?"

"Think about it," he says.

"If I admit that I'm privileged, then you would have to do the same."

Matt looks at me begrudgingly.

"Besides, how did this become about me being privileged? I didn't even get to finish my presentation on the nomads living outside the Lexicon walls. I had props and media."

Matthew smiles. "Why are you obsessed with people who live by no rules and travel from place to place?" he asks.

"Imagine not having to answer to a rigid social structure, to not have to sit in one place and be what the world thinks you need to be. I want to debate the unnecessary Lexicon social hierarchy. I have so much I don't understand. Why must we only talk to and marry people within our social class? Why must it be in place outside the protection of these walls?"

Matthew laughs. "Because people needed structure after so much destruction."

"You sound like a text book," I tell him.

"Well, luckily for you, your dad views things differently. He makes his own rules, and Axis is his world. Why do you constantly bring up the subject?"

"Matt, I didn't mean to make you feel uncomfortable."

He looks away. "You didn't. I just forget sometimes that I am a groundskeeper's son." He rubs the back of his neck, and I instantly know he's upset or uncomfortable but would never admit it.

He is my best friend. I have grown up with him and know every one of his nonverbal cues. I hate offending him or making him feel inadequate because he understands me better than anyone else. I've never seen him as not being my equal, by Lexicon standards, because we live in Axis and are sheltered from the harsh realities of a Lexicon social class. Here, we live and work among each other equally. It's my father's philosophy.

By Lexicon standards, I am President John Lewis's daughter of the Vitae Corporation, and Matt is merely a groundskeeper's son. We are by no means of equal standing and cannot associate outside the protection of the Axis walls. Tevan and I have ample opportunities for success. We could choose a career in science, because of our father, or a career as a professor, because our mother. Other people within the system, however, such as Matt are doomed to a life of service.

As Matt rubs the back of his neck, all I can do is helplessly stare at him. I want to tell him that he never has to feel that he isn't my equal, that many people around Lexicon are not compliant with the laws. It is a system that was doomed to fail from the beginning. It was set in place after years of turmoil and wars by people so consumed by fear of losing control of the populace that they set up a government that dictates our lives.

I want to scream and tell Matt that people are rioting, and I know this because while out shopping in Lexicon our mother, Tevan and I were approached by a woman with a pamphlet on freedom ideas. She was quickly arrested, and the people in her group were dispersed, but I hid the literature and am secretly planning on sneaking outside of the Axis walls to attend a rally. It has secret codes to type in for meetings and dates. I keep the pamphlet with me at all times.

"Kaya," Matt says, breaking my train of thought. He touches my arm but then quickly puts his hand down. "Do you want me to wait with you so you can argue with Mr. Leer?"

I shake my head. "No, I don't feel the need to do so any longer."

"Lunch?" he says.

I nod. "Yes. Lunch."

"So do you want to discuss the subject of nomads after lunch? Mr. Leer hates when you bring up the subject," Matt says as we walk.

"Possibly."

He smiles. "Do you want to be a nomad, or have you read one of Tevan's romance novels on a Lexicon woman forsaking her place in society to wed a nomad lord?"

I bristle at his comment. "How dare you? You know Tevan reads nothing of value in her spare time. I am just fascinated with their lifestyle." I pause a moment and then say, "You know, my grandparents live on the very outskirts of Lexicon."

Matt looks at me strangely. "Yes."

"Once, when on one of my grandpa's crazy camping trips, I found an opening in the wall, and I went through—I saw some nomads camping."

Matt gets wide-eyed, and he scolds me. "They could have killed you or held you for ransom! If you had been caught going through the wall, you would have been killed or imprisoned. It is forbidden."

"I know," I say quietly.

Matt remains silent for the remainder of our walk to the cafeteria.

"Matt, please don't tell anyone," I say, breaking the silence.

"Sometimes, Kaya, you are reckless," he says.

I nod. "I promise I won't do it again."

Matt and I enter the cafeteria, and I quietly pull out a chair across from him. He begins eating a sandwich, as he always does. His mother packs him the equivalent of three normal lunches because he is her "growing boy" and always is eating.

For a few years, Matt went through a somewhat chubby phase. A few of the other boys in the upper grades would tease him, and I secretly threatened them when it got out of hand. At the beginning of this school year, though, Matt began getting tall and skinny. He was so tall that when he would hold my pencils over my head to play keep-away, I wasn't able to jump up and knock them out of his hand.

As I quietly pick at my sandwich, I notice he is again going through yet another growth spurt. He has been helping his father with the grounds, now that Axis has downsized, and he also has taken an extra interest in sports. I have spent hours doing my homework on the grass as he practiced and lifted weights, waiting for him because I hate walking home alone. I can't believe the size of his arms.

He has to read at lunch to keep up with assignments, and I think for once, rather than our having the same grades, my grades might be better. His presentation on the history of Nambitus was a bit lacking, but he never argues with Mr. Leer, so he probably did get a better grade than I did. He always has been so smart and doesn't even have to try. We both have reading as a hobby, as well as a competitive nature and wanting to outsmart the other. Just as I decide I might bring up his new interest in sports and that I might have the upper hand in grades, now that he is the ultimate jock, I hear giggling from the next table.

It's Tevan and Emily Watson. They're looking at Matt as he reads. No one has ever paid attention to Matt or me; we are invisible to the world. Tevan, who is eons older and whose heart belongs to Jonathon Talbert, is looking at Matt and giggling with Emily.

As if Tevan needs to flirt for a boy to notice her. She's perfect.

She has smooth blonde hair, like my mother, and long legs. I think she and my mother secretly are goddess fashion models. I, on the other hand, haven't combed my hair since the last family Christmas pictures in eighth grade. I find my daily outfits on the floor of my room, and chances are it's an old shirt that depicts an unknown band and tattered jeans. How did she get her hair so perfect? My hair is brownish-red and crazy, like my dad's. Tevan's clothes also are absolutely perfect. Although she's a senior, she dresses like a high-powered business executive, ready to tackle Lexicon.

I then look at Emily Watson. Why as she giggling at Matt? I quickly pull out a book and pretend not to care. I question why I am even having this internal debate on why I am bothered that someone is possibly giggly and flirty with my forever friend Matthew Larkin.

Emily is smitten with Jay Overcast and has been for some time. Emily, like Tevan, always looks like a paradigm of perfection. I wish Jay and Jonathon were here at this very moment to see how foolish they are acting, or I wish I had a laser gun to make them disappear from the planet.

I wonder what is accomplished by wearing such ridiculous shoes. I think, staring at them out of the corner of my eye. If I do attend the rally I received literature on, I can always blame Tevan because we were out shopping in Lexicon, trying to find her stupid heels that she had read about in a magazine. They get so loud that Matthew raises one eyebrow, as if he is enjoying the attention. I hate all three of them.

Just as I am about to leave and find a nice quiet corner to sit in solitude, my mother enters the cafeteria. Why does my mother have to be a professor of education over the entire school?

I sink in my seat as Mr. Leer follows my mother and then points at me. My mother shakes her head, seemingly apologetically. Then Tevan gets up from her seat to join my mother's conversation. Matt had said this conversation already took place. I wonder if Tevan is going to be an ally or throw me to the wolves. Why is she always called upon to be a witness?

"You know your behavior would be deemed unacceptable in Lexicon public schools," Emily says, breaking my concentration.

"Why?" I ask.

"My cousin who attends says you are not allowed to question, and that is all you do."

I roll my eyes.

"You are going to end up arrested," she insists.

I become angry. "Why don't you shut your face and mind your own business?" I say as politely as possible.

Emily gets a strange look on her face and whispers, "It must be nice to live in a walled city built by my daddy, where I can tell everyone how I feel about a fantasy life that will never change, no matter how much I have feelings for a certain individual. You never can have him." She points at Matt.

"First off, we are merely friends. And if you want to point fingers, what about living a fantasy about a dream world in which you love Jay Overcast?" I quickly look away, knowing I have gone too far because Emily's mom works in a store. Her dad is in retail as well. Jay's parents are scientists in my father's lab.

"I hate you, Kaya," she snaps. "I hope Tevan gets you into so much trouble this time."

I narrow my eyes.

"Let it go, Kaya," Matt says as he tugs my arm.

Emily smiles and gently pushes in her chair and leaves the table.

I watch quietly as Tevan talks to my mother and Mr. Leer. I think of how high she's set the bar and that I will never measure up to that standard of perfection. She never argues or questions authority. Even as she stands there, either defending me or calling for my demise, her posture is perfect. She looks like a lawyer. I just don't know if she, as a jury, determines my fate.

I try not to look at Emily as she stands on the opposite side of the lunchroom, whispering to everyone, probably telling them cruel tales of how I think I'm better than everyone because of what I said to her after she provoked me. At least her other victims are getting a break, and then tomorrow she will be on to her next one, possibly a junior or freshman. My turn comes more often now that the school is dwindling.

Emily always knows what to say to back me into a corner so I'll say the wrong thing, and she can play the victim. She's the ultimate mean girl. She has learned the entire playbook from Tevan and used the playbook on me when Tevan isn't around.

I hope she falls off a cliff or is eaten by wild, rabid wolves, I think, smiling a little.

"Kaya, quit,." Matt says. He throws a grape and hits me in the side of the head, and I snap back to reality.

"Quit what?"

"Quit picturing Emily's demise. It's unhealthy."

I pick up a carrot and toss it, and he catches it in midair. "I wasn't. I love Emily. She is my dearest friend."

He laughs. "Liar. I will turn you in to the guidance counselor."

"Fine. I'll stop thinking about Emily's demise, but if you turn me in to the guidance counselor, I will say you were the one you drilled a peephole in the girl's locker room."

Matt gets wide-eyed. "That was three years ago, and it was Jonathon Talbert and Jay Overcast."

I smile. "But I can tell by your reaction that you took part in the peeping." I stare him down.

"Let's drop this entire conversation," Matt says.

I nod. "Deal."

Matt begins reading again, and I stare at him.

"You owe me," Tevan whispers in my ear.

I freeze momentarily, distracted from my staring at Matt. "Am I in trouble?" I try not to get my mother's attention as she and Mr. Leer watch me.

"No, but Mom might have a chat with you. The usual lecture," Tevan says. "Why are you watching Matt read?"

"We are playing a game." I say.

Tevan rolls her eyes. "Well, everyone is watching, and it's awkward, so stop."

"I don't care," I insist, but I turn a bit red because I know Emily is at work.

"Kaya, you have to promise not to argue in class. You know Grandpa is not the authority on Lexicon, past and present," Tevan argues.

I agree with her. I wanted to argue, but I knew I was on trial. "You are absolutely correct."

She smiles. "See? How hard was that?"

Matt chuckles a bit. I kick him, ever so gently, from under the table, and he stops.

"Are you being serious, Kaya?" she asks.

"Yes, and it won't ever happen again."

She smiles again, as if she has somehow made me conform. "I knew you'd come around."

Matt bursts out laughing.

"Why is he laughing?" Tevan asks, and my mom and Mr. Leer take notice of us.

"He's a bit possessed," I say through clenched teeth as Mom approaches.

"Kaya, I need to speak with you," my mother says without greeting.

Matt straightens up, and I look around the cafeteria at the audience.

My mother has that authoritative teacher presence. Even though she's my mother, the sound of her voice in this particular tone means disaster is on the horizon.

"Yes, ma'am," I say, nearly choking on my words. I notice Mr. Leer's look of joy as everyone leaves to gather outside for the remainder of the lunchtime. As I watch my mother walk out, I cringe a bit.

"Clear out!" she snaps, and everyone stops staring at me.

"I'm sorry," Matt says, seeming at a loss for words as everyone awkwardly piles through the doors.

"Save it," I snap. I grab my bag, dropping most of my books.

"Kaya, please. Come and watch me practice after school. Afterwards, I'll make it up to you."

I shake my head. "What if I don't want to? What if I am tired of following you around and being a part of the Matthew Larkin Fan Club?" I sneer at him. "It seems to be gaining new members."

"Don't be ridiculous. You are the longest running member," he says, trying not to laugh.

"Stop laughing at me. You always laugh at me when I get mad, and frankly, I hate you for it." I drop a few more items out of frustration. I kick them out of my way, but judging by his face, I've hurt his feelings.

I haven't been this upset with Matt since the third grade. As I walk away, awkwardly dropping and kicking things, I want for us not to be fighting and for everything to go back to normal, but I can't make myself. As I walk to my mother's office down the long, dark hallway, I see a few strange people. At first, I'm tempted to follow them, but knowing what awaits me, I would rather get my punishment over with so that life can continue.

In the past two years, I have had to write extra research papers because of my insubordination, as well as do community service projects and apologize repeatedly. I have caused four teachers to quit. *I hope Mom remembers all my redeeming qualities*, I think as I push up my glasses. I'm kind—well, in most instances. I'm a humanitarian, even when not assigned numerous community service projects. I'm loyal, even though that makes me sound like a dog. I'm passionate— this very altercation proves that. I hold my breath and knock on my mother's door.

"Come in, Kaya," my mother says in an exasperated tone.

I quietly walk in and take a seat in front of her giant desk. It feels like an eternity goes by as my mom rummages through paperwork instead of acknowledging my presence. This is clearly a new tactic, and it's working. I want to explode.

"Kaya, Mr. Leer has turned in his notice," she says, and I smile a bit. He has taken the longest to break. "Are you smiling? Are you proud of causing a man to end his career?"

I shake my head. "I don't know."

"Kaya, your father and I have raised you to think for yourself, but there comes a time when you do not always have to argue and disrupt class for everyone else. Lexicon is different from Axis. Maybe your father and I have encouraged you to be open-minded and express your opinions in too open of a fashion." She becomes distracted once more, getting a box and piling in papers.

I want to ask her if she's cleaning, but I don't want to stay any longer than I have to. "I don't understand," I say.

"Maybe we should cancel your summer trip with Grandpa if he is encouraging such insubordination. You might not always be in a situation where your father and I can fix your convictions and how inappropriately you voice them. I don't want to see you carted off to prison, and that is what happens outside these walls." I stare at her because this clearly is a new tactic. "You are going to be sixteen, nearly an adult. Learn to cooperate cohesively. You are not the teacher. It isn't your classroom. Make amends."

I nod. "Yes, ma'am."

She signals for me to leave. I slowly get up from my chair. My mother has never dismissed me or lectured me so harshly. As I close her door, I try to think of ways to correct the situation. On the other hand, she seems preoccupied. What if I do nothing at all? Maybe she's so busy, and my offense is so minor that she won't give it another thought.

"And Kaya," my mom shouts from her office, "I will talk to Mr. Leer before he leaves." She slams her door, and I cringe a little.

I enter Mr. Leer's room to find him packing. "Mr. Leer, might I have a word?" I ask. He continues frantically packing. "Why the rush?" I look through his books.

"I've got to get out of here," he says. I smile a little to myself, thinking that I might have caused him such anguish after a year and a half of his torture, but he says, "Don't flatter yourself," and yanks a book from my hands.

"What can I do to make things right or to even keep you on here at Axis?" I ask through a forced smile.

"You could be a senior," he says, and I stare at him. "Fine, you can start by apologizing."

I cringe. "But you called me privileged, which basically implies I am a spoiled brat."

He smiles. "And?"

"Fine. I apologize," I snap.

"Mean it," he says, as large group of men wander through the halls.

"Okay, I apologize with all my heart," I say, trying not to grind my teeth.

"You know what, Miss Lewis? It doesn't matter. In fact, it all seems trivial. I forgive you," he says as he looks toward the men.

"What? Why? So you will tell my mother I apologized?"

He nods. "Of course. I can't wait until you grow up and life happens, and maybe that will happen sooner than later."

I look at him strangely. "All right."

He goes back to packing. I stand there as various people fill the halls that I have never seen and try to piece together both his and my mother's behavior. "Will there be anything else Miss Lewis?" he asks.

"No, best of luck," I answer as I walk slowly to the door.

"And to you," he says, laughing.

As I watch the workers measure and bring in equipment, I can't help but be curious. Ever since my father closed his labs worldwide, our school has downsized significantly. I don't think our student body could get any smaller. Since my dad doesn't have the world's top minds creating, stopping diseases, and inventing in his labs now, we don't have their children in our schools. At one time, there were waiting lists to work for my dad's company, lists so long that top scientists were willing to be janitors until spots opened in the labs.

I know we can't afford upgrades, so the fact that technicians and workers are filling the halls makes me panic.

Axis is quiet and self-sufficient with top-notch security. Granted, our security guard, Slow Sal McCoy, is older, but we haven't had a breach in years. We have our own stores, doctors, and schools. Some people, such as Ms. Larkin, Matthew's mother, haven't felt it necessary to leave in ten years. So the entrance of these people has to make a ripple. I wonder why everyone is still out for lunch as well.

As I walk outside, everyone is laughing with one another. "Did you get in trouble?" Tevan asks.

"No," I answer quietly.

"Matthew has been talking to Emily," she says.

I shrug my shoulders. "I don't care," I say, as I creep around to the side of the building to watch yet another truck of workers unload equipment. "Tevan, do you find it strange that so many workers and so much equipment is being unloaded into the building?"

She tugs on me. "Maybe Dad has come out of his funk." She tries to focus my attention on Matt, but I pull away to spy on the workers.

"Tevan, don't say Dad has been in a funk—he is the greatest. And stop trying to make me look at Matt. I don't care if he and Emily get married next week."

We get into a tug of war. She pulls harder on me, and a book flies out of my hand—and hits Emily in the back of the head.

Everyone freezes as Emily slowly turns around and picks up the book. She looks at the inner label. "Property of Kaya Lewis," she reads out loud.

I frown at her.

"Emily, it was an accident," Tevan says.

"No, it wasn't," Emily insists. "She didn't like me talking to Matt."

Matt and everyone else is watching, their eyes wide.

"*Was* it an accident?" Emily asks.

I secretly want to slap her for what she said about me caring that she was talking to Matt. "Even though I've dreamed of this moment for most my life, yes, it was," I answer.

"Always something witty to say," Emily snaps. "You think you are so smart and the rest of us idiots, and I am going to pulverize you."

I laugh. "That's a bit harsh."

The words are barely out of my mouth when she slaps me in the face. I stand there in shock for a moment, but then, without even thinking, I jump on Emily. We both fall on the ground and begin rolling and hitting each other. I hit her like I've wanted to hit her for years. She scratches me as we roll all over the courtyard. Matt, Tevan, and everyone else tries to pull us apart, but they get injured in the process. As Tevan tries, I rip her perfect pantyhose, which makes me feel a little better about life.

"Kaya Lewis and Emily Watson!" my mother shouts. We both freeze, but her voice echoes. The silence in the courtyard is deafening. "I expected more from both of you. Both of you, get your things and go to detention. Everyone else get to class."

Everyone stares at us. Emily and I slowly get up, and everyone follows us into the building.

I look over at Emily. I have ripped her skirt and sleeve of her shirt. We both have cuts and are filthy. My hair is a mess.

As Emily and I sit in detention, my mother walks in with Emily's parents. "Kaya, why did you throw a book at Emily?" my mother asks. Everyone knows Emily and I have a complicated past.

I don't want to say it was an accident, which will put my mom in a difficult situation because she is my mom, and she'll go into mom mode and defend me. I know Tevan already spoke on my behalf about the situation, and for once, I don't want to get out of trouble. I want Emily to think I did it on purpose. She slapped me in the face.

"Well, I have had to put up with Emily Watson and her garbage my entire life, and I thought, why not?"

Emily scowls at me. "So, you decide to assault me with a book?"

I nod. "I thought, why not help you retain knowledge in some fashion? Everyone knows you never are going to study, so it needs to get in your mind somehow."

Her parents gasp. "Are you saying our daughter is stupid?" Emily's mother asks.

"Precisely," I say. "She is also a conniving little witch."

"Kaya ..." my mother says.

"Well, she is a cruel person," I insist.

"What do you intend to do about her behavior?" Emily's dad asks.

"You've always encouraged her to say whatever she wants and run around with that Larkin boy. He's not of her class," her mother says.

I try to control my anger.

"Be careful, Mother," Emily says. "Kaya cares deeply for him. He's her only friend, and that is why she assaulted me—because Matthew and I were chatting." I almost lunge at her but catch myself. Still, she says, "See how violent she becomes over him?"

"I hate you Emily," I snarl at her.

"Julie, you should really make them spend some time apart, especially if he's corrupting her," Emily's mom insists. "Emily has been attending classes in Lexicon with her cousin to teach her to be a proper young lady."

I sit down and roll my eyes. "Maybe I should enroll if it has taught Emily to assault people not of her class and to roll around on the ground in a dress. Speaking of spending time with those not of our class, Emily likes spending time with Jay Overcast."

Everyone looks at me.

"Kaya, that was completely inappropriate, and I apologize," my mother says.

Mrs. Watson hands her a pamphlet on classes and says, "We'll talk to Emily."

"We'll see you tomorrow," my mom says as they leave. She then turns to me. "Kaya, I know that you didn't mean to throw that book, yet you were so rude. Tevan explained everything." I cross my arms but don't answer. "Your father has an Axis meeting for everyone tonight, and then we are going to discuss this together. I know you. Only you can choose how you will react to another person's behavior. Kaya Lewis is a good person."

I try not to make eye contact because she is not only giving me a mom speech but a teacher one as well.

"I'll see you at the house," she says. "Now get home."

I gather my things, and as I leave the school, Matt is waiting for me outside. "What are you doing here?" I ask.

He shrugs his shoulders. "I don't know. Maybe I want your autograph."

I narrow my eyes. "Don't be funny. It was completely disturbing when you went through that girl-fighter phase."

He smiles. "I know, but the way you were pounding Emily's head into the pavement brought back those memories. Please sign my notebook." He tries to hand me a pen.

"I'm still mad at you," I insist, looking away.

"Are you going to pulverize me like Emily or like you did Zach Hanson in third grade?" he asks.

"No, I'm not going to talk to you, Matthew."

He cringes a bit. "'Matthew.' When you call me Matthew, it's serious. Plus, I get the silent treatment."

I nod. "You got me into trouble today by bringing attention to me, and the only reason I beat up Zach was because I was defending you."

"I know. I hated Zach. He was cruel. He was my Emily," Matt says as he takes a seat next to me.

"You get me, Larkin, but I'm still mad," I say.

He laughs. "I know, and I feel horrible about today. That's why I'm skipping the first part of practice to make amends."

A few trucks drive by, and I ask him, "Do you find all the workers and tonight's meeting strange?"

Matt digs through his backpack. "I find many things strange lately, but before I forget—amends." He hands me a book.

"My favorite book," I say as I run my hand over the cover.

"Mr. Leer confiscated it when you refused to do anything but read, when you said his teaching was a joke. When he was packing, I snuck in and swiped it."

I throw my arms around him. "Thank you! You know this was my favorite copy, an original. It means so much."

Matt freezes as I hold on to him. "You really do love your books," Matt says. Then he coughs, and I pull away.

"Yes, you thief!" I say.

"Mattipoo, we have track practice," someone says. Emily walks up in the shortest shorts I have ever seen.

"I'd better go. I'm already going to have to run an extra mile," Matt says.

Emily laughs.

"You coming?" he asks me.

"No, I need to get home," I answer. "And Mattipoo, thank you for the book."

"You're welcome," he says, as Emily gets in her ridiculous vehicle.

"You know, you could get one better than Emily." he says. I nod, and Emily gives me a look.

"What would be the fun in that when I have Tevan to chauffeur me and you to walk with?" I say.

Emily honks at Matt.

"I'd better go; she's my ride," Matt says.

I wave good-bye and walk home. For once I feel lonely, and the closer I get to my house, the farther it seems to get away from me. I know my father has built a society based on the idea of equality, sequestered from the rest of the world, but the ideas from the outside always creep in and cause people to be viewed differently. Everyone knows the families within Axis who are mixed within the hierarchy. As I walk past the Patterson house, I remember that Mrs. Patterson is a scientist and her husband a contractor. I remember Tevan commenting that he is not even an architect.

I pull the pamphlet from my backpack about the meetings in Lexicon because I want to be a voice of change. As I watch Mrs. Patterson water her begonias, I wonder what her fate would be outside these walls.

"Kaya! Kaya!" Tevan shouts as I stand in front of the Patterson house.

"What?" I snap. Mrs. Patterson stops her task to look at me.

"I've been shouting and honking at you, and you've been standing there in a strange daze for two minutes," Tevan says from her car. "I thought for a moment you had become a stalker. Get in."

I walk toward her car and tuck away my pamphlet.

"Why have you been so strange today … and for most of your life?" she asks.

I roll my eyes. "Genetics. You should see my sister."

She gives me a look. "You were supposed to be home ten minutes ago, and Mom is worried since you have been a bigger basket case than usual. Of course I had to take a break from my studies to find her precious. You do realize I am trying to get into a good college next year."

I just stare at her. "Yes, I hear of nothing else. I don't know why you even bother studying. You know the Axis school is prestigious."

She agrees, and then says, "Anyway, we have the meeting. Mom has no idea what Dad is going to discuss, which is strange, and Dad seems stressed."

"You know everyone's business within Axis, and you call me a stalker?" I say.

She seems irritated. "Speaking of stalking. I heard you were talking to Matt a minute ago. Did he set you straight?"

I glare at her. "What is that supposed to mean? Set me straight?"

"You have such a bad temper, and he tends to help you see reason where no one else can. I know he made you mad today, and he felt bad," Tevan says.

I don't like the tone of her voice. "Shut up, Tevan. What are you? The voice inside his head?"

"Observation," she says. "He was moping around. He cares about making you mad." She rolls her eyes.

"It is none of your business. I don't want to talk about it," I insist, and she laughs.

"I know you will not be in nearly enough trouble for what you pulled today, as usual. It must be nice to be the baby of the family," Tevan says.

"I have to be awful to make you look so good." I say as we pull into the driveway.

"Kaya, could you at least work on getting your driver's license?" she asks.

I shake my head. "It's bad for the environment. Plus, if I got my license, Mom wouldn't send you to find me when I was late, and we wouldn't get a chance to have our little talks. I would be clueless as to Axis news and never get lectures on how big of a loser I am."

She glares at me. "If it weren't for my intervening, you'd be in a boarding school," Tevan says as we get out of her car. "Mom's cooking, so Kaya be nice."

My mouth drops open. My mom only cooks when she's stressed, so that means things are bad. "Tevan, no." I shake my head.

"Eat whatever she makes," Tevan orders me.

My mom is a horrible cook. As we get to the front door, the odor wafts out, and it is horrifying. "Now I know why you volunteered to get me." I say.

She nods. "I was getting sick from the smell. It was interrupting my studies."

We both hold our breath. The neighbors look over at us from their yards, and I wave at Mr. Jenson. "You first," I say as I shove Tevan. "A quick dinner, Dad's meeting, and then a trip to the ER."

Tevan shoves me back. "Shut up." Tevan smoothes her hair and practices her fake smile. I roll my eyes. "Get it together, Kaya." She pops my arm, and we walk in. I didn't realize things were this bad.

CHAPTER 3

After my mother's dinner, she, Tevan, and I arrive at the community building to find every Axis worker and their families seated. My father ordered the gates and walls placed on lockdown so everyone could be in attendance. I look around and find Matt, and he does our special wave.

"Tevan, this is serious. Everyone is here," I say as we take our seats. My father promptly comes out to the center of the stage. Tevan grabs for my hand, and rather than push her away for once, I grip it tightly in mine.

"Members of Axis, for years we were at the top of our field. We have seen entire tribes and civilizations worldwide cured of diseases released during the Great Wars, all because of cures the Vitae Corporation created. I am proud of my scientists. We have had the top minds in science, medicine, technology, and other areas too many to mention. We have made Axis a model for the entire world, and for that I am proud. Years ago, we had a rift in the family, and we felt that it couldn't be mended. Many parted ways, and since then things have changed."

I knew who he was talking about—the evilest person on the planet, Rebecca Dean, one of my father's leading scientists. She weaseled her way in and then rose to the top within his same mission. My father provided her with labs, but her agenda changed as soon as his back was turned. She began experimenting with chemical warfare and disease, backed by large companies in several countries.

Her tactics threatened peace treaties and everything Nambitus had fought for, causing her to go off the grid for almost a decade after being forced out of the Vitae Corporation. I had heard my parents talk in private that once she was caught by an ethics board for experimenting on human subjects after she left, but she paid off the right people and went unscathed. When she left the Vitae Corporation, she created the Thantos Corporation, taking some of my father's top scientists and causing the rift my dad never got over. Every year, more and more people slowly slipped away from the Vitae Corporation to her various funded companies.

In the past few years, we even lost the Talberts, who are Jonathon's parents. I know it crushed my father when they left because Jonathon and Tevan were so close. The only good thing that came from Rebecca Dean was her son, Talon, who was my age. When we were younger he, Matt, and I were inseparable.

"Kaya, Dad is about to make his big announcement," Tevan says. She grips my hand, and I snap back to reality.

"I know we have had our troubles in the past years," my father says, "but it is time to make amends. It is time for a new era in Vitae history. With that being said, just like science, life is always changing, and I have made a decision to better life for all of us. I have accepted merger terms with Rebecca Dean and the Thantos Corporation. We will once again be family. I know this comes as a surprise, but I expect all of us to accept the Thantos family with open arms."

Everyone begins looking around in disbelief.

"Wait!" I say, standing up.

"Kaya, sit down," Tevan whispers.

Rebecca Dean begins making her way on stage.

"This can't be happening!" I shout. Tevan begins pulling on my arm. I turn around and face everyone. "Is everyone just going to sit here and let this happen?"

"Kaya, sit *down*," Mom says.

"It seems you have a fan, John," Rebecca says, pointing to me as I take my seat. "Are you finished? Don't stop on my account. I didn't think John had a friend left in the world." Rebecca laughs, and I start to get up again.

Tevan pulls me down and places her arm over my lap. I look over at my mom, who has tears in her eyes as my dad exits the stage.

"There will be more details and new protocol to follow," Rebecca says, "but I can see this has been an emotional ordeal. We'll reconvene tomorrow evening after you have had time to absorb this passing of the baton. It isn't the end of the world. I feel we have come full circle, and I am once again home. I might tease John, but I have the utmost respect for the Vitae Corporation and look forward to working with you all." She slams a gavel. Everyone remains quiet and in their seats.

My father quickly finds my mother and comforts her. Everyone is somber, and some are sniffling. I see Matt signaling me from across the room.

"Mom may I walk home?" I ask.

"Not too long," she says. "You have school tomorrow." My dad leads her and Tevan out.

I walk out of the building and onto a dark basketball court. Someone quickly comes up behind me and covers my eyes. "Think fast. What would you do?" Matt asks.

"Using my self-defense, I'd stomp on your foot, throat-punch you, and I might kick you in a few uncomfortable places before deciding on whether to annihilate you," I say.

Matt starts laughing and drops his hands. "I did that to Emily, and she started screaming."

I squint at him.

"What?" he asks.

"Did you ask me here to talk about Emily Watson?" I ask.

He shakes his head. "Absolutely not." He quickly looks down and rubs the back of his neck. "What do you think about everything that has happened?"

I try to keep my composure. "I'm horrified. We should have been prepared to stop her."

"Wasn't it Rebecca's goal, as she left, to destroy your dad and take over the world in the process?" Matt asks.

"I think you are mocking me and making a joke about our entire world crashing," I say, but he shakes his head.

"If you would have done your homework, Miss Lewis, you would have seen Rebecca's contacts reach well beyond Nambitus. Her network is worldwide, with large and small companies like your dad once …" Matthew stops.

"Like my dad … what? Say it."

"You know she does nothing the right way. But she has a network in place and has practically won the Nambitus elections. She has political intentions as well as business motives. I do my homework, Kay," Matt states. "I'm surprised you don't know this."

I roll my eyes. "Why would I research a psychopath?"

"She's a political candidate and a business guru. Granted, her techniques test boundaries, but there was no substantial evidence," Matt says.

I take a step back to study him. "Where is this coming from?" I ask.

"Your dad's speech. We have all seen the media, and he reassured us that we are going to benefit from the merger. You were sitting there."

I make a fist. "I can't sit idly by and let this happen."

"It's been happening for years," Matt says, shaking his head, "and your dad must have a good reason to finally give in, or else it wouldn't have happened. Axis is her new headquarters. Accept it."

"So are you trying to make me see reason?" I ask.

"What are you talking about?"

"Tevan says that you are the only one able of making me see reason," I say, not meeting his eyes.

"How flattering." He laughs.

"It wasn't a compliment," I tell him. "I don't like this."

"You don't have—"

I pick up a rock and break out a window.

"What are you doing?" Matt asks.

"Vandalizing," I say. "I need to blow of some steam, and it is technically not my father's property any longer." I pick up another rock and break another window.

"Stop it!" Matt snaps.

I refrain from throwing a third. "You steal books," I argue.

He rolls his eyes. "I retrieved it and gave it back to the rightful owner; that's not stealing. But I do want to give you something. Tomorrow is your birthday, and I have a gift for you."

"I thought my gift was the stolen property."

He ignores my comment and hands me a small box. "Shut up, and open it."

"This must be serious. You haven't gotten me a real gift since we were ten."

"Forget it, Kaya," he says, trying to take it back. We get into a tug-of-war.

"Matt, I'm only teasing." I carefully open it. "A necklace." I say.

"You hate it. Give it back," he says.

I shake my head. "No, I don't. Is it vintage?"

"Yes, I know you like items with a past and mystery. So last year, on vacation, I saw this particular piece and thought you'd like it."

"You went on vacation? I thought your mom hasn't left Axis or Lexicon in ten years."

He shrugs his shoulders. "Maybe we saw some Nambitus sights in secret."

I smile. "Mysterious. Will you help me?" I ask as I hand it to him.

"You really like it?" he asks, placing it around my neck.

"I love it. Thank you for thinking of me."

"So you accept my necklace?" he asks.

I start laughing. "Why would you ask if I accept it?"

"Just answer the question," he says.

"Of course, and I swear to never take it off, Matthew Larkin."

He smiles.

Matt walks me home, and I take his arm, as always. He tells me about his practice, and I make fun of Tevan until he laughs.

"I feel bad that Tevan is always the source of our entertainment," he says as we reach my porch.

"Don't. She thinks she is my second mother."

He stifles a laugh. "She's so sophisticated."

I roll my eyes. "She's not that complicated. Do you want me to take a picture of her without makeup?"

Just then Jonathon pulls up in his car. He walks past Matt and me and knocks on the front door. He and Tevan have a short conversation, and then she kisses him.

"Matt, have you ever thought about kissing anyone—not one of your weird, fake kisses that you tried when you tricked me when we were kids?"

He shakes his head. "No, never, and you promised to never speak of that incident."

"Would you kiss Tevan or Emily?" I ask.

He grins. "In a heartbeat." I give him a shove. "I don't think about girls," Matt says as I make a strange face. "I mean, I don't think about kissing. I focus on school. Do you think about kissing?"

I shrug my shoulders.

"Of course you do. You sneak Tevan's books," Matt says.

Before I can respond, my mother flashes the porch light, signaling me to come in. "I'd better go in. We have another Rebecca Dean meeting tomorrow."

Matt starts to hug me but then pulls back. "Good night, Kaya."

I walk in and lean up against the front door.

"What's wrong?" Tevan asks as she watches me slide down and hit the floor.

"Adolescence," I tell her. "Leave me alone."

"Why is Kaya on the floor?" my mother asks, glancing over at me as if everything is normal.

"Where's Dad?" I ask.

"He's downstairs in his personal lab," Tevan says. "It's going to be nice having him home more. Not so many hours now."

"What? Were you not at tonight's meeting?" I ask.

She sits down on the floor beside me. "While you were out trying to get Matthew Larkin to kiss you, we had a family meeting. Mom was so upset; she came in screaming. I have never seen her so upset. He left her out of the loop because he thought she would talk him out of his decision. Thantos has taken over the world, and we were the last stop."

"I don't want to talk about it." I insist, taking off my shoes.

"He held out for as long as he could, Kaya. Don't be angry. Dad feels bad enough."

I go up to my room and throw myself on my bed. I turn my music on loudly to annoy Tevan. It's what she deserves for telling me how to feel. I fall asleep, staring at the ceiling.

I wake up with my mother, father, and Tevan standing over me.

"Happy Birthday!" my mom exclaims.

"Good morning," I snap, rubbing my eyes.

Tevan is already dressed for school and looks perfect. As my parents sing "Happy Birthday," Tevan studies my filthy room. I watch as she eyeballs a dirty plate with pizza crust. My parents finish singing, and my mom says, "Blow out your candle on your birthday muffin."

"We'll have a family party after tonight's meeting," my dad says.

I cringe a little, thinking of yet another meeting. "Thanks," I say. I blow out my candle and nudge a pile of dirty clothes toward Tevan. She takes a step back, falling over a mound of shoes.

"I have to get out of here," Tevan says.

"Presents at dinner. Hurry up and get ready for school," my mom says as she kisses my forehead.

I meet Tevan downstairs. I have to ride with her; Matt has early practice and can't walk with me. "Five minutes—a record," Tevan says. I try to ignore her. "Where's the horrible music player that you and Matt pass back and forth?"

I grab it off the counter, and we leave the house. "Why do you look so good today?" I ask as I cram my birthday muffin in my mouth.

Tevan scowls. "Word is that we are going to have new students since Rebecca is rejoining us."

"And?" I say.

"I just want to look my best," she insists.

"Wait a minute," I say. "It all makes sense. Rebecca Dean is bringing in all her back-stabbers. Are the Talberts back?"

"Possibly," she answers.

"Is that why you're supportive of this merger? Where is Jonathon right now?"

"Kaya, it was going to happen regardless. He's doing a professor internship and might be at our school today."

I glare at her. "Disgusting. You're a student."

"He graduated early," Tevan says, clearly irritated with me.

I try not to vomit. "So it just sweetens the deal that Jonathon is coming back. That's why he was here last night. For you to sell out Dad and call yourself family sickens me. And the thought of Jonathon being one of my teachers makes me want to kill myself. And for you to be with him after everything his family has done … Aren't there laws against a student being with a teacher?"

Tevan grips the steering wheel until her knuckles turn white. "At least he's worthy of me," she snaps.

"Meaning?"

"He's my equal and not beneath me. He wouldn't get arrested outside Axis walls for associating with me."

I laugh. "I'm not arguing with you. Jonathon is your equal. You are both stuck-up monsters. As for Matthew and me, I didn't know we were anything other than friends—not that it's any of your business. Obviously, if you are so happily-ever-after with Jonathon, you wouldn't need to pry in my or anyone else's business, as you constantly do."

She suddenly slams on the brakes. "Out."

I roll my eyes. "Don't, Tevan."

"I have a physics and a calculus exam, and I'm not in the mood for your nonsense," she says. She refuses to move the car and reaches across me to open my door. "I want you out."

I grab my backpack. "Fine," I snap. I barely have time to get before she speeds off.

I think of about ten more horrible things to say about her and Jonathon, but I want to scream. Even if I run to school, I'll still be late. *I hope Tevan fails both her exams and ends up a janitor*, I think. I place my earpieces in and listen to my and Matt's music.

I walk to school, taking my time. It's my birthday, so I decide to take the scenic route. Everywhere I turn, I see upgrades and changes being made. I walk past the orchard and see the apple trees in bloom. The ducks on the shrinking pond are particularly chatty this morning.

By the time I get to parking lot at school, it's full of cars. I walk into the building, and realize it's almost lunch. The bell rings, and the hall fills with students, who begin laughing the second they see me. This lets me know Tevan has used me to entertain the masses, both old and new.

"Kaya, it's lunch," Matt says as he signals me toward the cafeteria.

"What's going on?" I ask. He grabs me a seat; Tevan, Emily, Jay, and a couple of new kids take a seat at our table.

"New schedules, strict rules, and very few electives," Matt says, handing me my new schedule.

"How was your walk?" Emily asks sweetly.

I glare at her. "It was refreshing. I didn't have to hear your voice or see your face."

She smiles. "I would have kicked you out too."

Matt covers his mouth, signaling me that I shouldn't talk to her.

I ignore his advice. "That seems funny, Emily, because I wouldn't be caught dead in your vehicle. I might catch a disease from your back seat."

Everyone gets quiet, except one person who laughs from the back of the cafeteria.

"Has anyone seen these schedules?" I ask. "They're a travesty, meant to mold us into scientists for a corporation to which I refuse to give my loyalty. I refuse to take these classes." I wad up my schedule and throw it toward Tevan and Emily. At this moment, you could hear a pin drop in the cafeteria, except for the laughter growing from the back.

"Kaya, maybe you should take the day off," Matt suggested. "Go home and come back tomorrow. You need to read your orientation packet."

I shove my papers at him. "Not interested."

"Why are you embarrassing yourself and the rest of us?" Tevan asks.

I glare at her. "I don't know. Why did you find it necessary to kick me out of your car so you could impress these sell-outs?" Matt tries to pull me out, but I refuse to leave.

"I don't think the lady wants to leave," someone says. He comes forward, and everyone stares at him.

"We don't want any trouble." Matt says.

I smile at the familiar face. He's older now, but in many ways, he is much the same. He still has blond hair that keeps falling across his blue eyes. It's Talon Dean. I know a ridiculous argument over me is in the works, just like when we were kids.

"Maybe she needs to cool off before she makes a spectacle, breaking the school policies she has yet to read, resulting in expulsion," Matt explains. "She's already been a target of bullying."

"Maybe she wouldn't be a target of bullying if you'd stop speaking for her, and let her make her own decisions," Talon says. He takes a step toward Matt.

"She made those choices yesterday and beat Emily to a pulp," Matt says. "She can't even cover the bruises with makeup. Did you not hear during orientation about a fight yesterday and how there is zero tolerance because of certain people and scenes such as this one now? It could lead to consequences we don't even know. That's because of Kaya. It's always because of Kaya." Matt finishes his rant, and Emily looks around, embarrassed.

Talon rolls his eyes. "Idle threats made by people wanting to mold us into a box of conformity. I say we protest." Talon jumps on a table, and I laugh.

"Why do you always have to act like a fool?" Matt asks as Talon jumps down.

"And why do you have to be so upstanding?" Talon asks as they begin getting in each other's faces.

"Boys, boys," I say, pushing them apart.

"He tries to control you," Talon says.

"He tries to make you a criminal, like he is," Matt says as they start shoving each other.

"I make my own choices." I slam them apart.

"Matt—always the pretty boy who does the right thing. How will you react to *this*?" Talon squirts mustard all over the top of Matt's head. "Oh, that's right; you won't do anything."

Matt stands there frozen as everyone watches in horror. Then Matt picks up a soda, shakes it up, and points it toward Talon, saying, "Hey, Talon, criminal this."

I get in between them as Matt pops it open, covering me from head to sneaker in sticky liquid.

"Kaya!" Talon gasps. Matt tries to touch my arm, but I push him away.

"Don't. Both of you." Everyone begins laughing.

"And I thought *I* was going to be embarrassed and have a bad first day. At least I'm not Kaya!" Emily says.

That was too much. I shake up a soda and spray it all over her. I see Talon trying to sneak out of the cafeteria. "No, you don't!" I call to him. "This is for Matt." I grab some cheese and run it through Talon's hair.

"Well, this is for you. It's for your birthday," Talon says as he takes a spoonful of stew and thumps it at Tevan, hitting her in the back of the head.

"Oh, my God!" Tevan exclaims. She's acting as if someone has shot her with an actual bullet, and I begin laughing hysterically.

"Happy birthday." Talon says. Everyone begins having a food fight, with Talon tossing spoonfuls of applesauce and cheese.

"You remembered my birthday," I say above the noise. "I think this might be the best gift anyone has given me."

Everyone is running around, screaming. Just then several teachers come in with megaphones and yell at the entire student body.

"Is that Jonathon Talbert?" Talon asks, pointing to one of the teachers.

"Yes, I despise him," I say. Talon quickly scoops up a heaping spoonful of stew and pops it at the back of Jonathon's head.

"How do you hit the target so precisely?" I ask, laughing hysterically.

"Everyone, back to classes!" Jonathon shouts. "I don't care if you are covered in food!" Talon and I sneak into the crowd. "I need to see Kaya Lewis and Talon Dean," Jonathon announces, and everyone looks at us.

Jonathon walks out, and we follow after him, but he refuses to acknowledge us. "Always the two of you," he mutters.

When we get to the office, a new secretary hands me the phone.

"Where's Beverly?" I ask.

"Who?" the secretary asks.

"Beverly. The secretary who's been here for ten years."

Talon takes the phone and dials his mom.

"Gone, dead—how am I supposed to know?" she says.

I look around the office for my mother.

"She's gone too," the lady says.

When I call my house. my mom answers. To my amazement, she's eager to collect me.

A strange man comes of my mother's office, grabs the phone from me, and begins talking to my mom. All of a sudden, I feel as if I'm in another world—there are so many new students and faculty, and Mom is no longer in charge.

I quietly take a seat next to Talon and try to absorb the situation.

"My mother always cleans house when she takes over a place," Talon whispers. "Out with the old, and in with the new." He pulls a piece of food from my hair. "It's good to see you."

I smile. "You too."

"I knew you would be the one to stand up for your convictions. I just didn't know it would be so immediate," he says, making me blush.

"Stop," I say as I cross my arms awkwardly.

"And the riot you tried to ensure last night? Beautiful as well," Talon says.

"You saw that?" I ask.

He nods and grins at me. "I was so moved; I took notes."

"Shut up, Talon. I sometimes get carried away." I slouch in my seat.

"And that is the Kaya I have missed," he says.

Just then Rebecca Dean throws open the door to the office. "I made it clear to not bother me at work," she says to Talon, who smiles a devious smile. "I told you if you started any trouble, there would be repercussions, and this does not surprise me in the least, especially when you get around this monster."

Talon stands up and blocks her from pointing at me. "I started the entire thing," Talon admits.

"I know you did. I was sent the footage, but *she* was ranting like a thoughtless rebel. Not going to take classes, and you agreeing and encouraging her." She glares at us.

Just then my mom walks in.

"Well, if it isn't Julie Lewis," Rebecca says.

"Rebecca," my mother says, narrowing her eyes. Talon and I just stare at them.

"It seems these two started a food fight and are encouraging inappropriate political behavior," Rebecca says.

"That sounds familiar. Kaya questions society," my mother says.

Rebecca quirks her eyebrow. "Maybe she shouldn't, and she should be punished. We will no longer facilitate such ideas." Rebecca gives me a look and then turns her attention back to my mother.

"John and I will have a talk with her, but it seems she is not the only one with ideas." My mom looks at Talon and then back at Rebecca.

"What to do with such children. You have a good day. Make sure you bring Kaya to tonight's meeting. It will be enlightening," Rebecca says, tapping the counter.

"Wouldn't miss it," my mother says as she signals me to go.

"That was the coolest thing you have ever done," I say as we get to the car.

"Rebecca is a bully and is trying to assert herself. Kaya, there will be repercussions."

I lower my eyes. "I'm sorry, Mom."

She nods. "Let's go home."

My mom sends me to my room to think about my behavior for the rest of the day, which isn't such a punishment for me. She insists that she and my dad will talk to me about my recent behavior after tonight's meeting.

I don't think she's ready to be a stay-at-home mom. I listen at my door as she struggles with the vacuum and sneezes, presumably while dusting. I look out my window to see her watering the grass. Our grass hasn't been watered for a decade. When I hear her in the kitchen, I turn on my music player, hoping it will all go away.

She comes and goes throughout the day, lecturing me. Tevan will be graduating soon, and I'm sixteen today, but let's face it; she has her work cut out for her with me. I can tell from her actions today that she'll spend more time ensuring my behavior will improve. I place my pillow over my head and scream.

When Tevan pulls up and gets out of her car, her hair is still caked with food. I can't help but smile as I see her scraping crusty food from her clothing. She looks horrible. She walks in and immediately starts crying.

I slightly open my door and listen as she tells the story of her humiliation. She then does something unexpected and tells on herself for kicking me out on the side of the road, forcing me to walk to school, thus setting the stage for my behavior.

"I know we are in the process of a stressful transition, but both of you are behaving unacceptably. Reflect, Tevan," my mom lectures.

"Mom, she broke all the rules as soon as she got to school." Tevan pouts.

"She might have known the rules if someone had gotten her to school on time. The ride to school wasn't that long, and Tevan, you have an attitude as well."

Tevan sighs. "I know; she just never shuts up."

"What exactly happened when Kaya got to school?" Mom asks.

Tevan finally confesses, and my mom lectures her on how we represent Axis, that we're failing my father miserably with our behavior, and that we're acting like anything but family. When I received the same lecture earlier, I blocked my mom out, but Tevan cries.

"You and Kaya have such strong personalities. Kaya sees the world and wants to take it by storm and change it at any cost. She doesn't know when to keep her mouth shut, and she gets that from me. You, on the other hand, want to change the world by infiltrating the system. You have such a heart. You remind me so much of your father. Imagine what the two of you could accomplish if you worked together."

Tevan gets huffy. "Okay, Mom. I didn't need a lecture. I wanted you to kill Kaya." Tevan pouts again.

"And isn't it such a lucky coincidence that the two of you are sisters?" my mom says, talking over her.

"Fine, I'll forgive her but not until I have a shower, and you should at least have her clean her room." Tevan stomps up the stairs. I quietly close my door as Tevan comes down the hall.

I decide to clean my room before my mother demands it of me. I put all the dirty dishes in a pile, I separate dirty and clean clothing, and I find all my shoes. I even find my retainer from two years ago.

"Kaya, Tevan, it's time to go," my mother shouts from the bottom of the stairs.

"Meeting time," my father says.

"It's nice to have you home now, Dad," I say.

"One of the perks of being a Thantos employee, rather than the Vitae president," he says. Tevan and my mom start out the front door, but Dad holds back and tells me, "Kaya, I need to talk to you for a moment." He insists I wait. "We might hear some things tonight that none of us will like, but it comes with being a new company. We're not under my leadership any longer."

"What are you trying to tell me?" I ask.

"Kaya, you are going to have to fall in line. You might not agree with how Axis is being operated, but I'm no longer in charge."

I try not to get angry. "So what you are saying is I need to keep my mouth shut."

He looks away. "Kaya ..."

"I got it, Dad. From this moment on, we have no control over our lives."

He nods. "You're not a little kid anymore, and I'm not going to treat you like one. I had to sell my company or be destroyed. I was able to keep everyone within Axis. I hate having to admit my failures to my own child, but act accordingly during this meeting."

"Fine," I say.

He holds the door open for me.

As we walk to the community center, we see it's already undergoing changes. The seating is being ripped out, and new carpet is being installed. I watch as workers throw out artwork.

"Come on, Kaya. Don't take it personally," my dad says as

he guides me inside. The entire place is packed. The lights begin flickering to let us know to take our seats. "It's time," my dad says.

"Is this seat taken?" Talon asks as he points to the seat next to me.

Everyone stares at him. "No," I say, "it's not."

"Good, I get to hear one of Mommy's speeches. I see she's already instilling fear," Talon whispers.

"I'm not in the joking mood," I say.

"I saw your moment of nostalgia back there," Talon says.

I glare at him. "Are you stalking me?"

"Yes."

I roll my eyes.

"Here we go," Talon says as his mom comes on stage.

"Axis family, it has been an honor to come back home. I have missed all of you," Rebecca says.

"Lies," Talon whispers. When I give him a look, he says, "What? Are we playing nice now?"

I try to ignore him.

"The way in which you have welcomed me and my fellow employees has made this transition seem like a homecoming rather than a merger, but more changes are on the horizon. As you know, the Nambitus elections are months away, and I am within inches of a victory as president. This, as well as our technological advancements within the labs, makes security here at Axis our highest priority. I have installed extra cameras as precautions. I am also issuing each person, young and old, a tracker. Lexicon is not a safe place, and citizens living within Axis are prime targets for kidnapping due to the Thantos name. Each one of you is valuable, and I will not have a competitor ransom you as a way to steal data to unleash harm on Nambitus."

Talon laughs. "Lies again. Each one of these people has the potential to betray her, so she monitors."

I begin feeling uneasy.

"Your tracker will alert us if you ever need assistance in the event of an attack, so security can come in an instant. We have hired the best militia in all of Nambitus. You will be able to come and go through the gates, but no outsiders will be allowed within these walls." A few guards step forward. "Next, we will address labs and schools. Children in Axis have lived a sheltered existence. Outside these walls, that life does not exist. We have two weeks of school left and then the summer. Next year, the children of Axis will attend Lexicon Public Schools. They must learn they can speak to those only within their circle and must practice this now because outside these walls, that act is punishable. Axis, new experiences await you." She winks at Talon.

"Well, I guess I know what the repercussions to our behavior are," Talon whispers. Several students begin whispering and pointing at us.

"I didn't," I say.

"During orientation we were warned of such behavior," Talon explains, "and then we broke all the rules during lunch. Everyone is blaming us."

Several parents give us a look, but Talon shrugs.

Rebecca then says, "The school will be turned into labs to further Thantos productivity so everyone wins. Thantos will provide bussing for all Axis students. The Lexicon schools will provide life experience, which, in the end, is priceless." Everyone applauds. "Thank you, and please get your trackers on the way out. We will also be installing state-of-the-art fire alarms and security equipment in all of your homes within the week. Remember, Thantos loves each and every one of you."

I watch as Rebecca exits the stage, and they take a sledge hammer to the Vitae sign. I wanted to scream. I looked around the room at everyone applauding, and I wondered if they were ever loyal to my dad for one day. Now, he pulls me towards the door, saying, "Come on; let's go home."

I see Matt from across the room, and he quickly ducks his head, not even making eye contact with me. It suddenly hits me—Matthew

Larkin, my best friend, won't be able to speak to me. I feel like someone has hit me in the stomach and sucked the oxygen out of the room. I can't breathe. He is in my every memory. He was at every birthday party I had, and even when I didn't want him around, he was, because he is Matt.

"Kaya," my dad says as he tugs on me.

"Right," I say as I watch Matt leave with his parents.

We get our trackers and exit the building.

"Kaya, you're quiet," my mom says. Everyone looks at their trackers, which are small and can be placed behind any small piece of jewelry. I place mine behind my watch.

When we get home, my mom says, "Kaya, can you run down to the store for milk?" I know she wants to send me on an errand so she and Tevan can set up for my birthday, but I can't make myself leave the house.

"Not in the mood," I insist. I sit in front of the TV and flip through the channels.

"Kaya, this is depressing," my mom says, licking frosting off her hand. "The missing total is up to thirty within the last two weeks."

"Who's missing?" Tevan asks.

"Kids, elderly, people of all types," my mom explains as Tevan tries to hide balloons.

"Isn't this the conspiracy channel? If people were really missing, wouldn't it be on the Lexicon news?" Tevan asks.

"They would never report it because it's a mystery. Bad things happen outside the Lexicon wall, Tevan," I insist, as Tevan tries to take the remote.

"Kaya, we need you to be gone for at least thirty minutes," my mom explains.

I turn off the television and toss the remote. "Fine. Where's Dad?"

"Try his personal lab," my mom says, which means the basement.

I walk down to the back part of the basement. The front part is my and Tevan's lounging room, which we rarely use anymore.

Usually, I would find my dad pouring over research or testing samples but not today.

"Dad. Dad?" I say. I feel the wall vibrate. I snoop around my dad's lab. I haven't been down here in years. I see a book on genetics and some samples that are of no interest to me. Just as I am about to abandon my search, I hear a distant popping sound and feel vibrations. I feel along the wall, trying to see where the vibrations are coming from. I find a strange handle with a keypad. Out of curiosity, I begin typing in codes containing birthdates and anniversaries, and then I type in my mom's birth date. It opens.

I discover a damp-smelling cement room. Just then, I hear another loud sound echo off the walls. It is so loud I have to cover my ears.

"Kaya, what are you doing down here?" my dad asks as he walks toward me, carrying a gun and wearing ear covers and strange goggles.

"What are you doing?" I ask loudly.

"I'm shooting."

I stare at him. "Shooting who?" I ask and then scream when a target pops up. "What is this place?"

He shoots the target and pushes a button. "It's my other lab. Can we talk?" When I nod, he says, "I'm not having a good day. I hate what I had to do. She makes my skin crawl." My dad continues to shoot. "Do you know who I am talking about?"

"Rebecca Dean," I answer. "Did she fire Mom?"

"Yes, but your mom has a job lined up for next year at a college. You know it kills her to stay home. She just doesn't want you and Tevan to know."

I feel relieved about that, but then ask, "Why do we need trackers? Is she going to monitor us?"

"Yes. People previously have sold secrets to her about competing companies, so she is going to be keeping tabs on us so we don't sell secrets."

"What happens in her labs?" I ask.

"She has levels, and she has made me her saline boy, along with her trainees." My dad blasts another target, which catches me so off guard that I nearly fall. "She has me sterilizing Petri dishes. It's insulting." He starts shooting once more. "She turned all my investors against me, but I had you, Tevan, your mom, and all my employees to think about."

"Dad, I thought you hated weapons."

I follow him to a blank wall. He pushes a button, a wall opens, and guns I have never seen pop up. Some look like space guns from movies.

"Have you seen the people who carry guns in Lexicon?" he asks. "Most of these that I make are not to be used on the street. Some of these could destroy city blocks."

I touch one, and he swats my hand. "Grandpa would be so proud," I say.

He rolls his eyes. "Don't get me started on your grandfather."

I ignore the comment and look through his collection. I know he and my grandpa believed differently, and I'm not in the mood to hear a lecture on old way of thinking versus the modern. "Why would you make such destructive items?" I ask.

He smiles. "It relaxes me." He chooses another and begins shooting.

"Let me shoot one. It's my birthday, and it's been a crummy day."

My dad laughs. "It has." He walks over to the wall and pulls up a small handgun.

"It's so small," I say as I swing it.

"Kaya, be careful. It's powerful." I gasp as a laser pops up, and my father steadies my hand. "Look at the target."

I focus. "Can I shoot it in the head?" I ask.

"That's worth the most points, but you do know the value of life and that taking a life should never be taken lightly, right?"

I pull the trigger. "Yes, and relax, Dad; it's only a target. I don't even kill animals when I'm out with Grandpa." I hit the target in the eye.

"Grandpa allows you kids to shoot?" he asks.

"Yes, but if you kill it, you skin and eat it. I've never been a fan," I say as he gives me a face. "May I go again?"

He nods and smiles. My dad and I shoot guns for over thirty minutes. I get to try high-powered bows and arrows, which I am a master at because of Grandpa.

"Kaya, John," my mother calls as she walks in through the secret door. When she sees us, she places her hands on her hips in a very mom-like fashion. "John, really?"

I quickly place the high-powered bow and arrow behind my back.

"Too late. Busted," my mom says. "We discussed this, John. The girls were not to know of this and especially Kaya."

I sigh heavily. "Mom, I'm right here." I hate it when my mom talks about me as if I'm a little kid.

My dad shrugs. "I know, but she came down here and let herself in. I thought she could handle it."

"We've talked about her week at school and how my father influences her. This was anything but a good idea, John," my mom scolds him. "Did you at least talk to her about her behavior?"

My father shakes his head, looking sheepish.

"Unbelievable, John. You know what? Tonight we are going to celebrate Kaya's birthday, and tomorrow both of you are in trouble."

My father and I quietly put away our weapons.

"Sorry, Dad," I say, but he laughs.

"It's all right. I wonder what our punishment will be."

I stare at him, and he grins. When we get upstairs, Tevan and my mom have balloons, streamers, food, and cake ready.

"I rented your favorite movies, Kaya," Tevan says. She pulls out a seat for me and places a birthday hat on my head. This is the first year Matt won't be here. I look at an empty chair. Tevan notices and immediately starts singing, and my mom lights my candles. Tevan and my mom had hit all my favorite stops for food—the Thai place and pizza place.

"Let the party begin!" my mom says, and Tevan wipes frosting on my nose.

The gifts were unique. Tevan got me a couple of outfits like hers and shoes to match.

"Thank you. I will treasure them, as I do every year," I say, and she smiles.

"Maybe you can wear them next to school year," she suggests.

I open the gifts from my mom and dad—a few gift cards to my favorite stores in the mall and some faded jeans.

"Do you like them?" Mom asks.

"I love them!" I say, smiling. Tevan looks irritated.

We eat tons of food and watch movies well into the night.

CHAPTER 4

I wake up at eight o'clock on Saturday morning. My mother is standing over me with garden tools.

"It's punishment time. Start planting flowers," she says.

I cover my head with my pillow. "Can't I write you an essay on the economic development of an impoverished third-world country and offer possible solutions to develop it further?"

She rips my covers off. "No, you did that one last year." She lets light into my room by undoing the blankets I have strategically placed over the window. She coughs from the dust that's released. "You need to wash these," she says as she tosses my blankets on the floor.

"You do my laundry. Remember? I'm your baby."

"You're sixteen now, and next year I'm going to be a full-time professor, so it is time for my baby to do her own laundry." She picks up a dirty spoon from the floor and flicks it at me, hitting me in the head. "And to do her own filthy dishes. Soak that."

After getting dressed, I make my way to the backyard to find my father beginning the demolition on my old tree house. "Dad, what are you doing?" I yell.

He pauses to look at me. "Taking this down. It is practically falling apart."

I run up the rickety old stairs. "No!" I say, throwing my arms out as if to protect it.

He tries to move past me. "Kaya, it is an eyesore, and your mother has been after me to tear it down for years."

"Too many memories," I say.

He looks at me strangely. "Kaya, you haven't been up here in eons."

"You can't!" I wail as I hold on to both sides of the rails.

"Kaya, don't be silly."

"I can't let you do this today," I insist, trying to take the saw out of his hands. "See that trunk? It contains plays and costumes that Matt, Talon, and I would write and act out during the summer. See that indent in the table? Matt and Talon got in a fight over who would be the prince, and Matt rammed Talon's head into the table. We painted this wall with leftover garage paint and got into a paint fight. After Talon would leave, Matt and I would do our homework here. We collected dinosaurs in this bin and then carved our names with some knives I took from the kitchen." I run my hand over the names. "I'm not ready to be told I can't speak to him. I saw him as we were leaving the community center last night, and he wouldn't even look at me." I am trying not to cry.

"It's going to be hard for him too," my dad says, giving me a hug. "Don't cry. We can leave the tree house up and plant flowers around the bottom."

"That would be nice," I say.

We climb down and begin our "punishment" gardening.

After Dad and I finish our chores, Tevan and Mom come outside.

"Are you ready for more birthday fun?" my mom asks.

"No." I say, shaking my head.

"Go change your clothes," Tevan says excitedly. "We are going for manicures."

"Oh … goody," I say awkwardly as Tevan looks pointedly at the dirt caked under my nails. I slap at her hands. "That means we will have to leave Axis."

"As long as we have our trackers, we'll be fine," Mom insists.

I draw out the process of getting ready for as long as possible. I know manicures are Tevan's idea. I slowly make my way downstairs and put on my tracker. Tevan and Mom are waiting in the car.

As we leave Axis, I see all the new security people. They have huge guns and are dressed all in black. "This isn't scary," I say flatly. "This isn't scary at all."

We are ushered through extra checkpoints.

"Jonathon says they have high-priority top-secret spy things they work on within the labs, and this is all a necessary precaution," Tevan says.

I roll my eyes. "So we have chemical and germ warfare in our labs with security guards on steroids. I feel safer already. At least we know Tevan will be safe because of who her friend is."

She glares at me with angry eyes. "You will as well. Everyone knows you are practically a Dean."

I return her angry glare with one of my own. "I do not believe in the sanctity of marriage, nor do I encourage Talon's friendship." Tevan and my mom begin laughing. "Laugh all you want, but I am merely friends with Talon, just as I have been friends with Matthew," I say. "I hate both of you."

Slow Sal McCoy ushers us through the final gate and waves at us.

"I thought Rebecca terminated or found new jobs for everyone upon taking over," I say. "Why is Sal still working?"

"He and Rebecca's father were in the Great Wars," Mom explains. "She must have a heart. Rebecca's father didn't survive."

"Did you see Sal's hand?" I ask. "All the markings? Each mark commemorates his fallen comrades."

"That's a lot," Tevan says. "I always thought he had a skin rash. Is that why Grandpa has the markings on his hand as well?"

"Yes, and you'd know that if you didn't ditch going to their farm for basic training," I say, and Mom laughs.

"Kaya, I just outgrew the hunting, farming, and survival

training. It was great when we were kids, but who dumps their grandkids six miles from civilization and tells them to sink or swim? He made us survive for three days and get back home. Aunt Karen refused to let the boys go back after that." Tevan sticks out her lower lip in a pout.

"He said it would separate the men from the babies. And Stevie still goes occasionally," I say.

"Have his challenges become harder?" Tevan asks. Mom looks at us in disbelief.

"Last year he made me camp near a known site of a rabid boar, but I never found it," I say. Mom gasps, nearly stopping the car. "Grandpa wants us to be ready for anything, and he gave me and Stevie a big knife."

"I told you Grandpa has lost it," Tevan says.

We see a wall covered in pictures, and my mom stops the car.

"What is that?" I ask. Along the wall are candles, bears, and all types of mementoes. "This is bad. Look at how long the wall stretches."

"What is it?" Tevan asks. She begins reading the signs and posters.

"Missing people," I say.

"Why is this not on the news?" Tevan asks, and I roll my eyes.

"Censorship of a corrupt government," I say. "You'd think the candidates would bring it up with possible solutions to help as their platforms. Some of these date back years." I take out my phone and snap a few pictures.

Just then, a few of the Axis militia take notice of us.

"What are they doing this far outside of Axis?" I ask Mom, as she tugs on Tevan and me.

"I don't know, but we need to leave," she says.

We continue to the nail salon, and for the rest of the way, we are all quiet. I review the pictures of men, women, and children. Tevan and my mother begin to quietly talk once more.

When we stop for lunch, I notice a few familiar cars from the wall. "Mom, are we going to be followed everywhere from now on?" I ask.

"I don't know, but life is changing, and as your father said, we are going to have to adjust."

"At least we will be safe from such tragedy like those on the wall," Tevan says.

"I thought you said it was a conspiracy," I snap.

"Let's go, girls," Mom insists as guards from Axis pretend not to watch us. We go to a few stores, but everyone is quiet, and we look over our shoulders uneasily for the rest of the day. My mother wants to get back into Axis before nightfall.

When we get home my mother immediately speaks to my father privately, and Tevan begins primping for what I assume is a date with Jonathon.

"Kaya, can I borrow the shoes I bought for your birthday?" Tevan asks as she walks into my room without knocking.

"No, they are a treasured gift," I say as I turn on music.

"Kaya, be serious." She turns off my music.

"I adore those shoes. It would break my heart to see them on another person before I wear them." I decide to try them on but quickly realize she bought them in her size. "Why do you even buy me gifts?" I ask

She smiles. "Because Mom takes me out of Axis to shop. I say I'm trying to help you, which is impossible, and I get a new outfit for my efforts."

I roll my eyes. "You are evil." She looks at the clothes adoringly. "Night out with Jonathon?"

"Just a friend," she says.

I mime throwing up. "You are such a bad liar. Do Mom and Dad know you are dating your teacher for grades?"

She looks horrified. "The last of my exams will be Tuesday, and I hate you."

The phone rings, and she answers it.

"Who calls the house anymore?" I ask, picking up a magazine.

I hear her say, "You want to speak to whom? Kaya, as in Kaya Lewis?"

I peek over my magazine and give her an inquisitive look.

"Kaya, it's for you." Tevan hands me the phone.

When I answer, the person on the other end of the line says, "Hey, Kaya. What are you doing?"

"Reading a magazine." I look at Tevan, trying to figure out to whom I'm speaking. "Did I win something because I can't order anything. I don't have credit cards."

The person on the other end laughs. "This is Talon," he says.

"How primitive to call on a landline. I thought only grandparents and telemarketers did that. Oh, and politicians during election season. So if this is a call on behalf of your mom wanting my vote, she wouldn't get it."

Tevan hits me and whispers, "Don't be rude." I slap at her.

Talon laughs. "I wouldn't vote for her either. I was calling you on this primitive device because I didn't want to just show up at your house unannounced, and I didn't have any way of contacting you. I was wondering if I could take you out for dinner this evening."

I just freeze. "I think I'm grounded," I say.

Tevan begins jumping up and down excitedly. "Say yes," she whispers. "I'll talk to Mom."

I shove her face away.

"It would just be two old friends, catching up," Talon says.

"Just two friends," I say.

"Yes."

"Okay."

"I'll pick you up at seven," he says.

The second I hang up the phone, I shove Tevan. "What is wrong with you? Are you a lunatic?"

She ignores my questions and tries to put makeup on me. "You have to let me do your makeup and hair. You should wear this outfit."

I toss the outfit she bought me for my birthday on the floor. "No!" I snap.

She starts yelling at my mom. "Mom, Kaya has a date."

"With who?" my mom asks.

Tevan touches my hair. "Talon Dean."

"It's not a date," I insist as my mom joins us.

"How nice," she says in a strange voice.

Tevan's eyes get dreamy. "Just when I thought we were upper level since Dad sold out Axis, Kaya begins dating Talon. His mom is almost president of all of Nambitus, and then there's his car. This is sure to put us at the top again."

"That's it. I'm not going," I say. Tevan stomps her foot, and Mom laughs. "I wasn't going for any of those reasons."

Tevan continues fussing with my hair. "Every girl throws herself at Talon and for some strange reason he is drawn to Kaya. It must be her smart mouth. You should see how he dresses. He is so mysterious," Tevan gushes.

"Don't you have your own date to prepare for?" I ask.

"I do, but this takes precedence."

I shake her off and I grab a pair of jeans.

Tevan looks aghast. "Kaya, please, for the future of our entire family, do not wear those jeans; they look worn."

"They are new, Tevan. Mom bought them for my birthday." I finish dressing and do a spin.

"Why won't you cut your hair?" Tevan asks.

"Mom, tell Tevan to find a hobby," I beg as I begin to put on my favorite pair of shoes.

"Kaya, those are ancient," Tevan says.

"*Mom*," I say.

"Tevan, focus on your date, and let Kaya have hers." Mom says as she makes a face at me.

"It's not a date!" I snap. They quickly leave my room.

I can't believe I let my mom and Tevan get in my head, but for some reason I am nervous. I look in the mirror, adjust my necklace, and try not to think about how badly I want to talk to Matt about what I saw in Lexicon today. He probably already knows and has a well-researched theory. As I place on my tracker, the doorbell rings.

"Kaya, you're up!" Dad yells.

I smooth my hair and then almost slap myself because that was a Tevan move. I walk downstairs to find Talon visiting with my dad and Tevan drooling, which makes me want to slap her. My mom has one of those *I'm going to remember this moment for the rest of my life* looks. Whether I like it or not, this is a date.

Talon holds the door open for me, and Tevan looks about to faint.

"Sorry about my family," I say as we get outside.

"They're nice," he says.

"Tevan says I should be impressed by your car."

Talon laughs. "Most people are."

"I'm not."

He chokes. "Okay." I look around. "Do you want to get in?" he asks.

I shrug my shoulders. "I don't know. It might be nice to rub it in Tevan's face."

He smiles and opens the passenger door. "I'll let you drive it sometime," Talon says. "You look nice, by the way."

"Tevan did it."

He smiles. "So Tevan thought this is a date?"

"She loves fairy tales."

"Jonathon better be careful or she'll nail him down quick," Talon says.

I laugh. "She's been planning their wedding since junior high." I realize suddenly where Talon is driving. "We're leaving Axis?" I ask.

"Yeah, there's just not a lot of eating options within the golden gated city," Talon says. I start to panic a little. "Is everything all right?"

"Yes, I noticed there were quite a few people missing, even more so than the conspiracy channel has reported."

Talon nods, smiling and trying not to laugh. "The conspiracy channel. I'll let you in on a secret. We live in Axis, so we are under constant surveillance so that we're protected. You're safe." He taps on his rearview mirror.

I turn around to see a car changing lanes to get behind us. "I noticed that as well. It's awkward." I slump in the seat.

"My mom has goons everywhere. You have to learn not to take it personally." When I get quiet, he asks, "What are you thinking?"

"I don't know whether to feel safe or violated."

"Quite the conundrum," Talon says, smiling. "What did you do on your outing?"

I hold up my hands and wiggle my fingers, showing off my manicure.

"I didn't take you for that type," Talon says.

"I'm not, but Tevan will do anything to get a manicure, even on my birthday."

He laughs. "So where would you have gone if you could have chosen?"

I think for a moment. "No one has ever asked me, but ...well, I've always wanted to try this crazy international place, ten streets over. I read about it three years ago. I think four or five different people have owned it, but they have kept each person's recipes while adding their own. They say is has a creative culture all its own."

Talon laughs again. "Let's do it."

As Talon pulls up to the restaurant, his eyes get wide. "Interesting," he says.

"Let's have some fun," I say, pulling him inside.

"So, what do you read?" he asks.

"Classics, and you?"

"I prefer modern. In which areas within the hierarchy do you see yourself majoring?" he asks.

"Many, but I plan on being an activist," I answer.

"I plan on the taking a political route," he says as he crosses his arms.

"Interesting." I say.

We study one another.

"Right behind you," Talon says as he points to Axis security.

"I didn't know your mom was so protective," I say.

"She's more protective of her secrets. Business is everything, and now that she has a political future at stake, look out, world." Talon takes a sip of his drink. "What's in this?"

I shrug. "I don't know what anything is on the menu." I point to the guards. "What do they do?"

"They spy and report back. One time I had a few weeks off from school, and I set up a kidnapping to see what would happen. I think her guards spend more time with me than she does. Once, I set it up to look like I was selling her secrets. She was more upset over the possibility of her secrets being dispersed."

Talon laughs as the servers bring us our food. I look at him strangely.

"What?" he asks.

"So you stage kidnappings and sell secrets to get your mom's attention?" I ask.

"I'm complicated," Talon answers, and then he asks, "What is this?"

"Adventure."

"Don't think I am weird. I usually don't talk about my mom."

I laugh. "I don't think you're weird, but it tells me so much," I assure him. He squints at me. "So where have you been the past six years?"

He cringes. "Well, let's dive right in. I've been in boarding schools. One after another. Not so fun. When Mommy Dearest hops the globe, I do as well. She doesn't like to deal with me, and she doesn't like to share me with my dad, so off to a new boarding school I go, if I'm not kicked out first."

When I laugh, he asks me why I'm laughing. I can only shake my head. "I don't know. That is horrible. I'm so sorry. I just have this thing—I laugh at the worst times."

He grins at me. "Well, stop it. I need you to feel sorry for me. Girls never laugh or try to analyze me. The sad stories, car, and clothes all work for me."

"You mean girls buy into the facade?" I ask, and he nods.

"Yes."

"Oh." I try to compose myself.

"Are you finished?" he asks.

I try not to laugh. "Yes. I truly am sorry about the boarding schools and your mom."

He glares at me.

"So, you are a ladies' man?" I ask.

"I didn't mean to say that."

I begin laughing once more, and reach across the table to try something off his plate.

"Kaya!" Talon snaps at me. "I'm glad you did that. I wanted to try this." He grabs something green off mine.

"We are merely two friends, catching up," I insist.

He seems suddenly flustered. "Do you know you are a difficult person?"

I smile. "Undoubtedly. Not many people can put up with me— or so I'm told."

He quirks his eyebrow. "So who puts up with you?"

"Well, usually just Matt. You saw how many friends I have at school."

"And Matt? This friendship?" Talon asks.

I quirk my eyebrow in return. "Oh, you want to know if there's something more between us than friendship?"

"No. Well, maybe."

"But Talon, you know so many ladies. Why would you be bothered with me?"

"You happen to be different than most girls. Most girls are like Tevan and want to go to expensive restaurants and are impressed by my car. You couldn't care less. Plus, Matt always tries to keep you for

57

himself. He's had you to himself for six years. I've dated hundreds of girls. I should get to hang out with you too."

I just stare at him.

"What?" Talon asks.

"I don't know if you want me to be grossed out or impressed by the fact that you've dated hundreds of girls since you've traveled the world with so much money. And I don't know if I should be flattered or insulted that you are offering to share custody of me with Matt, rather than fighting it out like you usually do, so kudos on the step toward civilization. I think the only compliment you gave me was that I wasn't like Tevan, but you probably meant you could save money on showing me a good time."

Talon shakes his head, and I start to stand up.

"Kaya, stop. I knew I'd do this. I always mess up when I am around you." When I pause, he says, "You make me nervous. I tell you things I'd never confess to another living soul. I'm sorry. Please sit, and I'll act like when we were kids. I won't put on a show. I'll be myself."

I glare at him. "You promise?"

"I promise."

I offer my hand for him to shake, like when we were kids. "Best behavior," I say as I edge my way back in the booth.

"Of course. It's me. Best behavior."

I study him through narrowed eyes. "Last time you promised best behavior you tried to play doctor with me."

He smiles. "Then I promise nothing because I always offer a good time." As I get up once more, he says, "All right, I promise best behavior."

I sit down again, this time next to him.

"So what did you see today at the wall with the missing people?"

I pull up the pictures to show him.

"Do you mind if we drive by after dinner?" he asks.

When we get to the Wall of the Missing, it is beautifully lit up with candles. Loved ones are mourning and placing items. A dark-haired woman kisses a picture of a child and then lovingly places it on the wall. A block down, an elderly woman, escorted by her children, places a flyer of an elderly man, last seen watering his yard.

"This is surreal," Talon says as we watch.

I see a man with a computer to the side. "Excuse me—are you a reporter or policeman?" I ask

He keeps typing but answers. "No, I'm a statistician." He looks up at the new flyers and posters.

"Is it an illness, nomads, or some type of enemy?" I ask.

He looks up at me over the rim of his glasses. "We don't know, and many people are not reporting their missing to the police because of distrust. Private agencies are handling the cases. Either way, no one ever comes home. Bodies are never recovered. It has been going on for years, but the media won't cover it."

"Will this ever be made public?" I ask.

He closes his computer. "I am not at liberty to discuss that."

Talon pulls me toward the car.

"Are you all right?" I ask, as Talon seems somber.

"Why would my mom want to be in Lexicon?" he asks.

I shake my head. "It is the most powerful city on earth."

"With the highest crime rates on the planet. Some of the kids missing were last seen in the area where we will attend school. It's like she's using our going to Lexicon schools for her political gain."

"Talon, just like tonight, it will be an adventure."

He quirks his eyebrow. "It's my fault we're going to school in Lexicon. My mom told me I had to be an upstanding student, and the first thing I did was pick a fight with Larkin, ruining it for all of us. I always let my temper get the best of me. I'm sorry."

"I think your mom had plans for the schools. She needed labs. I overheard my dad ranting."

Talon nods. "Of course, but because of the changes she had in the works, she needed me to be me so I would walk the line out of guilt."

I place my hand on his. "We'll get through it. All together," I say.

"Some of us can't even speak to each other. Matt and Emily can't speak to us any longer. I'm sorry, Kaya. I never wanted this. As much as I fight with Larkin, I don't think I'm better than he is. He's always been Matt."

I nod. "I know."

We begin the process of getting through Axis security.

Slow Sal McCoy doesn't want to let Talon through, which amuses me.

"He's with me, Sal." I say, and Sal waves us through.

Talon scowls. "Does he not know who I am? I own this place."

I roll my eyes. "But *I* did last week. I should have said you were trying to invade and were my kidnapper."

Talon laughs.

Later, when he takes me home, Talon gets quiet.

"I had a nice time," I say as we pull up in front of my house.

"I did too," he says. Just then, Talon tries to kiss me.

"What are you doing?" I ask.

Talon freezes. "Nothing."

"I don't think we are to that point," I say.

He intentionally hits his head on the steering wheel.

"What's wrong?" I ask.

"I have humiliated myself this evening. Just go."

I slowly get out of his car. "Good night," I say as I close the door.

Talon slowly drives away.

As I walk up to my door, I hear a rustling in a bush. I know it's a kidnapper that somehow breached security and followed us into Axis. Rather than push my tracker, which contains an alarm, or scream for help, I grab a rock, take aim, and throw it at my assailant. The dark figure doubles over. I run at the shadowy figure and punch him right in the face.

"Ouch!" he says. I grab his hair. "Kay. Stop."

I let go of his hair at the sound of his familiar voice. "Matt, I'm sorry." I pull him inside and try to sneak around my kitchen. I get a wet cloth to clean his face.

"Why are you cleaning my face?" he asks as I dab around his eyes.

"The rock I grabbed apparently was muddy," I explain. "Stop moving."

He dodges me. "It hurts. You are so violent."

I smile as I finish cleaning his face. "I know. You know I loved self-defense class." I open the freezer, take out some frozen vegetables, and place them over his eye. "Did I hurt your stomach?" He refuses to let me look, but I lift his shirt to inspect. "Let me see."

He pushes at me. "Did you sneak me in because I'm not allowed to talk to people of your stature any longer?" he asks.

"No, I'm late for curfew." I say.

He lowers his eyes. "It's all right. I shouldn't be here." He tries to get up, but I push him back down in his seat.

"Matthew, always so analytical," I say. Mom comes in from the living room, and I say, "Sorry I broke curfew. Matt is here."

My mom smiles. "Hey, Matt." She then addresses me. "Don't be late again." She tosses Matt his favorite soda and walks back into the living room.

"You are right. You shouldn't be here. My mom is livid."

Matt looks embarrassed.

"Do you want to make out in the streets to see what the people of Axis will do?" I ask.

Matt shakes his head. "What would Talon say?" Matt asks.

"I don't know."

Matt rubs the back of his neck. "You went to dinner with him. Are the two of you a thing?"

"I'm not a thing with anyone," I answer.

Matt gets flustered. "I didn't even get to tell you happy birthday this year because of the new enforcement."

I sit next to him. "You didn't miss much." As I tell him all about my birthday dinner, I lean my head on his shoulder.

Matt then tells me all about practice and his weekend.

When he's finished, I tell him, "I felt like I was going to explode when I didn't get to talk to you. And the way you walked out of the community center ..."

He shakes his head. "The guards were watching like they wanted us to make a mistake. The seating was already segregated when we went in."

I clench his arm because I am so upset. "Since you are the king of research, you might want to know that I found something today in Lexicon." I show him the pictures of all the missing people.

"I'll look into it. Since we can't talk, I'll have more time on my hands," Matt says as he looks away.

"Don't say that. Nothing has to change," I insist. "We are here and talking now. We found a way."

"It felt like an eternity without talking to you. When they said we couldn't talk, I expected you to jump up and argue, but you didn't," Matt says.

"My dad asked me not to," I explain.

"Just think—in two weeks we will be out for summer."

Matt averts his eyes again. "I bet you forget me now that Talon is back in the picture."

"I won't. Who will argue with me and try to set me straight?"

Matt smiles. "I'd better go. I snuck out of my room."

The second Matt leaves, I sit down at the table, which is covered in huge piles of Tevan's graduation announcements and her college applications. All I can think of is how quickly life is spinning and how out of control and unsure I feel about the future. I have to be careful to whom I speak. I will be entering the Lexicon schools, and Tevan will be gone in the fall.

I rest my head on the table. I feel so overwhelmed and anxious that I can't even lift my head, so I just stay there until I fall asleep.

CHAPTER 5

On Sunday morning, I wake up to someone banging on the back door. My neck is stiff from sleeping face down on the table. I can barely lift my head. I slowly open the door to find an entire crew here to install an alarm system within our house.

"Mom, Dad!" I shout as my parents walk into the kitchen. They sit us down for orientation on how to use the system in the event of an Axis breach. Buttons are placed all over. We are then grouped with several other families on the block. We are to use the buddy system in the event of an emergency. Our family was buddied with the four-member Riven family. We are to check on one another, do head counts, and remain in our basements on the off chance security cannot come due to an emergency. We are told horrifying scenarios that include terrorists, gunman, nomads, and even wild animal attacks—all before 9:00 a.m. We are given kits to set up in our basements or safe rooms, with items that include food, first aid supplies, water, and some strange communicator. We are told to expect drills to prepare us in the event of an attack.

I haven't even combed my hair and have mascara under my eye from the night before. To make matters even stranger, Mrs. Riven is a tactical guru and one of the heads of security. As she takes care of our block with extra precautions, all I can do is stand there with my mouth open, in shock at all the what-ifs and buttons hidden around the neighborhood. Suddenly, Axis feels like a hidden-camera reality show, and we were the stars.

"Kaya. Mom told you of the meeting. You look like a train wreck," Tevan says as she smooths her hair.

"I know." I try to recall being told of a meeting.

"This adjourns your safety orientation. Anticipate drills in the near future. If you have any questions, there is a number next to your phone for Axis security," a workman says as he stares at Tevan.

"Thank you," one of the neighbors says. Everyone applauds, and I stand there. As one of the workman gives Tevan extra numbers, my mom smiles.

"Why are you smiling?" I ask.

My mom laughs. "Because I'm going to miss her." She hugs me.

"Me too," I say.

Tevan flips her hair, and we laugh.

For the rest of the day, we finish stocking our basement for the apocalypse and get Tevan's graduation announcements ready.

Monday morning fills me with dread. For once, I don't know how to act or to whom I can speak at school. I slowly get ready.

"Hurry, Kaya!" Tevan shouts from downstairs as I finish brushing my teeth.

"Good morning," I say as I grab my backpack.

"Next year you are going to have to dress for success. You won't have me to smooth things over when you get mouthy," she says.

I tear up and hug her. "I know."

"Wow. You love me," she says.

I nod. "Just a little."

We make our way to the car.

"So how did your date go?" she asks.

"I didn't even have enough time to close the door," I say.

"Details."

"It was all right. Talon got frustrated. I wasn't impressed by his car or stories, and then he broke down and tried to kiss me. When I left, his head was on the steering wheel."

"He likes you," Tevan insists.

"But I'm not relationship material. Why can't we be friends?"

She laughs. "Because you, Matt, and Talon grew up. Matt couldn't stand it, so he stayed outside in the trees."

"Matt is acting so weird about the rules," I say.

"I'm sorry," she says.

We arrive at school, and I ask her, "Who am I going to talk to and fight with next year on the way to school?"

"I was just thinking the same thing. You didn't ask about my date with Jonathon. I adore him."

I shake all over. "Then stop flirting with every guy you see."

She giggles. "I can't help it." Tevan flips her hair.

As I walk into school, I try to flip my hair, but I look as if I am convulsing.

To make matters worse, everyone is awkwardly grouped. Even though we're kids, everyone knows his or her place. Matt, Emily, and a few others chat together, and Tevan and I stand alone.

"Why does it have to be this way?" I ask. Emily is making a huge production of chatting with Matt.

"It should have always been this way to make things easier on the outside. I'll take care of Emily," Tevan says. She's now flirting with Jay.

"This is insane," I say. I take out a book and begin reading.

"Why so glum?" Talon asks. He yanks my book out of my hand, checks the title, and then tosses it.

"I was reading that," I snap.

"Why are you so moody?" he asks.

I point to everyone. "This feels wrong."

"Dramatic," Talon says.

"We're not allowed to speak to one another. The second I walk up, Emily grabs Matt like he's an entrée. Tevan thinks it's a game and in turn goes after Jay. Why would you throw my book? I'm trying to study for my driver's license." I clench my fists.

"It wouldn't bother you unless you have feelings for Larkin. Just like it wouldn't bother Emily unless she has feelings for Jay." Talon says.

I try to pick up my book off the ground, but he runs and grabs it first.

"Stop analyzing me, and leave me alone," I say.

"Admit it. That is why you wouldn't let me kiss you. Plus, I deserve the chance to analyze you because you traumatized me last night."

"I merely listened to your life stories and questioned you," I insist.

Talon laughs. "These driver's manuals are stupid. Let me take you driving." As I try to get my book back, Talon says, "Why does Larkin have a black eye?"

"I gave it to him by accident because I thought he was an intruder," I answer.

Talon laughs. "Who needs guards?"

"Don't tell anyone I talked to him."

Talon shakes his head. "I think Lexicon rules are stupid. If it helps, when we go to the Lexicon schools next school year, we won't even notice each other." Talon hands me my backpack.

"Thanks," I say quietly. I try to wrap my mind around being in school with so many new faces.

"Remind me to never make you mad. I'll pick you up for driving lessons after school," Talon whispers in my ear as we walk into school.

Lunch seems strange when everyone sits segregated. Tevan and the other seniors get out note cards and begin studying.

"Why are they like robots?" Talon asks. He takes a seat next to me as I look up from my driver's manual.

"Because Axis kids get into the best colleges. Look at the juniors; they are a little more relaxed," I say.

"You don't seem concerned," Talon says.

"Nor do you, and frankly, I couldn't care less."

He grabs my manual and begins quizzing me.

"Watch Tevan move her seat away from Jay and Dave when Jonathon walks into the room," I say. "She is such a flirt."

"Is that bad?" Talon asks.

"She's predictable." I say.

"You aren't, and it tends to drive me a bit mad," Talon says.

I make a face at him and eat my apple.

After school, Talon picks me up to help me practice driving in a vacant lot.

"Now you move to shift like this," Talon says as he places his hand over mine.

"Talon, I've been driving all over Axis since I was ten. I took my parents' old car."

"They didn't mind?" he asks.

"They were dedicated to their professions, so I ran the streets," I say. "Can we drive by the library, honk at Tevan, and go into Lexicon?" I ask.

Talon hits his head against the back of the seat.

"I promise I am a good driver," I say.

"All right," Talon says.

I get excited, and I hug him.

"We have to do this right," Talon says. He places sunglasses on my face and then on his. "Music is key." He turns up the volume.

"How do you stand this?" I yell.

"Act cool, and when they see us, pretend not to notice!" he shouts as he rolls the windows down.

"Why?" I ask.

"Because that is the cool thing to do, Kaya. I don't make the cool rules."

I laugh.

"Now let's roll," Talon says.

When we get to the library, everyone is outside, taking a break from studying. I drive by, music blaring, and then I get in the lane to leave Axis. The last thing I see is Tevan's jealous face, which is glorious.

"Where's your friend Slow Poke?" Talon asks as we get through the gates.

"Monday has always been his day off. He sometimes goes to the Axis park and feeds the pigeons, and other times he visits his daughter in Lexicon."

Talon just shakes his head. "Do the people in Axis know everything about one another?" he asks.

"We are like family. After our scary safety meeting, I know about my new imported neighbors. Even though I am a recluse, I feel it's important. My dad said people were more than just employees."

Talon nods as I change a lane quickly and weave in and out of traffic.

"You are a professional. Are you a secret race car driver?" Talon asks.

"No, I play race car video games in my spare time," I say, as Talon begins laughing hysterically. "I am also a skilled assassin. Feel like robbing a bank or scaling a wall?" I ask as I make fake guns with my fingers.

"Oh my God, Kaya!" Talon says.

I make my way into heavy traffic, and Talon grabs the edge of his seat. "I might have road rage," I say.

"How do you know?" he asks.

"I don't know. I've just always wanted it."

I begin yelling at cars, and he laughs. After I weave in and out of rush-hour traffic, go on and off highways, and yell to my heart's content, Talon and I decide to make our way home.

"That was so much fun," I say as we approach Axis.

"That was something I will never forget," Talon says.

Guards with lights cover the entrance to Axis.

"What's going on?" I ask.

"I don't know," Talon answers. His mom stands on the curb, and a reporter seems to be trying to interview her. I quickly park the car, and Talon jumps out.

"Do you deny there is a problem within Lexicon? Surely,

Candidate Dean, you will voice your concerns on the situation, since it is now at your front door," a reporter says as she chases after Rebecca.

"No comment," Rebecca says, and one of her guards pushes the reporter away.

"What happened, Mom?" Talon asks.

"Get rid of her!" Rebecca snaps, and the guards place the reporter in her van.

"Sal McCoy hasn't answered calls from his daughter since last night, and then when he didn't show up for their weekly visit today, she contacted law enforcement and the media," Rebecca says.

Her guards run out and begin fighting with the various reporters as they try to get a comment.

"I told her I was looking into the matter, but apparently that wasn't good enough. With my being a candidate, the media jumped on the story. This is all I need right now," Rebecca says as she takes out her phone. "What are the damages?" she asks into the phone. Then she turns to her son. "Talon, a word." She pulls him to the side. "Why are you with Kaya, and why is she driving your car?"

I don't hear his response, but he begins arguing with Rebecca. Talon angrily leaves as she continues her call. We get in his car, and he drives me home without talking.

"That wasn't awkward?" I say.

"So, you caught that?" Talon asks. "My mom feels that there is tension with her and your dad, and I'm possibly into you because of those reasons."

"Is it true?" I ask.

"No matter the reason. It sweetens the deal."

I stare at him. "Thanks."

We pull up in front of my house. "Why do I always say the wrong thing with you?" he asks.

I shrug my shoulders. "I don't want to be some pawn in a game you use to get back at your mom."

"I just can't help myself with you," he insists.

"I'd better go." I get out of the car.

The next day, I walk downstairs slowly before school. It was going to be Tevan's last day.

"Kaya, I have my last final!" she exclaims. "Am I taking you to school, or is Talon?"

I roll my eyes. "We're just friends."

"She was driving his car, Mom," Tevan says.

"That sounds fun," my mom says as she pores over books, trying to get ready for her new job.

"Mom is like me, Tevan," I tell her. "She could not care less that Talon's car cost more than this block."

"Kaya, be careful in that death trap," my mom says, and Tevan seems irritated.

"I will." I stick out my tongue at Tevan.

"Make sure the two of you are wearing your trackers. No one has seen Sal," my mom says; his daughter's interview is on the news. "Do well on your examines today," she calls after us as we run out the door.

"I can't believe Mom doesn't care that Talon drives a one-of-a-kind car from a magazine that was designed just for him," Tevan says when we get outside.

"Why don't you date Talon?" I ask.

She shakes her head. "The Talberts founded Lexicon."

I roll my eyes.

When we get to school, I decide to stay by myself.

"When's the big driving exam?" Talon asks as he takes my manual.

"Any time I want. I'm ready."

He hands me a small box. "I didn't get you a birthday gift, and I'm constantly putting my foot in my mouth, so ..."

I open it. "A rabbit's foot keychain," I say as I hold it up.

"It's for luck—for when you take your driving exam. The lady at the gas station insisted it's lucky."

I begin laughing. "Thank you," I say. The bell rings, and I walk over to show Tevan.

As I latch my gift on my backpack, Emily says, "Why would he give you a gas station key chain? It's fitting he would spend as little money as possible on you. He bought a czar's daughter diamonds. I read it in a tabloid."

"I guess we should be proud of you for reading, Emily," I snap.

Matt gives me a look, and a few people laugh.

One of the new teachers approaches us and asks, "Is there a problem?"

I shake my head. "No more than usual."

"Was one of our students out of line?" she asks, looking at Emily.

"No," I answer.

"Good," she says.

Emily walks to the opposite side of the hall, and I quickly go to class.

"You could have gotten Emily in trouble," Tevan says.

I pick up a book. "I know, but it is no one's business what we say to one another. Plus, if anyone is going to get Emily, it will be me on my terms."

After lunch, I find a note in my locker. I know exactly who it is from and where to meet by the handwriting. I just can't believe Matt wants to meet during school hours. I wait until class starts and double-check that he has indeed skipped. I walk behind the back of the school through thick grass and trees until I get to a field where Matt and I would go camping when we were kids. At one time, there was a pond, but it's a puddle now.

"Kaya, were you followed?" Matt asks

"No, were you?" I ask, laughing.

"No. I had to get out of there," he says.

I take a seat next to him on the ground. "I can't believe you ditched school. You even begged your mom to go when you had chicken pox."

"I had a mini-project, and I couldn't let you present it without me," Matt explains. "I've noticed a change in you."

I wait for him to elaborate. When he doesn't, I finally ask, "What do you mean?"

"Talon and you are disastrous," Matt says.

I smile. "We do have fun, but I have fun with you as well."

"Have you even started studying for finals?" Matt asks.

I begin digging through his bag. "No, Dad, but I bet you made me note cards." I find my copies.

"I found information on the missing people of Lexicon on many conspiracy websites," Matt says as he hands me a few stacks of papers. "I had to research in Lexicon because all the sites were blocked throughout the Axis server. As soon as I began at the Lexicon library, I had company from some tech guys that shut me down on every computer, but here's what I found."

I begin looking. "As you ordered," I say, as I throw him a player with music on it.

"Thank you. Did you ever find my other music player?"

"I told you I gave that back, Matthew."

We each take an ear piece, and I begin going through all the theories, which range from aliens, to big company abductions, to nomad ransoms resulting in death, and possible acts of terrorism related to another Great War.

"Matt, there are so many theories and no answers," I say as the music runs out. "I hate this."

"I do too, but now, since Sal went missing and with all the media attention around Axis, maybe we can get answers. This is life now. With cameras everywhere, we need to take this chance to talk."

I stare at him. "Is this about that thing with Emily? I hate her, but I would never get her in trouble."

"She still got in trouble," Matt explains.

"I said there wasn't a problem."

"But she is lower than you."

"I don't think like that," I say.

"You don't, but everyone else does. We are going to get caught Kay. There are consequences, and between the cameras and the media watching Axis, we can't keep this up."

I try to think of a way to stop him from making a decision we'll both regret. "I would say it's my fault," I say.

"I know, and I wouldn't let you do that. You have a good future, and mine isn't so bad."

I start to get upset. "Don't, Matt. You are my best friend, and your future is just as good as mine."

He looks away. Matt hesitates for a moment and then takes my face in his hands. "Kaya, don't make this any harder than it has to be. You have Talon, and I don't mean that in a mean, jealous way, even though I am jealous because he gets to be around you. It will all be all right."

"You are not good at this," I say.

"Is it better than the time you broke your arm, and I had to comfort you until Tevan got your dad?" he asks.

"Please don't try to sing a strange folk song to me," I say.

He smiles. "Promise."

"Why do you always do the right thing, even though it hurts?" I ask, getting upset.

"Because there is not a way to win this. There never was. We got to be friends longer than I thought we would, and it was great."

I try not to cry. "Maybe not speaking up is wrong. I love a fight, and you are worth it."

He shakes his head. "Sorry, this is my decision, and I'm going to stand by it. You could be arrested, or they'll make an example of you."

If there was one thing I knew, it was Matthew Larkin, and when he made up his mind, he was the most stubborn person in the world. "Matt," I say through clenched teeth.

"Kaya," he says back.

"You can't expect me to go along with this," I argue.

"People could get hurt. Most importantly, you could, and then

73

I'd never forgive myself. I'm not good enough for you. We both know I never was," Matt whispers.

I fall to the ground and he sits down next to me. I lay back to look at the sky.

"Does cloud watching make it better?" he asks.

"I never thought I'd hear you say that, and it makes me angry." I say, and he closes his eyes. I lean over him. "Never say that again."

"We always knew," Matt says. He lifts a strand of my hair and tucks it behind my ear. "I'd better go."

I begin to take off my necklace, but he stops me. "Keep it," he insists.

"So never again will I talk to you? Matthew Larkin never existed?" I ask, and he nods. "What if we use our phones or meet late at night?"

He shakes his head. "No."

"You're killing me, Matt."

He gets up to leave. "I'll miss you every day," Matt says, and he does our special signal.

"Bye, Matt," I say as he walks away.

As Matt leaves, I try to keep it together. I want to scream, cry, and throw a fit about living in Lexicon. I don't even remember getting home.

"Did you get out early?" my mom asks.

I shake my head. "I was sick. So I just left."

Mom feels my face. "You don't feel warm, but you look a fright. Get upstairs, and I'll bring you some soup." She takes my backpack.

I throw myself on my bed and cry. How could someone I have known for so long decide to end our friendship? I was willing to risk everything—but then again, I didn't protest the verdict at the meeting when it was handed to us. I hate Rebecca Dean. I hate Axis. I envy Tevan for getting to leave and go to college after summer break.

Just when I think I might be finished soaking in my own

self-pity, I hear Tevan run in the house, screaming. I sit up and nearly fall out of bed.

"I am in! I got in, Mom!" she screams. She runs up the stairs and calls to me, "Kaya, I got into Silverton!"

I smile. "That's close and the best school in Lexicon," I say. I hug her and then throw myself back on my bed and pull the covers over my head. Tevan looks at me strangely but quickly starts making calls.

My mom tries to get me to go to school the next day, but I clearly do not care about seeing Emily gloat over my misery. I need more time to pout; plus, my mom made the best potato soup, even though she's such a bad cook. I suspect it came from a can, but I never question it.

On Friday our family is piling into Lexicon near Axis for graduation. This will be the first year that graduation is held outside Axis, due to safety. Talon stops by after school to bring me my study guides for my semester exams.

"Kaya," he says as he taps on my bedroom door. He pops his head in. "Oh my God. You look disgusting," he says.

I place a pillow over my head. "Leave me alone, Talon."

"I don't want to be in here any longer than I have to be. It smells."

I throw my pillow and hit him.

"Put the pillow back over your hair," Talon says.

"What do you want?" I ask.

"You have a driving test tomorrow, and then all your finals are next week. You were supposed to be my study buddy." He hands me a pile of books, but I shove them on the floor.

"I know. I can't," I say.

He tries to find a place to sit but eventually gives up. "I think I'll just stand," he says as he scrapes his hand on my television stand. "Please go to your test. I know you're ready. And call me on Sunday after Tevan's graduation, and we'll study for exams."

I wave my hand in his direction, signaling him to leave.

"Look, Kaya, I don't know what you're going through, but I'm here."

I hide my face and wait for him to leave.

No matter what I might do, I can't pull myself together. I need to focus on Tevan's big day and my exams. I have to quit thinking about Matt and every memory we shared—walking home every day, our phone conversations, listening to music, arguing, camping, and everything else. He was the one who ditched me, even though he felt he had to. I am so angry! I punch my pillow until the seams burst. Every time anger consumes me, sadness sets in, and I restart the cycle. I lie on my bed, looking at the ceiling, until I think I might go mad.

I finally get up and clean my room, and then I get ready for Tevan's dinner. I even put on a dress. I stay at the back during Tevan's graduation party. The only person I want to see is Grandpa. As I walk to the restroom, I hear a strange noise from a nearby room and follow the sound.

"What would happen if you were attacked after investigating this sound?" my grandpa asks.

"I'd grab those large candleholders and bash your skull in," I say.

He applauds. "Good job. Remember we ran out of ammunition and had to engage in hand-to-hand combat in the latter half of the Great Wars. Candleholders were a valuable commodity."

I hug him. "I've missed you, Grandpa," I say, and I cry a little.

"No tears; that is for captives. For my beautiful granddaughter, I will make an exception. Is everything all right?"

I nod. "Everything has been changing, and I just need familiar scenery."

He smiles. "Well, you are in luck because summer is just around the corner."

This excites me. "I need a trip to the farm," I say.

A look of relief spreads across his face.

"What's wrong?" I ask.

He nearly tears up. "Your grandma and I had almost counted

you out because you're getting your driver's license. Driver's licenses usually mean good-bye to summers with Grandma and Grandpa."

I hug him once more. "I'll be there," I say.

"Good, now I have to test Stevie. He's getting his license too. He's a blubbering baby and on his way to the restroom." My grandpa walks out with a candleholder. I wait until I hear Stevie scream. "Blubbering baby," I whisper as I walk out.

When I return to the party, it is quite alive. People are dancing and spinning. There are streamers everywhere, and music is playing.

"Kaya, you missed it," Tevan says, jumping up and down. "Jonathon asked me to marry him, and I said yes!"

Everyone stares at me to see my reaction. "You are just eighteen and about to go off to college. Why would you want to be engaged? Is there a reason?" I look pointedly at her midsection.

She rolls her eyes. "No, stupid. We are going to have a long, romantic engagement. It is all the rage." She runs off squealing with my cousins.

I take a seat by Jonathon. He's watching Tevan. "Are you sure about this?" I ask, pointing to all of my family running around.

"Of course I am. I just want you to have a good time. It's a party, Kaya, not school." Jonathon laughs.

"I've never seen you like an actual person," I say.

"It's because you don't like me," he insists, though he offers a smile.

"You're right," I say. Tevan is smiling and showing off her ring. "She's young and impressionable."

Jonathon looks at me strangely. "And you are so wise?"

I look at him and nod. "Why would you ask a little kid to marry you?" I ask.

"She's been dropping hints for two years, and it's not like we're getting married tomorrow. I still have four years left of college and a lab internship. Plus, look at her and look at me."

I laugh as I look him over. "You are right. She's beautiful. I would put a ring on her too."

"Tonight, we dance," Jonathon says. He tries to pulls me into a line.

"I don't like dancing," I say, but Jonathon rolls his eyes.

"Consider it payback for you and Talon throwing food at me."

I lower my eyes. "You figured that out?"

He pulls me into a dance. "Paybacks, Kaya."

My aunt tugs on me, but I refuse to move.

"For me?" he says. "I'll give you an A on your semester exam."

I grin at him and join in.

As we dance, a strong wind blows through the doors. People who are out on the balcony run in, and tables overturn from the impact. "What is happening?" I ask.

Jonathon pulls me behind an overturned table. "I don't know. I have never felt winds so strong."

People are shoved backwards, hitting walls, trying to get to safety. Glass breaks, and a piece of it hits my aunt in her arm. Within minutes, it is over. As we rush out to the balcony, we see people on the streets come out from hiding, confused over what has occurred.

The following day, the news reports offer no answers on the occurrence of the winds, and Lexicon tries to recover from the damages caused by the five minutes of terror.

I ace my driving exam—with my lucky rabbit's foot in my pocket—and I'm excited to tell someone of my success. I forgot my phone, so I can't call anyone. Since everyone at my house is getting ready for Tevan's graduation, I decide to stop by Talon's house. Maybe he will forgive me for my behavior from the day before.

When I get there, I am promptly directed to a guest house. His mom has already had a pool installed. I hear music as I knock; a strange girl answers the door.

"Can I help you?" she asks. She's wearing a tiny robe and the world's smallest bikini.

"I'm looking for Talon," I say, "but I can see he is probably busy."

She gives me a quirky smile. "I'll tell him you stopped by."

I hear rustling in the background, but I just thank her and walk away. As I do, Talon calls to me.

"Kaya!" As he approaches, he is wearing only a pair of swim shorts. "I see you met Elle," he says as a large group exits his guest house.

"Yes, she seems lovely," I say.

"I went to a concert last night and made some friends. After the windstorm, I thought, why let the fun stop, so here we are."

"I should have called first. I just wanted you to know that I aced my driving test."

Elle kisses him on the cheek. "Great party, Talon," she says as she winks at me.

"I'd better go too," I say.

"Why? We should celebrate," Talon says.

I get in my car to leave, Talon tries to follow but is preoccupied with guests, especially Elle, who wants his undivided attention.

For the rest of the day I focus on getting ready for Tevan's graduation ceremony. Tevan, as always, looks amazing. She is the valedictorian, and her speech moved the entire audience to tears. I expected nothing less.

My aunt Carol says to me, "I can't wait to hear your speech in a few years." I cringe a little. I didn't have Matt competing with me the past few weeks so my grades have slipped. I'm clearly losing my edge. After dinner I decide to study for finals. I have never studied by myself. Talon bombards me with messages, but I ignore him. I feel it's for the best if I stay clear of him.

On Monday morning I am ready to conquer the world. Tevan gets to sleep late, so she allows me to borrow her car. Talon tries to talk to me, but I ignore him. I pass all of my exams, and by lunchtime Talon clearly decided he's going to speak to me one way or another.

"Kaya, talk to me, or I will make a scene!" Talon shouts.

I look up from a book. "What?" I ask quietly.

"Why won't you speak to me?"

"I've been busy," I explain.

"Doing what?" he asks.

"Studying," I answer.

"You were supposed to study with me."

"I thought you would have a better time studying with Elle and your new friends. I wondered all weekend how you snuck them in."

"All you have to ask is how I snuck in people from a concert into Axis? You avoided my calls after I was so sympathetic to you."

I roll my eyes. "Well, after I went over to your house, I didn't feel like talking any longer, just like now."

"That's not fair. You pout over Larkin for a week, but I go out one night, and then you come over—unannounced, I might add—and I am crucified for getting together with a couple of friends." Talon says. Everyone turns their attention toward us.

"I went over to apologize to you for my behavior, and I would never pout over Larkin. I wasn't well," I say.

"You were a jerk and are still being a jerk. You won't allow me to apologize," Talon says.

"You call this an apology? Accusing me of weeping over Larkin? How were you to know I was even there when you were so hung over?" I accuse him, and everyone gasps.

I try not to look at Matt because I know he's giving me the *shut up, Kaya* look, but I need to get my frustrations out. If Talon wants to be that person, then I am willing to oblige.

"At least I know how to have fun," Talon says.

I laugh. "How? Getting drunk with strangers? You are so cool, Talon. Shall I take notes on your rebellious nature?"

Talon grabs the side of his head in frustration.

"Usually it's Kaya fighting with Matt. Now it's Talon," Emily whispers.

I cringe a bit and give her a look.

"I hate the fact that you have gotten to me. I don't even like you that much," Talon says.

I pick up my book and begin reading. "Well, then leave me be. Problem solved."

"She always has to have the last word," another kid says as Talon slams a chair into the table and leaves the cafeteria.

"What did you just say?" I ask.

Matt shakes his head and the girl gets wide-eyed. "Enough, Kaya," Matt says quietly.

I try not to quirk my eyebrow. I excuse myself.

The rest of the day seems like a silent film. No one talks, and everyone avoids me in the halls. I think that it has always been like that; I just never noticed. I take my tests and drive home. The rest of the week has the same melancholy feel. Before we even finish our tests and clear out our lockers, demolition begins on the building for the Thantos labs. I steal my mom's nameplate from the front of her office, as well as my and Matt's locker numbers as mementoes.

The second that school gets out, I get ready for my trip to my grandparents. "Are you sure you won't go overseas with us?" my mom pleads. "We'll be celebrating Tevan's graduating."

"I already have made plans," I say as I pack a huge knife.

"Kaya, this is alarming, and after what Aunt Karen told me, Stevie isn't even going back this summer."

I begin laughing. "Mom, Stevie is a baby, and the only reason he fell into that beehive last summer was because he couldn't read his map." I throw in my compass.

"I think I am going to talk to your grandpa," she says.

"No, because I am the longest running grandkid and that means this summer I get to actually train. I'll be fine," I reassure her. I dig out her nameplate from my backpack and hand it to her. "I stole this since they were destroying the place anyway. I love you, Mom."

She tears up. "I love you too, and I want you to have an amazing summer." She kisses the top of my forehead. "With that being said, you have a visitor, and he's just in time before Grandpa gets here."

It's Talon. "Are you going to boot camp?" he asks.

I grab my bag and boots. "No," I answer as I cross my arms.

"I came by to make things right before I leave," he says. I stare at him. "I'm going to be in Europe this summer, like you."

"I'm not going with my family" I tell him. "I'm going to the farm with my grandparents." "Why?" he asks. When I glare at him, he says, "I was just kidding. Being on a farm sounds amazing."

"I like hanging out with my grandparents. I have since I was a kid, and I thought, why break tradition?"

He smiles. "I'm sorry for being hungover and then an even bigger jerk at school," he says.

"I'm sorry for being one too," I say.

"I don't feel we're good," Talon says. I shrug my shoulders. "It will drive me crazy this summer," Talon says.

I smile, and just then my Grandpa pulls up. "Good," I say as I grab my gear and leave.

CHAPTER 6

Traveling through the layers of Lexicon with Grandpa is always an adventure. Grandpa yells at traffic and threatens people who pass by. He charts all the camera systems. At one point, I think we are going to get followed and killed because of Grandpa's road rage. We stay in flea-infested motels because Grandpa is cheap. It's just the same as it has always been.

"The cameras are increasing, even in the bad regions," he says.

"Who would monitor so much of Lexicon?" I ask.

"I don't know—the government or private industry. They're increasing at astronomical rates." He compares maps from previous years; I go back to watching television.

My grandpa allows me to drive the rest of the way to the farm so he can count cameras. As we pull up to the farm, I see it still is picturesque, like something out of a book. I dream about the two-story, yellow-painted farmhouse with white shutters and red barn every year when summer approaches.

"Unload the car, and give it a scrubbing," my grandpa says. He tosses me the keys.

My grandma runs out of the house. "Let me see my little Kaya!" She hugs me and grabs my bags. "I have cookies and milk," she says.

"Stop smothering the kids," my grandpa says, and she gives him a look.

"Come in and tell me all about your school year. We didn't get a chance to talk the other day," she says as I toss the keys back to Grandpa.

"Where's Stevie?" I ask, looking around.

"Well, he's not coming. Your grandpa took away his sunblock last year, and he got a little sunburn. You know how Grandpa overdoes it."

"What a baby," I say.

For the rest of the night we laugh, cook, and sit around the fire.

I wake the next morning with my grandpa standing over me. "Up and at 'em," he says. I pull the covers over my head. "Soldiers do not ignore their commanding officer," he says, and we get in a tug-of-war over my covers.

"Grandpa, it's not even light outside."

He dumps the water from my nightstand over my head.

"Grandpa! Really?"

He snaps his fingers. "Let's go."

I sit up in shock, but grab my gear and boots and go downstairs. I am so sluggish I almost take out a few walls in my path.

"We'll make a morning person out of you," my grandpa says. Grandma pours me some orange juice.

"I seriously doubt that," I say. He hands me a towel to dry my face.

When we get outside, Grandpa decides we need to run a couple of miles as part of basic training. I can barely keep up with him. Then, for a break, he makes me milk the cows. Since my coordination is so poor, he then decides to make me balance buckets of milk while walking across a log over a running stream. This process ends in disaster. I end up downstream, as do the buckets. The stream picks up into a much heavier current, and I can't find a place to get out.

Rather than help me, my grandfather finds it entertaining. "No one will help you out of life's problems, so you'd better get yourself out before the waterfall," he tells me. The scary thing is, I know he means it. Once I am able to get out of stream, he considers that my break because it was my swim time. I have never been more thankful for muddy, murky water with slime on the side. I have trouble finding my glasses because they ended up almost a half mile upstream. Grandpa says glasses are for the weak.

My day ends with foraging and preparing a forest lunch for myself and then getting a review as to what plants to never eat—I ingested a few inedible and paid the consequences. When we get home, we don't even get through the door before Grandpa blames me for dropping the day's milk. I did drop it, but that's because he made me balance over logs.

"It's all right. You know Kaya is uncoordinated," my grandma says. I never knew my poor coordination was family knowledge.

I barely get out of the shower before I fall asleep. I don't even wake up when Grandma calls me for dinner.

I have no choice but to wake up the next morning as Grandpa stands over me.

"Wake up, cupcake," he says.

I scream, "Grandpa, can't the rooster wake me or something?" I can barely stand.

"Sorry I threw you under the bus over the milk. Your grandmother would never let me live it down if I told her I was making you balance milk, and you dropped it. So don't drop it today, or she'll know something is up. I think knowing that Grandma will be upset is the right motivation."

I drop my head into the pillow.

For the rest of the week I run my miles and continue to drop buckets. By week two, Grandpa has added carrying logs to my runs, and water has replaced the milk in the buckets so Grandma won't be mad at us. By the end of week three, I am hauling bales of hay, feeding chickens, and have become a regular farmhand.

On week four, Grandpa goes to an army surplus sale and acquires knives, tents, and camping equipment. After chores, I am to practice my knife throwing and bow-and-arrow shooting on bales of hay.

"You have improved," Grandpa says.

"My dad has an underground shooting range," I say.

"I knew it," Grandpa says.

"Grandpa, he let me shoot, but you can never say anything."

"Bunch of blubbering babies," he says as he rubs his chin.

One evening as I am practicing, a group of black vans drive past the farm, which is strange because hardly anyone goes by the farm, except for old Charlie, who guards the wall, but he drives a beat-up brown car.

"Grandpa, what are vans doing out here?" I ask.

"I don't know," he says, documenting it, "but they are coming more frequently. Ole Charlie takes note too." He closes his notepad.

"So they pass clearance?" I ask.

He nods. "Unmarked. Charlie says his superiors called and told him to let them through."

That night when we get in, my grandma hands me my phone. "Tevan called, and you have been getting messages. She said they ran into a friend of yours, and they miss you."

Tevan sent me pictures of them in Europe. They had run into Talon, and he stopped for a photo. I can tell he's with a girl because although Tevan cropped her out, her hand is visible on his neck. On the girl's wrist is a diamond bracelet.

"I hope they are having fun," I say as I toss my phone on the table.

"What would you like to do this evening?" my grandma asks as we clear the table.

"Let's do the campfire," I say.

She smiles. "All right. The three of us will have a campfire."

Grandpa and I pull up logs in the backyard.

"Talk about the old days, Grandma," I say, and my Grandma laughs.

"The old days. In the United States, life was all right, but the tension over borders and population grew intense within North America and the rest of the world. It's sad how fast people can die because of man's destruction and desire for power. Grandpa and I probably went to war on this very land when we were just a few years older than you. We were recruited, and when the wars got bad and a resolution wasn't in sight, many were killed. They began drafting everyone who was eighteen." Grandpa takes her hand.

"I'm sorry, Grandma. Is it hard to talk about?" I ask.

She shakes her head. "I lost a brother and a sister. Grandpa lost a brother. Starvation, famine, and disease were issues. Other countries all over the world fought with one another. It was a domino effect." Then she points to Grandpa. "I met this one. Every night there were wild parties, and out of all the girls there, he found me."

"What kind of parties?" I ask.

She blushes. "The kind you don't ever need to know about. Let's just say we were all young, and there was a lack of supervision. Well, I wasn't into the party scene because I had sense. I would escape to find a tree, which were scarce because of bombings and fires. All of a sudden, there was this captain there, making it impossible for me to read. I would barter food for books. Soon he began leaving a book or a piece of fruit but never talk to me." She laughs.

"Was he handsome?" I ask.

"He was all right." She laughing again. "I knew that bartering and finding those treasures were not an easy task during a war, so I began leaving him items. We were married halfway through the war." Grandpa winks at her.

"When did it get better?" I ask.

"When the war was over, the government was in chaos," Grandma explains. "We just went to what we knew—planting. Big businesses began and, before too long, the rules of Lexicon. We became the top growers in Lexicon when most were pushed over to Magnis. We stayed in the city for the girls to go to school and allowed someone else to manage the farm, but we weren't cut out for the city life or politics."

"You went into politics?" I ask my grandpa, and he nods.

"For a couple of years," he says. "You didn't think your dad was the only Lexicon man in the family did you?"

"I did," I say.

"How did you think I made all the connections for your mom and your aunts to go to school in that ridiculous Lexicon system in which they've raised all you kids?" he asks.

"I never thought about it. I just always saw you as a killer," I say

He laughs and then says, "It's time to call it a night. Your grandma is insisting I take it easy on you tomorrow."

I give them each a kiss on the forehead. "Good night," I say as I head for the house to turn in.

When I wake up the next day, it is actually past eight o'clock. My grandpa is not standing over me but is downstairs having breakfast. I quietly creep downstairs.

"Grandpa, are you all right?" I ask.

He takes another sip of his coffee and looks over the top of the paper he's reading. "Yes, your grandma has claimed you for the morning, and I get you for the afternoon."

"More kidnappings," I say as I look over the paper.

He points to the conspiracy section. "Yes, nomads are uniting and planning attacks on us."

"What else?" I ask.

"It appears President Dean of the Thantos Corporation will be the next president of Nambitus."

I put my head down on the table.

"You don't like her? I thought you were sweet on her boy."

I lift my head up. "He's a friend … sometimes."

He smiles. "That's my girl. My grandkid hasn't fallen for the lust and lights of Lexicon. Your grandma is waiting for you outside. The next few days will be your vacation because the real test is coming."

I grab some bacon off his plate. "Love you, Grandpa." I leave, letting the door slam. My grandma and I go to the local market, which is much different than the stores in Lexicon. Most of the items are homemade. There are a few stands, animals, and fresh produce.

"So, Grandma, what was life like before the rules?" I ask as we walk.

"People had more choices and life was less structured," she says. "You could talk to whoever you wanted and be what you wanted." I stop to think, but then she says, "I've raised three girls. What are you running from, Kaya?"

"You noticed," I say, and we both smile. "Lexicon and change. I'm tired of everyone expecting me to be something that I'm not sure I want to be."

"My Kaya," she says as she hugs me.

"So what do I do?"

She thinks for a moment. "You can't avoid the change; you just have to conquer whatever challenges it brings with it." I nod. "Look at everything Grandpa and I have overcome that life has thrown at us, and we're still having adventures. Next season I think he wants to move to Magnis." I make a sad face. "It will be all right," she assures me. "You still come and visit. You can travel in between Lexicon and Magnis and fight nomads."

When we get back to the house, Grandpa and I go fishing.

"Grandpa, what's wrong with the sky?" I ask. Clouds have gathered, and there are lightning strikes.

"I haven't seen a tornado in years," he says as he ushers me closer to the house. "They have been obsolete since the wars."

For the rest of the day, Grandpa insists on continuing our assassin training and survival skills close to the house. I am a master at starting fires.

"Kaya, put out your fire," Grandpa says nervously.

I grab water. "What is it, Grandpa?"

He looks through binoculars. "Get your grandmother and get to the cellar!"

Just as I open the screen door, a tornado touches down right outside the wall of Lexicon. My grandma rushes out as it jumps the wall and heads toward the farm. Grandpa grabs us and throws us into the cellar, slamming the door. We wait for what seems like hours as the wind howls and the cellar doors shake.

The next morning the house is intact, but half of the barn is missing.

"My cattle, crops, and fences," Grandpa says.

"It's all right, Grandpa. I'll help you rebuild and find your cattle," I say.

He thanks me, and we begin picking up debris.

Most of the damage was done in the Nambitus wilderness outside the wall. Grandpa was preoccupied with collecting eyewitness accounts on what happened for his records. Charlie and the gate were lost to the tornadoes. The papers did not report the tornado, which ignited endless theories for Grandpa.

"Grandpa, I understand if you do not want to test me this year. I know Charlie was your friend, and you have been preoccupied."

"You have worked too hard, and a soldier never retreats in the midst of chaos. Do you accept your challenge?" he asks.

"I accept."

He places eye black under my eyes. "You have outlasted my other grandkids, and because of that, I'm giving you my military-issued dog tags from the Great War." My grandpa places the dog tags over my head; I'm still wearing the necklace Matt gave me. "Now get some sleep. I will see you at first light."

I give him a salute.

I awake to Grandpa standing over me. "This would be the test of all tests. You are the last standing. No sunblock. No whining," he says.

I sit up and rub my eyes. For a brief moment, I wonder what Tevan and cousin Stevie are doing while I'm being tortured.

"Be downstairs in five minutes," he says as he slams my door.

Grandpa loads me with gear and abandons me in the wild once again. He waits until rain is predicted in the forecast. He blindfolds me and lets me ride in the cab of his truck. Usually, we are forced in the back with our gear, like actual soldiers.

In past times he would try to scare us on the way to our campsite with stories of the forests being haunted. This stopped when my older cousin was so scared that he carried a knife with him for the entire campout. When he went to get water, Grandpa dressed all in black and snuck up to scare him. My cousin stabbed a hunting knife through Grandpa's boot, injuring him. Scott screamed so loud that we all ran in various directions into the night. It took Grandpa an entire day to find us because we scattered. I was the last one retrieved because I ended up in the tree for the night, gripping a knife. Grandma was furious that he scared us to that point and banned all ghost stories.

I hope this year will be relaxed since everyone is missing in action.

We drive for half a day to a new site. It's green from all the rain and filled with plants and wildlife—it was unscathed by the tornadoes. Grandpa helps me unload my gear, which consists of a knife, sleeping bag, and jug for water. He offers to stay with me since Tevan is absent, but I tell him, "No, I've worked too hard for this."

He pats me on the head and says, "That's my girl." He heads off, not knowing that I know he always stays nearby. Just to make things interesting, he stabs my water supply. As soon as he takes his leave, I set off to find water. The stream is beautiful. I pause for a moment to hear the babble of a brook. I decide the freshest water will be at this spot. I see a few foxes getting a drink. Grandpa always says to take advantage of any kind of meat, but they were too magnificent to kill.

For a moment, I wish I had paint and a canvas so I could capture this scenery. I gather water and create a fish basket to catch a few small fish. Within minutes, I have my water and dinner.

Upon reaching camp, I gather supplies to start my fire before sunset so I might cook my fish. I lay out my sleeping bag as my dinner roasts on skewers. The aroma of the cooking fish makes me appreciate my summer all the more.

That night, I enjoy the peaceful solitude of my surroundings. I rarely get to see this scenery in Lexicon. Lexicon is covered in buildings and fumes and piled with people. When Rebecca Dean took over Axis, she began building projects that eliminate what little nature Axis had preserved within Lexicon. Axis had small natural places, unscathed by man, and now those areas are being developed for labs. I lay on my sleeping bag, enjoying the twinkle of every delicate star this night has to offer.

About halfway through the night, as my fire has almost burned out, I hear the snapping of a twig under a heavy foot. Knowing Grandpa, this is going to be the big finale, or he has clearly lost his touch. *If this is him checking up on me,* I thought, *I'm disappointed in the technique.*

I grab my knife from under my pillow. I make no sudden movement. I slowly open my eyes. Grandpa is standing in front of the fire—with a knife up against his throat. Now I understand why he was making me learn self-defense tactics. I am to be ready for anything. I sit up to see who is behind this horrific act.

I see three large men dressed in tattered jeans, bandanas, and dark shirts adorned in chains. They wear heavy black boots. The thinner of the three has scraggly long brown hair and a beard to match. The other two are heavyset. The first—the one with a knife to my grandpa's throat—is wearing a tattered black vest. The man who appears to be the leader has an earring and is shooting orders at the other two. I wonder where Grandpa found these actors for such a scene.

"Let him go," I demand.

"Well, look, Scrap, we have a feisty one. Don't we?" He tries to come closer, but I show my knife.

"If you value your life, you will walk away," I snap.

They throw my grandpa toward me, and I quickly push him behind me since I have the weapon.

"Kaya, I'm so sorry," he says, keeping his arm around me to shield me as I step forward.

"What business do you have here?" I ask.

"We're looking for the black vans," the leader growls.

"Your business is not with us, so let us be," I snarl.

The one they call Scrap says, "You know, if we were outside

Lexicon walls, I'd take you to our leader. He likes a feisty woman, but the problem is, we're on a mission to find vans, and we can't have witnesses."

I know things are about to take a turn for the worse in Grandpa's test.

"Kaya, this is not part of your test," Grandpa whispers. It takes a moment for his words to register in my brain. *Not part of your test.*

"Yes, listen to your grandfather, you stupid girl," the chubby one says.

I stand a little taller. "All three of you will be dead by sun up," I say.

The leader laughs. "She doesn't stop. I love it." He takes a step closer.

"You won't touch us!" I snarl as I get in the leader's face. "My father works for the Thantos Corporation, and you might get a ransom for us."

"Your Lexicon money is of no value to us. Our business is with the vans," he says. He twists me around and holds a knife to my throat. "Well, it seems killing you might be worth your jewelry." He slowly uses the tip of his knife to unclasp my shirt and lift out my necklace from Matt.

"You may kill me, but you cannot have that. I'll die with it," I yell. As he holds a flashlight up to my neck, I stomp on his foot and then elbow him in the stomach. "Run, Grandpa!" I shout.

The chubby one grabs me by my hair. "Come and look at this live wire. Skall would be pleased." He twists my hair until they can hold my necklace in the light. He places the blade of his knife between his teeth.

I turn my head and close my eyes.

"Scrap, get over here!" the second one exclaims. "Wait! Before you kill the old man, look at this."

They grab Grandpa, and Scrap throws him to the ground. "What, Brogan?"

"It has our markings. Who gave you this?" he asks me, and Scrap begins to loosen his grip.

"That is my business. I told you; you cannot have it," They laugh. "Do not laugh at me! If you're going to kill me, do it, and be done with it!"

They throw me to the ground. "Don't worry, girl, you're safe." Scrap smirks. "We honor your symbol. We will commit no offense here, but we ask for your complete silence in return. We have ways of knowing if you break an oath, and we will seek revenge. This man—is he part of your clan?" Scrap points to Grandpa.

"Yes, and the lady up the road in the farmhouse as well," I say.

"Fair enough. They will not be harmed." Scrap says.

I nod in acceptance, and they do a strange hand gesture. I do not understand how my grandpa and I have escaped death this night, but I decide not to question it. With that, they hastily disappear into the night.

I help Grandpa to his feet. "Are you okay?" I ask.

"I'm fine," he assures me. "Are you okay?"

"I'm shaken but okay. Should we check on Grandma?"

"No. I know nomads; they're true to their word. Kaya, we can't let anybody know about this, especially your grandma or your parents. If word gets out, it could put the entire family in danger. When we get home, we have to pretend none of this happened. Promise me you'll never speak a word of it,"

"But, Grandpa—"

"Kaya, I've never been more serious about anything in my life. Promise me! If anything happened to you ..."

"I promise, but what should we do?"

"We'll get my gear. I'll stay with you until dawn, and then I'll start home first, and you can follow. It will be just like you did your test."

I agree, and we begin our hike.

"Kaya, did you think that was planned?" he asks.

"Yes, and then at the thought of them hurting you or Grandma, I lost it."

"Promise me you will never do something that reckless. You could have gotten hurt. Or at least promise me you will try." I nod. "I'm proud of you. You reminded me of myself."

"When I heard the twig break, I thought maybe you were losing your touch," I say.

He holds his lower back and grimaces but then says, "Me? Never."

I pretend not to notice that he might be in pain because he is proud. I want to find those nomads and make them pay for hurting him, but more than anything, I'm grateful to be alive.

We gathered Grandpa's gear and pretend to camp for a few hours. *I'd be dead right now if it weren't for a necklace*, I think, gripping it tightly. Matthew Larkin will never know because I can never speak of it, but he saved my life.

I wake up at dawn and head east toward the farm. I make it back a little later than expected because I walk slower without Tevan there to tell me to pick up the pace, or Stevie, who always offered some sort of competition. I don't realize how exhausted I am. I walk in to find my grandparents at the kitchen table, drinking coffee and chatting. My grandma is relieved that we made it back in one piece.

For the rest of the summer I get to be a normal kid on the farm. I help my grandpa rebuild fences and plant for fall. We don't see the nomads or the vans again.

I would wonder if the nomads completed their task that night, but then I would push it as far from my mind as possible. I focus on doing chores and staying busy.

It surprises me when, with a few days remaining of summer break, my mom and Tevan show up at the farm.

"Are you ready to come home?" Mom asks excitedly as Tevan hugs me.

"I don't know. I like it here," I answer.

"It's time. School starts in a few days," Grandma says as Grandpa places his arm around her.

Mom and Tevan spend the night and tell me of all their adventures in Europe. "Talon was a total mess in Europe," Tevan says. "Did you know he was kicked out of nine boarding schools prior to Rebecca's takeover? He has connections all over Europe—and girls, the girls. He asked about you at every stop."

"I don't care." I say.

She giggles. "This is going to be fun." Tevan sits back in a chair.

"What?" I ask.

Mom then explains, "Your father made some business connections, and Rebecca is busy with her political career, so she made him vice president of Thantos. We are back on top. I think we are better off now than before."

"And I care?" I say.

Tevan rolls her eyes. "Because we are well connected, and Talon is crazy about you. It couldn't be a more perfect match."

"Make her stop, Mom," I say as I fold my shirts.

"Mom, we have to get Kaya ready for school," Tevan says

I start to panic. "I want to stay and go to school here." I begin to unpack my suitcase.

"Tevan, stop it, and Kaya, you can be yourself no matter our circumstances," Mom insists.

Tevan laughs about my going to school in a rural area. "Staying here would destroy us, Kaya." Tevan takes over my packing.

"We'll all leave in the morning," Mom says. "Now get some sleep."

Tevan doesn't waste any time getting ready in the morning. She's sitting at table, telling my grandparents of all her glorious college plans and trip overseas and about Jonathon.

I feel sad about leaving.

Grandpa winks at me as he says, "Don't tell Tevan about all the fun she missed. Some things are better kept a secret." He loads our suitcases and shuts the trunk. Then he gives me a blueprint of all the camera systems in Lexicon so I can fill out the new ones on my way home and send him a copy. My summer with my grandparents is over.

"So how boring was it?" Tevan asks.

"It was amazing. I learned how to can, sew, and knit. And I learned military tactics and Grandpa had me train with buckets. He even made me an honorary soldier and gave me his dog tags because I'm his favorite grandkid," I boast as I show Tevan.

"Mom, she deserves a medal," Tevan says.

The car stirs up dirt on the old country road, and I look at my grandparents in the rearview mirror. "It wasn't bad. I'm going to miss them," I say.

We get deeper into Lexicon, and I pull out my map and begin looking for cameras.

"What are you doing?" Tevan asks.

"Marking all the new cameras within Lexicon for Grandpa. They put in more over the summer."

Tevan slaps at my map. "Mom, Kaya has contracted Grandpa paranoia?"

"He's knows the truth," I tell her, but Tevan rolls her eyes.

Tevan has to stop at the mall for an eight-hour shopping spree in order to get ready for college. Little did I know that she was shopping for me as well.

"This is the style you are going for," she says as she loads up with skirts and jackets.

"I haven't worn a dress since your graduation party, and that was only because you hid all my clothes."

Tevan shoves me in a dressing room. The shoes Tevan makes me wear nearly make me fall through a wall, but I maintain my composure as a saleswoman helps me up from a rack I have knocked over. By the end of the trip, I don't even have the same hair or eyebrows.

When we get near Axis, it is almost dark. I stare out of the window at the missing posters.

"Mom, did they ever find Sal?" I ask.

She shakes her head. "No," she says as people place more posters along the wall.

"Don't be sad. It's bad for your face," Tevan says.

"I'm sorry I can't be happy all the time like you, Tevan, but there is a bigger world outside our spectrum, with people who have actual problems and who can't even go outside because they risk disappearing forever. The weather thing is an issue too. Did Grandpa tell you we almost died this summer from a tornado, and then it wasn't even covered by the media."

"So someone is controlling the weather?" Tevan teases.

"Yes," I insist.

"Whatever, Kaya. You are insane, and I hope this conversation proves to Mom that you shouldn't be hanging out with Grandpa. If anyone is responsible for the weather, it's the soldiers who destroyed the earth in the Great Wars. We are living with their mistakes. Weather is part of nature and not controllable. As for the kidnappings, we are upper level and have trackers. The risk of our getting kidnapped is nonexistent."

I clench my fists, trying to control my anger. "I hate you."

Mom shakes her head. "Girls, let's stop before we say things to one another we will regret."

I lean back against the seat. We remain quiet for the rest of the ride home.

As we pull into the driveway, Jonathon and my dad are waiting with balloons.

"What's going on?" I ask.

Tevan beams, and my dad says to me, "We wanted to surprise you. Since you will be going to school in Lexicon, and you got your license, we got you a surprise." He opens the garage door to a new car.

"This is for me?" I run my hand across the hood.

"Yes, we saved on traveling expenses by your staying with your grandparents, so we thought, why not?" Dad shakes the keys at me.

"Well?" Mom asks.

"Thank you. I love it." I hug them and then get in.

"Take it for a spin," Mom says.

I pull it out of the driveway, and head down the street. I drive by the Axis schools, which have been replaced by labs. The tennis courts, football fields, and lunch areas are gone. I drive to the park and see that it's smaller. A swarm of lightning bugs hit my windshield, so much that I can't see. I pull over and try to clean them off.

"Need some assistance, ma'am?" a familiar voice asks. I didn't need to turn around to know it was Matt.

"I'm fine," I say as I hurry.

"Kaya, let me help you," Matt says. I refuse to make eye contact. "It's good to see you." He sprays cleaner on my windshield. "Do you remember when we were kids, and we loved catching these things?"

"I don't remember," I say. "How are you magically here with cleaner, and why are you talking to me?"

"I'm working on maintaining the park with my dad, and he has every supply you could imagine. Because I'm providing a service, I can talk to you."

I look up at him.

"Well, look who is so very Lexicon," he says as he looks my car over.

"It was a gift," I explain.

"I know. I was just giving you a hard time. Your mom asked me what type of car you would want. At first, I was tempted to mention one like Tevan's, only better, to drive her insane. Then, I thought back to you saying if you ever did get a car, you wanted one that was environmentally friendly."

I look away; he even chose the color I wanted. "Everything is different. Axis is now Lexicon," I say.

"We now have acres of crops. We've added more orchards and vineyards and livestock. I know my trade so well." He shows me his dirty boots and continues slowly scrubbing my window.

I want to get angry that Matt has accepted his position within society so easily, but I'm so happy to see him. I want my window to stay dirty. "How was your summer?" I ask.

"Football practice and work," he says. I try not to pay attention to how much Matt has bulked up. "You are tan, and look at those arms," he says.

"My grandpa gave me his dog tags," I say. As I hold them up, Matt sees his necklace and smiles.

"Seems you had a good summer," he says. I wanted so badly to tell Matt how his necklace saved me from death, but I couldn't. "Looks like you're all set." He taps my windshield.

"Thank you, Matt," I say and get back in my car.

"Have a good first day of school," he says.

"You too." I drive away.

When I get home, I begin getting nervous about starting a new school. I have a schedule and my classes won't be an issue because Axis schools are clearly superior, but the thought of new faces from all over the spectrum worries me. Just when I think my nerves are about to get the best of me, the phone rings.

"Kaya! Talon!" Tevan shouts.

"How was your summer?" Talon asks.

"Good, and yours?" I ask.

"I thought about you quite a bit. That's what brings me to this call. I was wondering if you'd like to accompany me to school on the first day."

"If I didn't, who would you take?" I ask.

He gets quiet but then says, "I only thought of you."

I was not ready to see Talon, but the thought of going to a new school all alone seemed terrifying. Maybe having him would make things easier, so I agree.

"All right. I'll pick you up Wednesday," he says as I hang up the phone.

"What did Talon want?" Tevan asks excitedly.

"To ride to school together."

"This is so exciting!" she says as she goes through my clothing.

"Don't you leave for college tomorrow?" I ask.

"I do, so we should talk."

"All right. I thought Talon and I were friends, but Matt is no longer allowed around me, and even he said I belong with Talon. Talon always has tons of girls around him, and then we had a fight before school got out," I explain all at once.

"Kaya, he was clearly miserable in Europe. Torture him all you want. The fight proves it. You have him."

I roll my eyes. "I don't want to torture him. I just want everything to be the same."

She holds up outfits. "But it's not, and here we are. Now help me pack."

She drags me to her room, and we stay up until 1:00 a.m., packing and laughing. The next morning, we wake up at 9:00 a.m. to take Tevan to her college dorm in the middle metropolitan Lexicon. My parents save their tears for the car and sniffle for the entire drive back home.

For the rest of the evening I nervously clean my room in order to keep my mind busy and not think of school in Lexicon the following day.

CHAPTER 7

I wake up the next morning and style my hair, as ordered by Tevan. I wear a suede skirt and matching jacket. *Tevan would be proud*, I think as I put on makeup.

"Kaya, Talon's here," my mom shouts.

I go downstairs, wearing impractical shoes. I see Mom is ready to tackle her first day as a Lexicon professor. "You look amazing, Mom." I hug her.

"You do too. Have a wonderful day." She snaps a picture of Talon and me and throws me a granola bar.

Talon does a double-take when he sees me. I pretend not to notice as I grab my bag.

"Hello, Mr. Dean," I say.

He holds the door open for me. "Hello, Miss Lewis."

"I'd just like you to know I was given a car, and if we are going to continue to carpool, I'd like to take turns."

"Of course," he agrees. "Variety is good."

When we get into the car, his radio is blaring campaign ads.

"Is that your mom on the radio?" I ask.

"Yes, and that was sweet of your mom to take a first-day picture of me. I don't think anyone has done that in years, except maybe a nanny. Do you have your tracker?" I pull it out of my bag. "They are checking for them at the gates now. I think it was a way for my mom to reassure our safety after Sal."

"Have they done any drills?" I ask.

"I couldn't tell you. I've been in Europe, but the neighbors say their kids panicked because of the loud sirens," Talon says as we get through security. "You look good, Kaya."

I try not to blush. "Thank you, Mr. Dean. You look nice as well. I didn't think you would be wearing a light-colored suit to match."

He laughs. "Tevan. Not that I wasn't a fan, but where did the glasses go?"

"Contacts, but I hate them," I say. "Where are your supplies?"

He laughs. "This year is going to be easy. We are just here so that my mom can be among the little people and get the vote."

As we pull into the parking lot, I notice that it's huge. Cars and buses pile in.

"Just act like we own the place," Talon advises. "We are the top of Lexicon. Well, if isn't one of our old classmates." Talon turns his music up, and we pass Emily.

When Talon opens my door for me, I want to take in everything. I have never seen so many people in one place for a single event in my life.

"No smiling. We are celebrities," he says.

I put on my sunglasses. Everyone notices Talon and me. We have the best car and clothing.

"Wow," Emily says under her breath, but I hear her.

We walk by kids banging on drums, some working on a protest. A teacher quickly confiscates their work. Boys are playing football. Some kids have wildly colored hair, and girls are dressed in clothing I have never seen sold. There are cheerleaders and too many others to even take note of. I wanted to do double takes, but I follow Talon's lead and pretend not to care.

The bell rings, and the hallways flood with students. and I pull out my schedule to find my locker, which is near Matt's. I try not to take notice of him as he watches me. I remind myself that this is Lexicon, and we cannot speak. I have to follow the rules or there could be consequences for both of us. I put my bag away and grab a few supplies for my first class.

I am almost tardy. The teacher has us seated alphabetically, and I am right behind Matthew Larkin. "Please sit," she says as I try to not make eye contact with Matt. The teacher begins passing out papers. All I can do is stare at the back of Matt's head. He looks nice.

He already has a football jacket. I want so badly to talk to him. I wonder if my presence has the same effect on him. Someone drops a book and brings me back to planet earth. The assignments for this class are going to be minimal.

I often wonder why Lexicon made so many people of the social hierarchy go to school together. My parents said is so we know our places within society yet learn how to work together cohesively while appreciating everyone's attributes.

As I looked at the various people, I saw resentment from some who looked at me and fear from others. I see some who would not get the opportunity for success. My grandpa said Lexicon schools gave us the opportunity to unite so we could find weaknesses within the system and overthrow the government. This theory made me anxious and attentive of my environment, as well as a bit more excited.

As my first class ends, I realize I haven't paid any attention.

"Kay, you look nice—not yourself, but nice," Matt whispers as the bell rings for dismissal.

"Thank you," I whisper as I gather my things.

The rest of the morning is tedious—full of rules, procedures, and assignments of papers and books to read that I mastered in junior high. No wonder Talon didn't bring supplies. Each class reminds us of our place and the actions that will be taken if we associate with those not within our spectrum.

When I get to the cafeteria, I am relieved to see Talon. He has already made friends with all the wealthy kids of Lexicon.

"I have your lunch, beautiful," Talon say. I stare at him. I don't want to play along with this.

"He is so sweet," one of the girls says.

Talon takes a book from my hand. "Come meet the gang," he says.

I hear Matt laugh from a table with the football players.

Before I can even lift a fork to my mouth, we are surrounded by Talon's new friends. Two boys ask Talon about his car. Their names are Jason and Chris.

Chris Ericson is a football player and the best athlete in the school because he plays every sport. His parents are professors in research, and he hints of their aspirations of living in the golden city of Axis.

Jason Johnson also is a football player. His dad is a public official and running for president against Rebecca Dean. His priority is to find information about Talon when not distracted by shiny objects.

Several girls welcome us. The first is Tiffany Beret, the richest girl in school. She's a tall, slender blonde. Both her parents are lawyers and have offices all over Lexicon. She knows where my and Talon's parents are from and about Axis. She makes it sound like we are in a cult.

Tia Spratt, a cheerleader, is more personable. Her parents are renowned doctors. She has long black hair and unwavering confidence.

Tia and Tiffany both are impressed by Talon and interrogate us during the entire lunch period. They want us to know they are worthy to be our friends as well. I feel as if I'm in a display window in the most popular store. It's suffocating. I have a newfound appreciation for popular kids. Everything is a competition in their world, and it's exhausting. The entire time, Talon was unshaken. He seems to be relaxed under the mounting pressure. I want to run and hide. I am relieved when the lunch bell rings, signaling us to go to class.

Talon is in my next period class. After another set of rules and procedures, we are allowed time to chat. The teacher carefully watches as we visit to ensure we group ourselves accordingly. Talon makes his way over to my seat.

"These people are pathetic. This is going to be a piece of cake." Talon smirks.

"They're acting like we're celebrities," I whisper in a worried tone.

"It's amazing. I hate Jason."

I try not to smile. "Why, pray tell?"

He grimaces. "Stop using phrases like that. It makes you look smart. I hate Jason because he's smug, and his dad is running against my mom. He's arrogant."

"Aren't those people the worst?" I say.

"Kaya, you know I adore your cleverness, but nerd is not the word here."

I take out a book to ignore him, but he then tries to take my book.

"Grow up, Talon," I say as I pull it back. People begin to stare.

"Come on, Kaya. We have a chance to get noticed. It's all a charade. Have fun with me. You can be nerdy and read all you want at home."

"Fine." I hand him my book.

"That's my girl."

By the time I get to my last class, I am exhausted. Once again, Lewis comes after Larkin. I take my seat and sit tall. This teacher is livelier than the others. I look around, and students are reading various pieces of literature. I make a mental note to get the titles. He gives us an assignment to get to know one another, not just people within our spectrum but the entire room.

At first, everyone freezes; then he snaps his fingers, and people begin with the questions on the board. Matt asks the person next to him what his ambitions are; then he turns to me.

"What are your ambitions … Kaya, is it?" he asks.

I try to stay serious. "To go to college and become the greatest in my spectrum. I mean, the world is my oyster."

He stops writing. "What are your real ambitions?" he asks.

I smile because he knows me. "To save the world but not through a lab coat."

He nods. "There she is, despite all that Tevan clothing."

"How do think others perceive you?" I ask, reading a question from the board.

"As a middle-class kid who has the potential to get into a decent college. I might be a football god as well."

I laugh a little. "You're wrong. I mean, you might be a football god. I never paid attention. You always get too hung up on rules, and rules often are meant to be broken."

"Then answer this: Why are you playing the part so well, Kaya?" he asks.

"Because all the world's a stage, and we're merely players—until one of us stops."

The bell rings, and Matt gets up without taking his eyes off me.

"Larkin, we have practice!" someone yells. He nods and grabs his backpack.

I am quiet on the drive home until Talon finally turns off the music and asks why I haven't spoken. I didn't want to tell him that I hate being tossed in Lexicon and having to pretend to be a snotty celebrity, so I lied.

"I am exhausted. I have to do everything you did but in heels," I say.

He laughs.

"My car tomorrow," I say as I wink at him.

The next day the interrogations deepen within our new social circle. "So, is Talon your boyfriend? Is he dating anyone or interested in anyone here at school?" Tiffany asks.

"Let me ask him for you," Tia says. "Talon, Tiffany wants to know if you're dating or interested in anyone here at school?"

She has interrupted Talon's conversation with Chris and Jason, but he answers, "Only one girl."

Tiffany gets excited.

"You know she thinks it's her," Tia whispers.

I shrug my shoulders. "You never know with Talon," I say.

Tia giggles. "So why don't you make it official with him?" she asks. "He does nothing but talk about you."

"Who is that girl?" Tiffany asks, pointing to Emily.

"She lives in Axis," I say.

She gets excited. "Is she one of us?" Tiffany asks.

"She's human at times," I answer, and Tia laughs.

"Her parents are retail." Talon says as he shakes his head. "She is someone we can have fun with."

Tiffany winks as she chases Emily.

"She is ruthless. She is going to torture her," Tia whispers.

After a few minutes, Tiffany returns.

"Were you nice?" Tia asks.

"Of course. I invited her to my party. I invite everyone within the spectrum so we can all socialize accordingly. It looks good for politics," Tiffany explains.

"You're hopeless," Tia says.

"Be glad I wasn't rude to you for once, Tia," Tiffany says as she passes out invitations. "Who is that new football player?" she asks.

Talon looks over. "Matthew Larkin, another Axis kid."

She grins. "He looks delicious." She walks over and hands Matt an invitation. "I'll take ten of him," she says as Tia whispers with Talon.

"He's a groundskeeper's son," Tia says, laughing.

"Tiff has it for a lawn guy," Jason says as Tiffany slaps him.

"I hate how Lexicon is stuck on labels. I need to go back overseas where I can have fun with no backlash." She waves to a couple of guys at different tables.

The bell rings, and Tia pulls her. "I have to go," Tia says. "Sometimes Tiffany is her own worst enemy. She is always like this at the beginning of the year when she gets back from vacation overseas."

Jason pulls Tiffany to the side and has what seems to be a serious conversation.

"Are you all right?" Talon asks me.

"What? Yes," I answer.

"You wanna go to a party?" he asks. I shake my head no. "Please?" Talon asks, putting his arm around me.

"What are you doing?" I ask.

"Sorry, please go." Talon drops his arm.

"No," I answer.

Talon glares at me. "This is the party of the year. You know we can't have parties in Axis."

"You do," I say.

Talon rolls his eyes. "I got in trouble for that."

Throughout the day, whenever Talon sees me, he either begs me or has a valid reason for why we should go to Tiffany's party.

By the time school ends, I am tired of arguing with him.

"It will give us the full high school experience," Talon pleads.

"Why do snotty Lexicon people have parties and invite people beneath them?" I ask.

Talon thinks and then responds, "Because it is custom."

I roll my eyes. "But they were terribly rude to people in the cafeteria," I say.

Talon agrees. "They have yet to learn to play their parts within society as humble leaders, which is why we are here for this social experience."

"That is crap. You will say anything to go to that party."

"Please, Kaya, I am begging."

"Fine, but you owe me."

He kisses my hand, and Tiffany gives me a scathing look from down the hall.

"It's like she's everywhere," I whisper as Tia walks by.

"Are you going?" she asks, and I nod. "Come by my house and we'll get ready."

When I get to Tia's house, I am wearing shorts, a T-shirt, and sandals.

"Oh no, we have to get you ready," Tia says. She puts on a short skirt and a shirt that shows her entire stomach. Tia gets me the same type of outfit and works on my hair and makeup for what seems like hours.

"We are going to be late," I say.

"That is a good thing," she says, laughing.

I look at my hair and outfit.

"You will get accustomed to Lexicon trends," she says and snaps our picture.

We drive to a gated community. Tia shows the attendant our invitation, and we are allowed entry. The music is so loud we can hear it a block away. Vehicles line the street from blocks away.

"Are these all here for the party?" I ask. Tia nods. The front lawn and inside of the mansion are full of people. Inside, people are dancing. The backyard is lined in lights, and even the pool is glowing.

"She has a waterfall," Tia says as she waves down Chris Ericson. Chris runs over, and they begin kissing and then take off together.

"Left all alone. I thought you stood me up," Talon says.

"Tia didn't think my party clothes were worthy of such an occasion," I say. I grab a drink off a platter. "Alcohol."

Talon smiles. I toss my drink into the pool.

"Did you bring your swimming suit?" he asks.

"And ruin this look, Talon?" I say in a dramatic voice. I make a funny dance move, and Talon laughs and places his hand around my waist.

"Kaya!" Matt calls from across the pool. "What are you doing?"

I look around and then grab some strange-looking food. "Eating and engaging in normal teenage shenanigans," I say. Talon laughs.

"No, what are you doing?" Matt asks. He speaks so loudly it seems the entire party stops.

"Matt, I think you're overreacting. Kaya and I are just having a good time." Talon says.

"Talon, I'm not talking to you," Matt says, his face becoming red. "Butt out. Kaya knows she is being ridiculous."

I get wide-eyed.

"Nothing here to see, folks," Talon says.

Tiffany comes out of the house.

"Talon. Matt," I whisper as I shake my head.

"Kaya is a big girl and can make her own decisions," Talon argues.

"Both of you, grow up. I can think for myself," I say.

Matt rolls his eyes. "Not when Talon is around," he says.

"Oh, like you have her trained not to argue and be compliant," Talon says.

Matt squeezes a cup. "We reason. She comes to her own conclusions."

"At least I don't have her hanging out with people of my choosing so I can polish her into my perfect Lexicon mold. It won't work," Matt says.

"It will never work for you either," Talon says.

They begin punching each other, and I scream at the two of them.

"Your friend Matt," Tiffany says to me, "will never recover from this."

I kick off my heels and slam Matt and Talon apart, ripping my skirt.

"Both of you are better than this," I say as I let them go.

I leave the party and can feel everyone watching me. Matt is escorted out of the party by security. Talon tries to follow me, but I push him away. I decide to walk home. If I have any real trouble, I have my tracker.

I walk for what seems like hours until Talon pulls over and gets out, trying to get me in his car.

"Kaya, please," Talon says.

I ignore him but then say, "No. You and Matt were once friends, but because of me, the two of you act stupid."

"You're right. We played fine and then you showed up to preschool."

"Don't you understand that there are repercussions for people who are beneath us when we make scenes in public?" I say.

"So what are you saying?" he asks.

"If you and Matt are going to be stupid, do it where there aren't witnesses. People at the party were saying things about Matt. People recorded the two of you fighting, and it made news sites." I continue walking.

"Why do you have to make it about Matt? He is a control freak," Talon insists.

"Because, Talon, it is about Matt when the two of you are being idiots over me, and he, in turn, could get punished. How do you think that makes me feel? I would rather avoid both of you." I begin to tear up and quickly turn away.

"I get it. If it makes you feel better, Matt and I made up, and he's home. I wouldn't let him get in trouble. We both have black eyes," Talon says as I laugh a little.

"The black eyes make me feel better," I say.

He tries to pull me closer. "Kaya, you are freezing." He rubs the sides of my arms and then gives me his jacket.

"Thank you, Talon," I say as he tries to pull me toward his car. "What if I want to walk?"

He looks at his car. "Then I would have to leave my 'baby' here and escort you." He looks as if he is going to tear up.

"Take me home Talon," I say.

A look of relief washes over his face.

CHAPTER 8

After the first week, school goes by quickly. I do an entire semester's worth of assignments in one weekend out of boredom. I am accustomed to a heavy workload at Axis schools.

After Talon and Matt had their falling out and then reconciliation, I saw less of Matt. He would nod as he passed my locker. As time marched on, I hoped it would become less painful for him, but it never did. Every time I found a new song or book, I wanted to call Matt, but I refrained. Still, I couldn't bring myself to delete his number.

The Lexicon schools embrace Matt, and because of his athletic skills, every student knows his name and football number. Talon and I never miss a game because Talon is a social celebrity.

When Talon is busy with Chris and Jason, I talk to Tia. She and Chris are social butterflies and know everything going on within school, as well as Lexicon. The beauty of our friendship is that I merely have to listen, as she does all the gossiping. I just have to change my facial features according to the news she relays.

Tiffany now is dating Jason but constantly keeps an eye out for Talon. She is in pageants or throws parties every weekend. Her entire existence is for the Lexicon spotlight.

Every morning Talon and I carpool to school, and I document the number of the missing as it grows. New posters with rewards are added daily. Those in mourning continue to lay trinkets and light candles as a vigil to their lost loved ones. I wonder if the nomads are responsible and that I was somehow spared because of my necklace.

"Still sad over Sal?" Talon asks as I play with my necklace.

"Yes, I am."

"My mom has a speech tonight. She's making it part of her platform to rectify the situation. She even has a plan of action. She thinks it might be outsiders. Possibly nomads."

"Really? Because I have thoughts on that theory." The words are out of my mouth before I remember I should stay quiet.

"What?" he asks. "Go on."

"Never mind," I say.

We get to the school parking lot and Talon opens my car door and hugs me.

"Kaya has a mysterious theory. I am intrigued," he says.

As I watch Talon walk into school, I see everyone take notice of him. He does well in the spotlight. I miss spending weekends at home or going somewhere unnoticed. I wonder what Talon would be like on a date.

"Why have you been watching me like a stalker today?" Talon asks as I stand by my locker, waiting on him.

"I don't know. I have forgotten what the real Talon is like as opposed to the Lexicon Talon."

He squints his eyes. "And you are the same, regardless," he says. "So … football game and party afterwards?"

I frown. "Something with just the two of us," I suggest.

"All right."

Talon picks me up at seven o'clock. "Are you sure about missing the game?" he asks.

"Yes, I'm tired of people and Lexicon clothes."

He laughs. "But we are so good at it now."

"I know, but I thought we could get a pizza or go to a movie," I say.

"Like a date?" he asks. I shrug my shoulders because he has

caught me off guard. "You are so adorable. Of course, just a Kaya and Talon night. I'd be honored."

"You know we haven't been out by ourselves in eons," I say. I take his arm as he gets movie tickets.

"I know, but you never ask, so like a gentleman, I don't push the matter," Talon says. I laugh a bit. "What?"

"I didn't know you were a gentleman," I say, and he responds with a snort.

As soon as we take our seats in the movie theater, the lights flicker.

"Attention citizens of Lexicon! This is an important message from candidates Rebecca Dean and Richard Johnson." The curtains pull back, and Rebecca Dean appears on the screen.

"Good evening, good people of Lexicon. Lexicon has seen turmoil in the past decade, but if chosen to be your president, I, Rebecca Dean, plan on making Lexicon live to its potential. We have a system in place, and it works. Ancient civilizations had this system in effect to pull themselves out of darkness. Since the Great Wars, we have risen out of those ashes into the most lavish nation on the planet, with the most advanced technology. We have a secure, sound hierarchy. All of us contribute to maintaining order and deterring us from the chaos that came after the Great Wars with a basis of tradition. Where some countries still struggle for their basic needs, we thrive.

"I know citizens are concerned about the missing within Lexicon, and I have personally assembled a team with leads for locating the lost. I will not rest until the culprits are brought to justice. Furthermore, as a nation, we need to improve security from inside, as well as against hostile forces and the chance of possible attacks from outside the protection our walls."

A few people start booing and throwing popcorn.

"Talon, what is going on?" I ask.

He looks around. "I don't know."

"Lies!" a person shouts. "She wants to control us."

"I keep photos from the Wall of the Missing, and I too make sure they are the last image I see before going to sleep. They also are part of my mission in the morning. United we will rise and conquer our foes," Rebecca says.

Some of the audience cheers and others boo.

"Thank you, Candidate Dean," the voice says. "Next we will hear from Senator Richard Johnson."

Senator Johnson now appears on the screen. "Good evening, Lexicon. Unlike my fellow candidate, I am not going to reassure you that things in Lexicon need to stay in order or that we need to maintain the hierarchy put in place by tyrants after the Great War. If my opponent will do some research, she will see it didn't work in history, and it is not working for the citizens of Lexicon. Citizens cannot work in a harmonious government when so many are divided by barriers that they cannot rise out of, due to inequality, poverty, and poor health care.

"If it was a success, then there wouldn't be daily riots in the streets because so many are opposed to the very system my opponent is dedicated to maintaining. She should be embarrassed because her very business is creating weapons that cause mass destruction and disease—or am I not at liberty to bring up such matters because I am a gentleman and not influenced by her payroll?"

People begin to cheer.

"Furthermore, diverting the attention from your misdeeds that have reached record heights since your arrival by mentioning the missing is a ploy. Yes, it is an epidemic that needs to be addressed, but it is not a platform in a presidential race. Rumors are surfacing she is kidnapping people, only to return them as part of the campaign to make herself look good. You are not our savior, Mrs. Dean. You are part of the problem. Are the missing being held behind your walls?"

Everyone in the theater goes wild. Before Rebecca Dean can speak once more, our trackers go off.

"What does it mean?" I ask.

116

Talon pulls me from my seat. "That we need to get back to Axis immediately."

"Look!" a man in the crowd says. "There is Rebecca Dean's son."

Talon gets me in the car as a mob chases after us, shouting.

"That was insane," I say as our trackers continue to light up.

"These things might as well be a beacon, reminding the world of who we are," he says. He takes his tracker off and throws it.

"Talon, it's going to be all right," I say, even as rioters line the streets.

Police quickly take the protestors down. As we get to Axis, the walls are lined with people holding signs. Some applaud Rebecca Dean, while others demand the return of the missing of Lexicon. People approach Talon's car and beat on the windows.

"Why couldn't we have just gone to the game, where her speech would not have been aired?" Talon moans. "She always causes dissension." Someone throws an egg at his car. "I can't go on like this. You have me so confused. Are we friends? What are we? I hate school—and stop throwing crap at my car!" Talon shouts. He glances at me. "You probably are wanting Johnson to win so you can be with Larkin—and why won't these people *quit*?" Talon shouts as we get to the Axis gates. "She put us in school, and I have to put up with pricks like Jason and play nice. I hate her. I haven't been able to see or talk to my dad in a year."

Talon punches his steering wheel and begins running his hands through his hair. I have never seen Talon so unraveled.

"I'm sorry for everything you've been through," I say.

Talon begins to laugh and then cry. "Don't apologize or try to figure me out. No one sees me like this."

We wait for security to let us through the gate. Just then a protestor slams a sign on Talon's car.

"What the *hell*, man?" Talon says. He jumps out of his car and begins punching the man. Several people begin punching Talon.

I get out of the car and try to get through the mob, and Axis guards try to get them away from Talon. By the time the crowd is removed, Talon is a bloody, mangled mess. Axis security take him away in an ambulance. The media swarms me as I try to get back into Talon's car.

"Look, it's Kaya Lewis, John Lewis's daughter, former president of the Vitae Corporation," one reporter says. "She is going to make a statement. What do you have to say about Mr. Dean?"

"He is a good person," I say. "You don't have to like a candidate, and you should have the right to voice your opinions, but this is wrong. Go home." I get in Talon's car and drive into Axis. Some of the protestors drop their signs.

My mom runs out of the house as I pull into the driveway. "There were mobs, Mom," I say.

"I saw you and Talon on the news," she says.

Once inside, I try to go to sleep, only to toss and turn.

I stay hidden from the world in my room most of Saturday and Sunday after I see Talon and me on several news channels. I want to crawl under a rock as some news channels insist I am siding with Senator Johnson because I insist people should have the right to voice their opinions. Other news channels are debating another statement, saying I am a hero, defending Candidate Dean by sending the attacking protestors away. After hours of going through channels, I don't even know what I meant by my own words. I try to call Talon, but it goes straight to voice mail.

On Monday, Talon does not pick me up for school. As I drive toward school, I am struck with an overwhelming sense of loneliness because I am so accustomed to our ride together. When I enter the parking lot, news trucks are lined along the street. I sit for a minute, debating as to whether I go should home. *I can do this*, I think.

The second I get out of the car, I am met with microphones and cameras.

"Is it true Talon suffered a nervous breakdown and is now seeking treatment?" one asks as I stand there, unable to form words. "Is it true you and Talon are engaged?"

"That will be all," Matt answers as he pulls me away from the cameras. One reporter comments on my relationship with Matt as she pulls up footage of his and Talon's fight the night of the party.

"I didn't know," I say as people pass by, staring.

"That Talon had a breakdown after being beaten to a pulp, you are engaged, or about our love triangle?" Matt asks.

"Any of it."

He quirks his eyebrow. "You should watch the news." He begins to take off, but I grab his arm.

"Thank you Matt."

He nods and turns to talk to a teacher in the hall.

At lunch, I watch the news to learn that Talon is seeking treatment at a top facility in Lexicon.

"Was it horrible?" Tia asks.

"I can't watch anymore," I say.

She tells everyone to put their devices away. The rest of the day, I can hardly keep it together because all I can think about are the videos.

The last class of the day is always the best one. The teacher, Mr. Fox, is progressive. He looks beyond society and wants us to be shaped by experiences.

Today, he brings a big fishbowl with names. He says we will be working with partners on a book report but won't be picking names. Everyone looks around the room, worried. "This is not the Lexicon we all know and fear. If you pick someone outside your spectrum, make it work." He passes the bowl.

Matt gets a fellow football player. I get a girl named Rachel Mendel. After drawing names, we are to find our partners and begin deciding on topics.

I scan the room, looking for Rachel. She's sitting in the back row. She has glasses and brown hair pulled into a low ponytail. She's wearing jeans and a blue shirt. Next to her desk is a stack of books, not including her backpack loaded with books. When the teacher calls her name, she nods and quickly ducks her head back down. She reminds me of myself. Everyone quickly teams up to begin discussing books and topics. I take my seat in the back next to Rachel.

"Hi, I'm Kaya Lewis," I say.

"Yes, I know. I've seen you on the news," she replies.

"Nice. Do you have any books in mind?" I inquire.

"A few," she says.

"Okay. Do you have a time you'd like to meet?"

"No."

"How about the library today after school?" I offer.

"Fine," she says.

The bell rings, and I get up. I can't understand why she hardly spoke, but maybe she's shy. Since English is my last class of the day, I think we might walk to the library together, but as I gather my backpack, I realize she's already gone. I make my way to the library, hoping to find her. I see her sitting at the main desk, chatting with the head librarian. By the resemblance, I can tell the lady is her mother.

"Rachel, did you want to start today?" I ask.

"You showed up?"

"Why wouldn't I?" I ask, a little offended.

She grabs her books and pulls me to the side. "Look, I thought I'd be doing the work. I didn't think you'd show up. Kids like you don't do school projects. These assignments are used to make the school think we can work and appreciate our places within society. I'll take care of it."

"Well, I'm not most kids, and I'm excited about this project. It is just what I need," I say.

"Is it because your lover, Talon, tried to commit suicide and will have nothing to do with you?" she asks.

I stare at her. "Sure."

She puts her hands up, not meaning to offend me.

"Do you have any suggestions?" I ask. "I have a couple."

"I was thinking either *Dr. Jekyll and Mr. Hyde* or *Frankenstein* in honor of Halloween," she suggests.

"Sounds fun. I vote *Frankenstein*," I reply.

"*Frankenstein*, it is." She smiles.

"So, is the librarian your mom?" I ask.

"Yes," she answers.

"Cool. I'd love to be around books all day."

"You read?" she asks.

"Nonstop," I say.

"Wow, you're the first popular kid I've ever had an assignment with who actually is smart," she says.

We dive into a discussion of report assignments and possible scenes for our poster.

"You have been more than I expected," she comments as we clean up.

"We still have two weeks, so imagine what other elements we can bring in about Shelley herself," I say.

"Tomorrow?" she asks, her enthusiasm clear.

"Tomorrow," I agree.

The hour we worked on the project was the only time I didn't worry about Talon or the media. I was a normal high school kid for the first time.

The first thing I do when I get home is call Talon, but I can't reach him.

"Will you please tell him I called?" I ask the answering service.

"Yes, as we do every day, miss," the woman says.

I pull out *Frankenstein* and read it, but the second I finish the book, I begin thinking again. I decide to walk over to the park to clear my mind. I know everything in Axis has changed, but at this time of year the orchards are beautiful. When Matt and I were kids, he would sneak me inside. I cut through the old field and over a couple of fences to get to the orchard.

I take a seat on a fence post.

"I knew you would sneak in here," Matt says.

"I feel safe here," I say, not at all surprised to see him. He takes a seat next to me. "I love the trees in the fall almost as much as I do in the spring. Look—there's the tree where we'd bury treasure." I jump from the fence and walk over to tree, where I see my, Matt's, and Talon's carvings in the trunk.

"Look at this one," I say

He blushes. "Why did you put our initials in that one?"

I shrug my shoulders. "Because I was eleven, and Tevan was dating Jonathon, and Emily was with Jay all the time. I assumed since we were inseparable that we were a couple. You didn't have to refuse to practice kissing with me when I carved that. That was cruel," I say.

"Now you have Talon, and from what I've seen and heard, he's had plenty of practice, so he can teach you," Matt says. "I am going to cut down that tree."

I push on it. "It's practically dead. Why haven't you?" I ask.

He shrugs. "I'm not in charge."

"Is it because it's our tree?"

Matt rolls his eyes. "Would you like for me to put your and Talon's initials in the tree?" he asks.

I shake my head. "Why do you have to bring up Talon?" I ask

Matt rubs the back of us neck. "I don't know." Matt sighs heavily. "Why him?"

I laugh. "We're friends."

Matt rolls his eyes again. "It's not that I don't want to be around you. I can't. I was reprimanded for talking to you in the halls today." He shows me a burn-like mark on his arm, and I get angry.

"You always do the right thing. I think we should fight this," I say.

Matt smiles and leans toward me until our foreheads touch. "You would do that to for me?"

"Yes," I say.

He looks away. "Leave, Kaya."

I shake my head. "You shouldn't be reprimanded for talking to me. Kiss me," I say.

He steps away from me. "No."

"You said Talon has had practice, and you know you are my dearest friend. I'll kiss you to prove how committed I am to this cause."

Matt shakes his head. "I won't do it. You are only here because your precious Talon is ill, and you want to prove a point to society."

He dodges me, and I roll my eyes. His evading me makes me angry. "I do not want you to kiss me, Matthew Larkin. Both you and Talon have ruined my life!"

Now he laughs. "Then why do you still wear that necklace?"

"Because it matches every outfit I own. I'm going to burn it when I get home," I snap. This only makes him laugh even harder. I hate when Matt laughs at me. "Don't ever talk to me again!"

He doubles over, still unable to control his laughter. "Deal! And don't try to kiss me for politics. I would never kiss you, Kaya."

I throw a rock at him, and he dodges it.

I walk home and read until I fall asleep. Being around people makes life a bit bearable, even though I have to dodge the media to get into school. I don't have to stay home and think about Talon. Tia is supportive and gives me the daily scoop from inside sources, since her parents are doctors. Tiffany, who's dating Jason, makes snide remarks about Talon's recovery and says that his mother is using his injuries for her campaign.

"If I were Talon and looked at the campaign, I'd keep myself in a facility," Jason says.

"Jason, what happened to Talon was a travesty," Tia snaps.

"He has enough going against him. With Rebecca Dean for a mother, those mobs might have done him a favor if they'd done him in. He should do himself in," Jason says, and Tiffany giggles.

"How dare you talk about him that way!" I say.

Jason laughs. "Calm down. I was only kidding. Talon knows how the game works."

"He might, but I don't play your games," I excuse myself and walk away from them. I spend the rest of the time reading alone on a bench.

Rachel and I talk books during the last class and then go straight to the library after school. We work on our project and are done within a few days, but we become fast friends and spend every day afterward visiting with each other.

"I saw you by yourself at lunch, not that I pay attention," she says.

I nod. "My friends are complicated."

"You mean jerks."

"Some are nice," I say.

She shrugs her shoulders. "If you'd like, we could eat in here," she says.

"Tomorrow?" I suggest, and she agrees.

For the rest of the week, Rachel and I have lunch in the library. We read, listen to music, and laugh.

On Saturday, Talon is home and feels good enough to accept calls. When I finally get him on the phone, he thanks me for calling and checking on him so often. Then he says, "Kaya, I'm sorry I went off. I wasn't myself."

"Let's put it behind us," I say.

"I thought I was going to go crazy in there."

"Do you think you will feel up to school?" I ask.

"Yes, I'll even drive," Talon says.

"All right but only if you feel well."

"Kaya, don't treat me like everyone else. If you are going to treat me like I am pitiful, then there is going to be a Halloween dance soon."

I laugh. "How can you think of a dance at a time like this?"

"Because it'll be a fun time. Say you'll go with me."

"Of course," I agree.

Before the end of the weekend, Tevan finds out I'm going to the Halloween dance with Talon. She calls me and spends an entire afternoon talking.

"Tevan, didn't we just drop you off a month ago?" I ask.

"Yes," she says, laughing, "but your first dance!" She continues talking, this time about college life.

"Where is Jonathon?" I ask, trying to get off the phone.

"He's getting out of school early and will be doing his internship at the Thantos labs," Tevan says. "He's a genius."

By the time I get off the phone with Tevan, it's midnight.

When Talon picks me up the next morning, I am exhausted. I try not to pay attention to the bruises on his arm, and he quickly pulls his sleeves down. "So did you miss me?" he asks.

"I did," I say, trying not to blush.

"I made Kaya blush," he says. "How was school?"

I don't mention Jason but tell him, "Talon, I don't think we should sit at the same table."

"Kaya, I've been in the spotlight my entire life. I'm fine," he insists as we pull up to school.

"I refuse to be around those people. While you were gone, we were given a new assignment to work with people outside our spectrum, so I made a new friend."

Talon gasps. "Shame on Lexicon schools for encouraging such rebellious behavior! My mom would be horrified. Stay with me today; I need your support."

I take his arm. "You've got it." We walk into school.

At lunch, Jason is already in his seat when Talon and I walk in.

"Well, Talon, it's good to see you are on the mend. Kaya was touchy about my joking on your behalf," Jason says.

"Kaya has a habit of seeing people in their true light," Talon says. He takes a seat.

"Are you saying I'm rude?" Jason asks.

"Well, your family does pride themselves on being called gentlemen, and you do fall short. Why insult me behind my back to a young lady? I mean, if you are going to insult me, have enough decency to wait until I am well and back at school." When Jason glares at him, Talon says. "You do understand what I am saying Jason? Your last report card was released to the media."

"Jason, remember your dad's campaign. This would make the papers, and you know Talon is unwell," Tiffany says as she gets in between Talon and Jason.

"You're right," Jason says. He looks around and then places his hand out for Talon to shake. Talon shakes his hand as the bell rings, ending lunch.

"Talon," I whisper.

"The Johnsons are gentlemen, and his dad would kill him if he hit me, especially after I almost met my end by protestors," Talon says. He takes a bite of an apple.

"You didn't have to start a fight," I say.

He shrugs his shoulders. "No one insults you on my account," Talon says. "You know you want to smile."

I take his arm.

As we get to our lockers, I see Rachel in the hall and realize I missed lunch with her. "Rachel!" I say. I try to catch up with her, but she keeps walking. "Rachel!" I say again, and she stops. "Rachel, I'm sorry. I should have messaged."

She looks around. "It's no big deal."

I shake my head. "No, it is, and I'm sorry."

Without responding, she ducks into a classroom.

"Well, that didn't go so well," Talon says.

"I'm going to make this up to her. I'll take her somewhere after school," I say, and Talon hands me his keys. "But your car is your baby."

He smiles. "Just be careful. I'll get a ride with Emily or Larkin."

I hug him. "Thank you." We walk to class.

Rachel isn't in our last class. After school, I go to the library.

"Mrs. Mendel, is Rachel here?" I ask her mom.

"Kaya, I didn't want to say anything, but Rachel doesn't make friends easily," her mom explains.

"I want to make it up to her," I say. Her mom points to a quiet area in the library. "Rachel," I say as I find her.

She glowers at her mom. "Traitor." She turns to me, saying, "I told you I'm okay

"I know, but I am sorry, and friends don't do that. Plus, I have a surprise."

Her mom signals that she should go with me. I drag Rachel out of the library and hold up Talon's keys.

"Is this the type of car I think it is?" she asks.

"Yes. Talon lets me drive it on occasion," I say.

She gets in. "It has so many buttons," she says as screens pop up everywhere. We drive until we are near Axis. "I have never been on this side of Lexicon," Rachel says.

We near my favorite library, but it's not only a library. During the Great Wars, it acted as a hideaway and protected historical documents. It was also the largest book store within Lexicon. It has copies of every piece of literature within Nambitus.

"I've read about this place," she says as we stand outside. "The art." She takes pictures, and we look for hours and collect books. I then take her to the restaurant where I first took Talon.

"I love it here," she says as she takes pictures of people.

When we finish, we drive by the wall. Rachel lowers her eyes.

"Maybe whoever gets elected will help," I say.

She shakes her head. "Not on my side of town. No one can help with the crime. We live in a vicious cycle." She keys her address into Talon's car and then gets quiet. I drive until I get into the innermost part of Lexicon. Flyers line fences and light posts. Men and women barter in the streets. Debris flies everywhere as children play. Several police speed past me.

"My stop is right here," Rachel says. "I get to go to your school because my mom is the librarian, but she lied about our address." She begins to get out but then hesitates. "Please don't tell anyone where I live."

"I won't."

I see a younger boy run out and hug her. Her house is a tiny, rundown single-story home. During the entire ride home, all I can do is think about the missing faces on the flyers in Rachel's neighborhood.

When I get back to Axis, I drive to Talon's house and cautiously ring his doorbell. His mother opens the door. "Yes?" she snaps.

"Is Talon here?" I ask.

She narrows her eyes as she looks at me. "No, he is at the park with the Larkin boy." She slams the door in my face without another word.

I get back in Talon's car and drive to the park. He and Matt are chatting like old times.

"Thank you, Talon," I say as I toss him his keys.

"Did you and your friend make up?" he asks.

"Yes," I answer. "Are you working, Matt?" I ask.

"Every day when I am not playing football."

"No fun?" I ask.

"I'm saving up for college, and football is fun," Matt says.

"Are you going to the big Halloween dance next month?" Talon asks.

"Working," Matt answers. I begin to edge away.

"Kaya and I are going," Talon says. I cringe and wait for Matt's response.

"Well, it is about time the two of you made it official. I'm surprised you're not wearing a ring like Tevan," Matt says, and Talon chokes.

"You should ask a cheerleader to the dance. I know a few," I say as I give him a look.

"They keep asking, and it's embarrassing how girls throw themselves at me. Isn't it, Kaya?"

"I'm going home. I'm tired," I say.

"I'll drive you," Talon says. "Good-bye, Matt."

I'm still fuming when we get into the car; still mad at Matt.

"Why are you and Larkin always using those underlying tones?" Talon asks. "It's like you have your own language, like when we were kids. You've never out grown it."

"I spent more time with him than anyone else and most of that time was fighting with him. He knows how to irritate me more than anyone on this planet."

Talon laughs. "So you're not mad I told him we were going to the dance?" Talon asks.

"No, I think it is a bit disgusting how conceited he is," I say. "I'm surprised your mom was okay with you being at the park with him."

Talon begins laughing. "I told her we were doing that progressive assignment you and your friend were doing just for fun." Talon says as I try not to laugh. "What did she say?" I ask. "Nothing. She just made a note." Talon says.

The next day at school, Jason extends an invitation to Talon and me for a party after Friday night's big game. Talon declines, but afterward, everyone seems relaxed and all is back to normal within our circle.

The topic then turns to Halloween costumes. Tiffany and Jason plan to wear designer costumes and have already had five fittings. Tia and Chris are having their costumes imported from overseas.

"It's important that the two of you match," Tia says to me.

"Tia's been planning for six months," Chris says.

Tia grins. "I have. So who are you two wearing?"

"We're going to start looking today at the mall," I say. Tiffany gasps. "Did I say something wrong?" I ask.

"You might choose something *they* will be wearing," Jason says, pointing to the other tables in the cafeteria.

"Would that be bad?" I ask.

"You could disgrace your family," Tiffany says.

I start laughing, and Talon nudges me.

"Promise you will take it seriously," Tia pleads. "There are cameras everywhere."

For the last class, everyone is working, and Rachel seems quiet.

"Hey, I had fun," I say, sitting next to her.

"I thought you wouldn't talk to me after you saw where I lived," she says.

"You know where I live and still talk to me," I say. "Want to have lunch tomorrow?" I ask.

She smiles, and we exchange books.

After school, Talon is waiting for me to go to the mall.

"Talon, do you think we'll look bad because we are not getting designer costumes for this dance?" I ask.

"Kaya, it is a high school Halloween dance."

When we get to the mall, we spend hours trying to find the perfect costumes.

"Talon, all of these cover so little," I say, holding a costume up to a mirror.

"Try one on, and I'll be the judge," he says. "Just one."

I reluctantly go into a dressing room. "Talon, I hate it," I say as I walk out and then go right back inside.

"Kaya, Kaya. That was beautiful."

I come back out, ready to leave. "I am not wearing that," I say.

"Fine, what would you like to wear?" he asks.

"Let's go to the old shop in the mall," I say.

Talon shakes his head. "Kaya, that part of the mall is dusty, and the clothes are used."

"I tried on something for you," I say, and Talon agrees.

We walk into a rarely visited part of the mall and to a store with stories of clothing. I quickly begin piling clothes on Talon.

"They smell musty," he says, coughing.

"Each piece tells a story," I say. I run behind a curtain and come out in a short dress. "Your turn."

He sniffs a shirt. Talon comes out in a gangster suit.

"I love it!" I say.

"My turn," he says as he hands me an outfit that reveals my stomach. As I walk into the dressing room, I toss him a pair of overalls.

"No!" he says.

"Yes," I insist. I walk out and do a dance as Talon jumps out in overalls and chases me around the forgotten floor of the store. He catches me and spins me around. He leans down and kisses me.

"I've been wanting to do that for so long," he says as he kisses me once more. As Talon and I are in this moment, someone begins tapping on the window of the store. It's the entire football team, including Matt. They are laughing and snapping pictures as Talon helps me to stand up.

"This is awkward," Talon says.

I try not to look at Matt. "Just a little," I say. I hand Talon a costume.

"So, we're settled," he says.

"Yes, we will be the envy of everyone," I say.

Just then, a few more football players tap the glass. "I am going to the checkout," Talon says.

I try not to get annoyed at his teammates. "Enough!" I say as one takes another picture, blinding me.

"Kaya, don't," Talon says as I walk out of the store.

"Are you having fun and enjoying the show?" I ask. "I'm talking to you." I walk toward the crowd of oversized football players.

"As a matter of fact, we are," one of them says. "The two of you are Lexicon celebrities, and these pictures will go for a high price, especially since Talon's mom is running for office, and your father is John Lewis."

"Get a life. You are pathetic."

He just laughs. Just then, Matt bumps into him, knocking the phone out of his hands so that I can grab it. "Nice going, Larkin," the goon says. "I hope you're not as clumsy for tomorrow's big game."

I smash his phone and then hand it back to him.

"Let's go," another one says as they give me awful looks. Matt hangs back as they leave.

"Thank you, Matt," I say. "So, tomorrow's homecoming, and the team hasn't lost because of you." He remains silent. "Matt?"

"Please don't come to tomorrow night's game. I don't want you there," he says.

"Is this about me and Talon?" I ask.

"No, I think it would be best if you backed off a bit," Matt explains.

"I was just supporting you as a fellow Axis classmate and getting the full Lexicon experience. Don't flatter yourself, thinking I go for you," I say.

Matt rolls his eyes. "Save it. Go out and party with Talon. He is an endless good time."

"Why do you have to be like this?" I ask.

He curls his lip. "I wish I'd never grown up around either one of you."

I squint my eyes as I look at him. "You are hurtful. Take it back."

"Never. The two of you are self-absorbed, spoiled little brats, and look what you subjected me to," Matt says.

"You are uptight and obnoxious. You don't have to save for college. You are just scared to have a little bit of fun because you might like it," I say

"I hate you," he says.

I smile. "Not as much as I hate you."

Talon walks out of the store and quickly gets in between Matt and me. "Everything okay?" he asks.

I nod. "Perfect." I uncross my arms, and the crowd we've attracted goes about their business.

"Good luck on tomorrow night's game, Matt," Talon says. "Here are your clothes, Kaya, and I paid for what you walked out in."

Talon hands me my clothing, and he and Matt talk. I stare at Matt, trying not to scream. I don't even pay attention to what they are saying; I just want to go home.

"So, Matt tells me you and I are not going to homecoming?" Talon asks.

"There is a silent picture that's leaving the theater after tomorrow. I'd rather spend my time watching a quiet film than supporting a bunch of Neanderthals who tried to make a profit off me," I say.

"Silent film it is," Talon says.

The next day at school, I do my best to avoid Matt. He is surrounded by swarms of jocks and cheerleaders. I even make an excuse to go to the library at the end of the day, rather than going to the pep rally. It's hard for me not to sulk a bit because fighting with Matt always makes me feel off balance. As he begins his speech as quarterback, it echoes in the halls, and I turn my music on so I don't have to hear his voice.

"You do realize you are not really here."

I look over my book to see Rachel. "I'm hiding," I say.

"Why?" she asks.

"It's complicated," I say.

"Boy trouble?" she asks.

"Yes, if you must know."

She laughs, and I look at her book as it slips out from behind another book that she has hidden. Rachel quickly tucks the book away. "You know what gets your mind off boys?" she asks. "Hanging out at your house."

"We're not allowed to have anyone at the Axis," I say. I see the look of disappointment on her face.

Rachel then gets up to get a drink. As she does, I look at the book she stashed away. I recognized the symbol. It's the same symbol from a pamphlet a woman gave me at the mall. In parts of her notebook, there is information about me.

"What are you doing?" she asks.

I drop her book. "You're one of them. A radical?" I whisper.

Rachel looks around and quickly tucks the book away. "Don't ever talk about the movement, especially you."

"Rachel, it's me," I say.

"Kaya, I can't trust you."

"Why? Why do you have things in your notebook about me?" I ask.

"Because you are one of them and took an interest in me, of all people. Your dad, John Lewis, designed and built the golden city of Lexicon. Axis is impenetrable."

I stare at her as if seeing her for the first time. "Are you and I even friends?" I ask.

"Wake up, Kaya, You don't even know who you are. You're a walking contradiction. You spout ideas on rebellion and then hang out with the top teens in Lexicon. You look like them, dress like them, and even wear a Thantos-issued tracker."

Self-consciously, I hide my tracker. "Judging by the biography on my life you have created, I am unable to defend myself. You made up your mind about me without giving me a chance."

She shakes her head. "You don't understand."

"Explain it to me because I am not the enemy, although you are treating me like one."

"It's just hard for me to feel bad for your boy problems when there are real Lexicon problems. People are starving and are planning revolts and secret uprisings. I can't even talk about them because it could mean death, but I can't help but be a part of it. I look at you, and I see the enemy. I hate that I can't talk to you publicly because you are a nice person. After this assignment, we can never speak again."

I hand her my pamphlet. "I took this."

She waves her hand at me. "It's just a flyer until you are a part of the solution. I'm sorry I was writing information about you. You are the coolest person I have ever met." She loads up her backpack. "I've got to go. We never had this conversation. We'll do our project next week." I look at the pamphlet. "Kaya some words of advice. For every person wanting to get rid of the system, there are two wanting to keep it. There are eyes everywhere. Watch who you keep close."

She leaves, and I'm overcome by an overwhelming feeling of panic. I look around the library, but it's dark. It's Friday, and I have stayed late. I walk out into the halls, where it's also dark. The pep rally must have ended hours ago. I can't find my phone, and the library door locked behind me. Fallen streamers line the hall. I walk outside, hoping to find Talon, but all I see is my car.

Rachel is walking down the cement stairs toward the parking

lot, but I don't know what to say to her after what she has told me. Can I trust her? Then, out of nowhere, a van speeds up and then slams on its breaks, blocking her path. I run towards her and the possible threat. Two men, dressed in black from head to toe, throw a black cover over her head. She begins to scream and fight. They struggle with her and take no notice as I approach. I reach them just they toss her in the back and peel out, leaving the back doors open.

I grab the inside of the van, holding on for dear life. One tries to pry my fingers loose as they speed up but then pulls me inside. They throw a black cover over my head and toss me next to Rachel, who's crying and no doubt scared. Someone binds my wrists, and I fight our kidnappers to no avail. The van speeds up and drives so erratically that I almost get sick. We are tossed from one side of the van to the other repeatedly. I listen to my surroundings as I was taught but hear nothing except the sound of the engine and tires on the road.

I hear Rachel vomit and whisper to her, "Rachel, it's going to be okay."

"Kaya? Is that you?" she asks.

"Yes, there was no way I would let them take you."

"Kaya, this is bad. I was working on an underground story, and somehow my computer got hacked. I knew they would come for me."

"Don't worry. I have a tracker. I'm privileged, remember?"

"Kaya, you don't understand. No one comes back from this. We will end up faces on the wall. We'll end up monsters."

I try to get my hands free. "I'm getting it from my watch right now. As soon as I push it, help will be on the way," I explain.

Rachel starts crying again, but I try to get free. I struggle but am unable to free the tracker from my watch with my hands tied.

The van stops, and I suddenly feel a sharp stab in my arm. I scream, and I hear Rachel do the same before I black out.

I don't know how long I've been asleep, but when I awake, I can barely see. I feel an IV in my arm with a cold solution. At times, the solution feels so thick I think it's going to burst through my veins. The cold sensation travels throughout my body and then burns. I can make out a hospital gown. I scan the room, looking for Rachel, don't see her. I look down, hoping to find my watch, but I've been stripped of most my personal belongings.

I began to move around, trying to get feeling back in my feet and arms. I can feel my necklace and then my watch. I clumsily feel for my tracker. I hear voices in a nearby room and hurry. I try to stand, but my feet are like jelly, and I fall to the floor. The entire room is cold and white. I quickly pull out my tracker and turn it on. It makes a noise and began flashing loudly. The moment my tracker activates, it alerts my kidnappers. I hear them burst through the door.

They try to deactivate it, but it's indestructible. They begin tugging on me like I am a ragdoll, and I'm defenseless in their hands. I lie on the cold floor, unable to move, and start crying as they argue how to kill me. They throw my tracker against the wall, but the tracker only gets louder. One of my captors towers over me, holding a syringe. The room begins to get fuzzy as he injects a solution into my IV.

I lose all control of my senses. I sit up and begin screaming because I have never felt such a pain in my body. I have vivid dreams that I pick up one of my kidnappers and rip him in half. The room begins to flash as if there is an emergency alarm sounding. The hot and cold sensations in my body are extreme and change in an instant, leaving me in excruciating pain.

At one point, I feel every nerve ending in my body stand on edge, and then I go numb to all my senses. I lose control of my limbs as they pour different fluids in my mouth and IV. I feel my chest burn, and it seems they shock me back to life numerous times. Each time I black out from the pain, I come back again.

"Do what you can. Vials A through Z if we have to. A-134. Hurry," one says. I feel myself foaming at the mouth. I sit up and scream as I come out of the darkness. "Her resilience is extraordinary,"

I hear someone say, and I am shocked once more. Everything then goes dark.

I want for everything to be over so many times. I embrace the darkness, hoping I will find the tranquility some speak of when one crosses over, but it never comes, only agony. I want the poison to end me; instead, I'm trapped in a recurring cycle. As the IVs and drugs enter my body, I remember coming up off the bed, convulsing, and then seeing the white walls before giving in once more to the convulsions that tear through my body.

As soon as I find solitude in the innermost corner of my mind, the torture reoccurs. Within my nightmares, I hear a monster as it stumbles around and gurgles. I hide within the corners, but it finds me. I hear it maim and kill, and I am afraid. It takes the entire facility to secure it. Someone comes in and saves us. The horror of this nightmare takes me into an abyss from which I cannot escape.

The remaining workers begin their torturous task of experimentation once more. I am pumped and filled to the brim with fluids that burn through my body like acid. I look down to what I later convince myself can only be hallucinations, as I see acid burn through my skin. I see people from the past dance in the room, and I join them. Then I am placed somewhere so cold I stop freezing altogether until all goes dark.

Once I'm revived, new techniques begin, involving new trials. These cruel people—monsters—do not care if I am conscious to endure the pain. Tears roll down my cheeks as I think of my family as the process continues. I do whatever I need to do to keep what remains of my sanity.

CHAPTER 9

"Kaya, wake up," my dad says, and I try to open my eyes. I know at this point I am dead or I am reliving a childhood memory. I've done this to try to escape the pain and torture.

"Her eyes are moving," my mom says as I struggle to control my eyes. "She blinked!" My mother begins screaming and shaking me, but I want to scream, for her touch is excruciating.

"Kaya," she says as they stand over me. Tevan calls to Mom as she walks in the room and drops a cup of water, and Jonathon follows close behind. Are my eyes open now? As the water falls to the floor, it's as if it's in slow motion. They all stare at me. I cannot talk or even signal that I am in here. Just then, my body convulses, and the nurses and doctors rush in, and my family is ushered out.

The next few days are marked with lights in my eyes and doctors insisting on speaking with my parents out in the hall. I hear the words "permanent damage," "facilitated," and "go home." I want everyone gone because in the few seconds I strain to open my eyes, the looks of fear and disappointment are enough to make me give up. I am too weak to keep my eyes open more than five minutes.

After everyone leaves late one night, I am awakened to someone reading aloud my favorite book. It is Lexicon's football god, Matthew Larkin. He gently squeezes my hand and tears up as he says how sorry he is to tell me not to come to the homecoming game. I scarcely remember the argument. I know I hated when we had arguments. I know we argued often, and I hated it yet loved it too. I just can't retrieve any of our past arguments. I just know he is Matthew. I can't console him; all I can do is lie here and listen as he tortures himself with regret. He continues to tell me that if I'd been at the game, none of this would have happened. I try to open my eyes to send him a signal and squeeze his hand in return, but I can't. He promises to return in secret.

The next day Talon and my family return. I hear their voices. I hear it has been weeks. Mom weeps, but Tevan tries to keep them in good spirits. All of a sudden, I feel as if electricity shoots through me, and I gasp for air. I can't get enough as I try to breathe. It's as if I have run a marathon. The nurses and doctors stand over me once more. I try to sit up, but I am too weak. They begin to take me from my room in such a hurry that I try to reach for my mom's hand and then try to scream, but nothing comes out.

My father quickly stops them. "What's happening?" I hear him ask.

"Sir, your daughter's labs confirmed last week that she would never awaken. She was never supposed to sit up. Don't you want us to find the source of this miracle or mystery illness?"

My mother holds me, and I feel safe and warm, but I know it's a false sense of security. I am limp in her arms, like a ragdoll.

Just then there's a ruckus down the hall. An ambulance pulls up with sirens blaring. People rush in screaming, and the hospital staff pulls out emergency equipment instruments. I hear gurneys being lifted out of an ambulance. I smell the rain, and I hear them prepare machines in the emergency room.

All the sounds are multiplied in my eardrums. They are intensified so that I swing my head. I try to bring my hands up to cover my ears, but I struggle. I finally pull my pillow over my head. The odor of blood and vomit burn in my nose. I feel sick because my entire system is overwhelmed by my heightened senses.

"You've upset her," my mother insists as a nurse rushes by and shoves my bed. As she did, I wanted to draw my arms up and tuck into a ball—except that I can't feel my lower extremities.

"My ... legs," I manage to say. A doctor reluctantly gives in and wheels me back into my room. He takes out a tool and pokes the bottom of my feet. I can't feel anything. I shake my head.

My mom begins crying. Talon gets a phone call, and the doctor pulls my family out in the hall. I hate this. I can hear parts of the conversation. It's cruel when people talk about you. Even though they have your best interest in mind, they treat you like you are broken. I want to panic; these are my legs. I look at my arms and see long incisions in my right arm and heavy needle tracks on both arms. The hospital has been pumping me full of fluids in their best attempt to rehydrate me and keep me alive. The thought of more needles and liquids in my body makes me go crazy. I begin panicking and pulling out IVs, setting off an alarm. The doctors and nurses try to place them back in, but I attack them.

Once again, a meeting is called out in the hall. Tevan and my mom come back; Jonathon and my dad hang back and speak with the doctors. I hate that Jonathon is here. He treats life as if it's a science experiment.

Before the doctor can even come back in, police officers fill my room.

"Excuse me, this patient is under my care and has barely regained consciousness," the doctor insists.

"She is part of a kidnapping investigation," the detective says.

"She has barely mumbled two words," my doctor argues.

"We are placing posters of missing people on the wall as we speak. She's the only lead we have. No one comes back from being missing in Lexicon, so I don't care if we interview her and she has to answer us with blinks." The detective shoves the doctor away from me. "Who abducted you?" the detective asks.

I begin shaking.

"She's not ready," my mother says, but the detective holds up his hand to silence her.

"Was it nomads? Was it random?" the other detective asks.

I begin crying.

"Who did this to you?" the first one asks again.

"Enough!" my dad says as he comes through the door. "When Kaya has had some rest, I'm sure she will be more than happy to answer your questions, but until then, I must ask you to leave."

"Fine. Here's our card, but remember—we were able to take *her* poster down," one says.

I try to hide.

"Oh, Kaya," my mother says after they leave.

"Where did you go?" Tevan asks. "You missed all the excitement."

Talon enters the room and says, "My mom called and was concerned about Kaya. Mr. Lewis, she said if there's anything you need, please do not hesitate to ask. She said you could bring her to Axis for her recovery and safety."

My father politely declines. My family and Talon stay by my bedside for days, hovering in shifts, noting every twitch and movement. The constant questioning if I'm all right makes me feel suffocated. The second they leave, I am visited by Matt.

"Did the party finally leave?" Matt asks as I struggle to sit up.

"Yes."

Matt takes a seat, handing me books. "You looked bored out of your mind."

"Are you stalking me?" I ask.

"Yes. I can always tell when you are a million miles away."

"Are you going to ask me if I am all right or if I need anything?" I ask.

He laughs. "No, you look like garbage, and if you were all right, you would be out of the hospital."

"I heard you the other night, and you don't need to feel guilty," I say.

He nods. "Good, because I put together a search party until you were found, so I feel we are even. I even worked with Talon." Matt pulls up a wheelchair.

"I am not supposed to leave," I say.

"Kaya, let's break a few rules. Pretend I'm Talon." As he puts me in the chair, I tense up.

"So how did your big game go?" I ask.

He laughs. "We won." He wheels me down the hall. "I saw an area that has a garden with the lights of Lexicon."

"I don't deserve for you to be nice to me. I upset you in the first place," I say.

We stop and he takes a seat next to me on the floor.

"I didn't have a right to be upset," Matt says. "Plus, you are my oldest friend. I don't want to rub this in Talon's face because his story is different, but I met you first." Matt looks around, and when he doesn't see anyone who might stop us, he sneaks me out onto the patio.

"The air feels amazing," I say.

"It stinks a little," Matt says, and I laugh. He points to my legs. "So when are you going to walk again?"

"Never."

"Kaya, don't give me that baby crap. I see everyone sniffling and hovering over poor little Kaya. You know it's time."

I get mad. "I almost died. You will never know what I have been through."

"I am sure it was horrible, but save it for television. The cameras are waiting outside," Matt says. "You do not accept defeat, and I am tired of your mom calling my mom with the sob stories. I can't handle it anymore."

I stare at him. "I hate you," I say. He responds with a smile. "Why are cameras waiting out there?" I ask.

"You are the hottest story in Lexicon, other than the presidential election. You were the first kidnapping victim to ever be recovered. They need to hear your statement so they can try to bring back the others. You need to be strong, like you were that night on the news. Plus, everyone is intrigued by the kids finding you nearly dead and naked in the field after a block fire."

I can feel my face turn red with embarrassment. "I was naked?"

"Kay, I thought you knew."

I cover my face and shake my head.

"I'm sorry," he says. "Hey, look at me. Every day you come closer to walking out of here and putting this behind you. You are Lexicon's hero. You're my hero, Kay." Matt hugs me.

"Did they find Rachel?" I ask.

Matt looks away. "Kaya, I don't know if you are ready for this conversation."

"Tell me."

Matt wheels me back inside and down to my room before he answers. "You are the only survivor to tell the tale, and so far, you haven't given any details." I close my eyes. "Let's get you some rest. I didn't mean to upset you with that naked stuff." He grins, and I roll my eyes as he helps me back into my bed. "Now, do you need anything?" he asks. "Oh! That reminds me: I brought you some things." He reaches for a bag he'd brought in earlier and takes out my glasses, some books, and a music player.

"You know me so well," I say, as he places my glasses on my face. "Matt, I'm already wearing my glasses," I say.

He looks at me quizzically. "Maybe it is still too soon," he says, placing my glasses on the nightstand.

"Good night, Matt, and thank you," I say.

He smiles and leaves.

Later that evening, I watch a news broadcast on TV. Rebecca Dean states that she has made it her personal business to see that crimes against me and others are punished. She gives an update on my condition. "Miss Lewis is a determined young lady and an inspiration to us all during these dark times." She stands in front of the wall and takes down my picture. Then she runs her hand over the other posters of the missing. This is followed by footage of her leading a vigil and search parties for me. I roll over and try to sleep.

That night I succumb to nightmares I cannot explain. I hear voices and suffer in my sleep, as if I am being tortured all over again.

I toss and turn. I see lab images. I wake up screaming and have to be sedated.

My mom is the first person I see when I wake up in the morning. "The doctors said you had a tough night. Do you want to talk about it?" she asks. She tries to wipe my forehead, but I pull away.

"Even if I could, I don't understand," I say.

She nods.

"What?" I ask.

"You are talking. You scarcely talk. You just stare. What changed?"

I shrug my shoulders. Before I can say anything, the detectives walk in again.

"She's not ready," my mother insists.

"It's okay," I say.

"Are you sure?" she asks.

"I need to do this," I say.

"I'll be right outside," she says. She makes sure the door remains open.

"What happened?" one detective asks.

I try to sit up and gain my composure. As they interrogate me, they ask how I became acquainted with Rachel, and they want to know every detail leading up to our kidnapping. I then have to admit that I had to fight to stay in the van, even though I was not the target of the kidnapping.

"Who do you think you are? Most people have enough sense to run from the black vans of Lexicon. Didn't you have a Thantos-issued tracker?" the female detective asks.

I hold my head in my hands to keep it from flopping. "I was bound so tightly I couldn't get to it," I explain.

"I'm sorry," she says.

The man helps me to sit upright. "Where did they take you?" he asks.

"I don't know. We had something over our heads, and by the time I got my cover off it was too late."

"What did they do to you?" he asks.

"As soon as we got there, we were sedated. When I woke up, I was wearing a gown. It was a lab—clean, sterile, and white walls. There were so many IVs." I begin shaking and find it hard to form words.

"Are you going to be all right?" one asks.

"I ... g-got to m-my tracker. I think ... I think I died a few times because I was brought back. No one came to rescue me. I guess my tracker didn't work." I sigh. "I woke up here, and that's all I remember."

"We'll be in touch," the detective says. "Wait—did Rachel mention anything to you?"

"As we were kidnapped, she mentioned a story, but I don't remember the details. We had an assignment for school."

After the detectives leave, Talon walks in with my mom. He hugs me. "You okay?"

"I want therapy. I want to walk," I say.

My mom gives me a pitying look. "Kaya, you can barely sit up."

"I'm ready," I say.

"All right, if you're sure I'll set it up," Mom says.

Talon gets a phone call and leaves the room. When he returns, he's carrying a large bouquet of flowers.

"Who are those from?" I ask.

He finds the card. "My mom. Apparently, she cares."

I stare at him. "I didn't think she was the caring type."

"She checks on your progress. She was upset your dad didn't want you at Axis." He takes my hand. "You are so cold. Are you sure you are ready for therapy?" he asks.

A woman comes in with a wheelchair.

"Be careful," Talon says.

"Did I miss the dance?" I ask.

"No, but there will be other dances," Talon says.

The lady helps me into the wheelchair.

"Kaya, do this at Axis," Talon pleads.

I dismiss his concern with a wave of my hand, and the woman wheels me to therapy.

My first day of therapy is almost as bad as coming out of the coma, with my body going haywire. I can't control anything and have little strength in my arms. I can't do anything with my legs and have to be carried. I hate depending on other people. I'm given small hand weights, which I flip and flop everywhere. I lose control of my face during facial exercises, but I refuse to stop. My mother leaves several times, crying. The only person who doesn't seem to panic is Grandpa, who visits. He watches me from the window, always signaling me to push onward.

"Hey, kid," Grandpa says. "I want you to remember the buckets."

"Okay, Grandpa." I say, trying to keep control of my head.

"I had your Mom get these," he says as he puts his dog tags around my neck. "Remember you are a soldier, and nothing stops a soldier."

"I won't fail you, Grandpa," I say.

"You couldn't if you tried," he says and kisses my head.

After an hour, I am forced to stop. I am in such pain within minutes that I know what hell is. The top of my body burns. My arms randomly convulse. When I'm not awakened by nightmares, I wake up when I feel my face pulling.

It takes every amount of mental power I can muster to continue, and by the end of the sessions, I am exhausted.

If only I could get the night terrors under control and interpret what they meant, I know I could make progress, but every night I succumb to the darkness. My levels drop, requiring medical attention. I don't know if nights with unexplainable terrors are worse than days filled with painful therapy.

My parents always offer to stay, but I prefer to be alone. By the end of the week, I am advancing more than anyone had expected and am able to pull myself up and down. I have a small amount of feeling in my legs. When I'm taken back to my room, I find a woman is there with a notebook in hand.

"Miss Lewis," she says, extending her hand to shake mine. I just stare at her. "All right, I will get to it. The hospital staff feel you have progressed physically, but they are worried about your mental and emotional states." She jots down something on her notepad. "Would you like to talk about what happened to you?"

The nurse helps me in bed, and then I say, "I have already talked to the police."

"What kind of facility where you taken to? What type of noises did you hear? Did you see any logos or symbols?"

I shake my head. "Why are you asking me about that horrible place?"

"Because we have been told of your nightmares, and the only way to deal with one's demons is to confront them."

I look away. "I do not remember enough to discuss it."

She seems to study me and then asks, "What about Miss Mendel? Was she in any kind of trouble or headed down an unlawful path? Was your abduction due in part to your association with her?"

I bristle at her questions but keep my voice calm. "Are you implying I was returned due to my station?"

"You are the daughter of an important person."

"I don't see how these assumptions could help me face my demons." Every time I speak, she writes.

"Do you think nomads were to blame?" she asks. "They have been seen within the city."

"No. Why would they experiment on people in labs? Should I say it was nomads to keep things quiet?"

"According to your statement, you implied they conducted experiments on you, much like an alien encounter." She laughs, although I'm not sure why.

"I know exactly what happened, and it is horrifying," I say.

"Interesting."

"That's the truth."

"Who do you think is responsible for these experiments?" she asks.

"Shall I say your employer?" I ask. "That's how you got in here."

The nurse returns and says to the woman, "Ma'am, we have no record of you."

The woman pulls out a knife and stabs at the nurse. They begin fighting. The woman grabs the nurse by the neck, striking a fatal blow. She then comes toward me, holds me down on my bed, and places her hand over my mouth.

"Such a shame you are in your right mind," she says. She taps the deep gash in my arm that is now stitched closed. "Such an ugly scar for such a pretty girl." She pulls out a syringe and takes off the cap with her teeth. "Sleep tight."

I grab the syringe from her and stab her in the neck, administering the poison meant for me. As the woman falls dead on top of me, as I pass out.

I wake up to find Talon watching me.

"Kaya, are you all right?" he asks.

I rub my eyes and look for the dead nurse and the woman.

"There was an attempt on your life. A woman tried to kill you, but a nurse saved your life. Unfortunately, she met her demise in the process," he says as he holds me.

"I don't remember it that way." I rub my head.

"Your mom says you have been under heavy sedation," Talon says.

I survey the room. "Why am I in a different room?" I ask.

"You are going home. It is not safe here."

My parents enter. "Mom, I can't leave," I argue.

"You were nearly killed," my mom insists.

"I'm sorry, but I killed the woman."

They stare at me, and my mom says, "John, we need to get her out of here. They have her so medicated she is delusional."

I shake my head. "What about my therapy? I am so close to walking."

Everyone avoids my eyes, and Talon says, "I'd better step out."

After he leaves, my mom says, "Kaya, they took you for a scan today, but we are not giving up."

I shake my head. "So I might never walk? I don't want to go to Axis. It's no longer home. I want to stay here."

"Kaya, we know you have been through a traumatic ordeal, but it is time," my mom says as she hands my dad my suitcase.

"What will we do if I have nightmares?" I ask.

"We will deal with it," my dad says.

"What about therapy?" I ask again, beginning to panic.

"We'll come here or hire someone to come to you," Mom says.

That calms me down somewhat. "What about food?" I ask.

Talon comes back in the room and looks at us all strangely.

"We will order take-out," Mom says. "Kaya, you do not have to insult my cooking in front of Talon."

"Sorry. I can't fend for myself."

They help me into a wheelchair and Mom asks Talon to wheel me out. She and Dad go ahead of us to get the car.

"I love that you hate Axis, now that my mom is in charge," Talon says.

"I can't help the way I feel," I say.

"I'm just trying to get you the best care. My mom has made it her personal business to ensure you have the best care. You even said that in Axis, we are family," Talon says.

"Talon, you get calls, and there is an update on me on the five o'clock news."

Talon stops pushing the wheelchair. "That was a low blow. I have never seen my mom so upset about a situation."

"Talon, I'm sorry," I say.

As we get to the elevators, his mom appears.

"Kaya, I heard you were getting released," Rebecca says.

Talon and I both stare at her. "How could you possibly have known that?" Talon asks.

"I have made it my personal business to care," she says. She takes my wheelchair from Talon as we see reporters and newscasters line

149

the hospital entrance. Then my parents' car pulls up. "Here's your ride," she says, wheeling me out and helping me into the car.

The last image I see is Talon standing on the curb as reporters take his picture with his mother. As we pull away from the hospital, the media encircle our car. I slide down in the seat as lights flash and people slap the windows with missing flyers, begging to know if I have seen their loved ones.

"I thought they said we would have no interruptions," my dad says, struggling to get out of the parking lot.

I pull my hood over my head and pull a music player out of my bag to drown out the sound. My parents can tell there is something wrong.

"Would Talon like to join us for dinner?" my mom asks.

I shake my head. "He probably won't want to talk to me for a while since I insinuated his mom is only providing me with the best care for her political gain."

My parents look at each other, seemingly dumbfounded, and then my mom laughs.

"Don't encourage her," my dad says. "I have moved up to vice president."

Axis is covered in news teams, curious people, and onlookers awaiting my arrival. Some people have even lit candles in my honor. "Please get us in," I say as people once again pile against the car windows.

At home, my dad takes me to my room, and there I hide for days. I can't bring myself to answer Talon's calls, read, or watch television. I sit in the dark when I'm awake, and I'm haunted when asleep. My dad takes blood samples and uses machines to monitor my progress. He and my mom take shifts to watch me, until my mom finally forces me to have visitors.

"Matt's mom and I were talking, and we decided you needed some fresh air," she says. "Since you are estranged from Talon and won't have anything to do with the Axis facilities, you can go with Matt on his orchard rounds."

I sit in front of the sink of my bathroom and look in the mirror for the first time since the entire ordeal began. I don't recognize the person staring back at me. She has dark circles under her eyes. She has no color to her skin and is gaunt and frail. Her eyes look dark and damaged, as if she is lost inside.

"It is a Lexicon rule that I cannot be around him. You are breaking the law," I tell her.

"Rebecca said all visitors are encouraged for your healing," Mom says. Just then, someone taps on my bedroom door.

"I can't leave. What is the use of my going anywhere since I am housebound for the rest of my life?" I sit in my wheelchair, and my mom pushes me out to Matt.

"She's so excited," my mom says as she throws a jacket over my head.

Matt wheels me downstairs backward, making faces at me. I ignore him.

We get outside just as Tevan and Jonathon arrive.

"What are they doing?" Matt asks.

"I bet Jonathon is coming to be nosy about my labs," I say, trying to shield my face from the sunlight.

"Maybe he can help," Matt suggests as he struggles with my chair.

"Maybe the situation is hopeless," I say.

Matt drags me along the back road. "And the Academy Award goes to Kaya Lewis," Matt says.

That makes me angry. "This ride is bumpy and uncomfortable," I whine, crossing my arms.

"Maybe your parents or rich boyfriend could invest in one of those motorized old-lady scooters," Matt says.

His remark only increases my anger. "How dare you!" I say.

Matt opens the orchard gate. "Come on, Kay; it was a joke. You are rotten company." I point to my legs. "And?" he asks as he spreads out a blanket.

"You have no compassion. I was told I would never walk. I can't wear my glasses." When he laughs, I throw my glasses at him.

"But you have some feeling in your legs, and if you don't need your glasses, why be mad about it?" He pinches my leg, and I rub it defensively.

"I know, but I had to leave the doctor and my therapy because someone tried to kill me. Matt, I think I killed her. It wasn't the nurse."

He smiles. "That is hot, like a secret agent."

I clench my fists. "I hate you, Matthew," I snarl at him.

He then dumps me out of my chair onto a blanket. "Shall I call Talon so he can console you or carry you? Your mom said you were having nightmares. And you are too weak to kill anyone." Matt lies on his back, looking up at the clouds.

"Why can't you ever take me seriously or be kind?" I ask.

He rolls his eyes. "Because you are a wreck and acting like a baby." When he laughs at his own words, I become further irritated.

I too lie on my back to look at the clouds. "Why would someone try to kill me?" I ask.

Matt looks over at me. "Have you met you?" he asks. I punch him in the arm. "Ouch. I don't know, but you are safe now."

"Why do you patronize me?" I ask.

Matt laughs again. "Because your reaction is priceless. People underestimate you. Talon says I try to control you, but I just try to curb your meanness so you won't look bad. Now I'm trying to curb the pity party so you'll toughen up. I hate this side of you."

"I am not mean."

"You *are* mean, but you are kind too, like risking your life to save a friend."

My irritation with him has not dissipated. "Thank goodness I have *you*, Matthew, because you have me and my life all figured out."

"You are welcome, Kay."

I watch him looking at clouds. This is the Matt I grew up with, the one who kept me on my toes and always challenged me. "Where have you been?" I ask.

He shrugs his shoulders. "Lost, like you and everyone else since becoming Lexicon."

"I've missed you," I say.

"I know."

"Who do you think the woman was who was trying to kill me?" I ask.

"Someone trying to shut you up. You might possibly know too much," he says.

"I can't remember anything," I insist.

"But eventually, you could."

"Matt, you mentioned Talon consoling me …"

"I nearly walked in on that one," Matt says, rolling his eyes again. "You crying about your disabilities and Talon telling you everything was all right." Matt throws an apple.

"Why are you so cruel?" I ask.

"Because that is not going to help," Matt insists.

I try not to get mad. Rather than have a fight with Matt, I just look at the clouds.

"Dog paddling a canoe," Matt says, pointing to the sky.

"No, elephant playing a banjo," I say.

"New one coming up," he says. "Crocodile carrying a purse."

"Clearly, a cat pushing a lawnmower," I say, and we both laugh.

Matt and I reminisce for hours as we watch clouds. Finally, he says, "I have to tend to the trees."

I sit up. "Do you want me to wait here?"

He laughs. "Do whatever you want to get home. Judging by the sun, you have a couple of hours of daylight, and your house isn't that far away."

I begin to panic, not sure if he's serious. "Matt, you can't leave me here."

He smiles. "I can, and I will. I told your mom I would lift your spirits and motivate you. Clearly, I won't lift your spirits by making out with you in store windows as Talon did, but I know your mom. She thinks after I tend the orchard, you and I will grab dinner and possibly watch a movie at my place. You could be out here for hours—and the sprinklers come on in three hours."

"You wouldn't dare!" I say.

"Oh, I would," he insists. "Call me when you get in so I know you're okay." He begins to walk away, and I start yelling. "No one can hear you," he calls over his shoulder. He turns to look at me, and I shake my clenched fist at him. "There's the Kaya I know." He walks away, laughing.

I wait for Matt to come back, but after ten minutes, I know he won't. He and I were cruel to one another. Talon would never do this to me. I army-crawl across the blanket to my wheelchair and pull myself back in. I'm surrounded by dense grass. *I hate you, Matthew Larkin*, I think as I try to stand and steady myself using my chair. I fall flat on my face. I continue the process until I manage to be steady on my knees. "I can do this," I say as I push my wheelchair while on my knees until I reach the edge of the grass.

I rip both knees in my pants as I drag my legs behind me, but I do it. As I get to the dirt road, the terrain is rough. I try once more to steady myself and pick myself up. I fall to the ground and get covered in mud. I push my chair over the mud and then crawl through the mud and over to my chair. I wheel myself along the dirt road for what seems like miles, even though I am just a block from my house. I have to stop and rest before reaching the pavement, but I easily wheel myself to my house by dark.

Matt is on my porch, chatting with Talon. "Three and a half hours. Pathetic!" Matt says as he puts away a timer. Talon looks horrified.

"How dare you, Matthew! When you dump me somewhere tomorrow, I'll be more prepared," I say.

Talon comes down from the porch and pulls a twig out of my hair. "You dumped her?" he asks.

"Her grandpa suggested it," Matt says.

"Look at her!" Talon says.

"I'll make half that time tomorrow," I say.

"He just dumped you in the middle of nowhere?" Talon asks as he examines me. "You are covered in cuts." He sighs as he pulls burrs off me. "There is a special therapist and a doctor who will see you."

"I was told there is no hope," I say.

Talon looks upset, but Matt pulls a face, mocking me.

"You will allow Larkin to abuse you, but you won't let doctors to look at you?" Talon asks.

"After what happened, I will never go back to a hospital," I say.

Jonathon walks outside. He tilts his head from side to side as he studies me and then leaves.

"What was that about?" Talon asks.

"I hate him," I say. "He treats me as if I'm not human."

Talon laughs. "Do you want me to fire him?"

I smile for a moment, but Matt gives me a look. "No, not necessary," I answer.

After the boys leave, I clean up and go to bed. The next morning my mom comes in early and pushes open my curtains.

"You have hibernated long enough. I know you have done all your schoolwork for the semester and have been through a horrific ordeal, but it is time to go to school again, starting next week."

I can tell Mom has been talking to a counselor on how to deal with me because she then mentions support groups.

"How can I join a support group when no one has ever survived this?" I ask.

"I know you are angry, and you are entitled to feel that way, but you are going to school."

"How do you know I did all my schoolwork?" I ask. "Matt came by and picked it up while you were in the hospital. He said it was in the blue folder."

"Blue folder," I say in unison with her. I pull the covers over my head, and she struggles to take them away from me. "Don't you have a job?" I ask.

"Beginning professors who take time off for personal reasons have to resign, but they want me back for the spring. This will give me time to focus solely on your healing."

When my mom leaves the room, I scream into a pillow. Now I know why Tevan has not been around as much. Mom has downtime and has been reading on how a family can overcome tragedy.

I sit and hit my legs, and for once, I feel them burn. They burn as if I have been sitting for too long and I need to get up and move around. I sit up and place my feet on the floor. I'm sore due to Matt's treachery the day before. I pull my chair over and wobble. "Yes," I say. I stand, terrified to move like a mannequin. I drag my foot and take my first step, causing every bone in the lower half of my body to crack. I fall, yet I am so happy. I get up and work all day at walking. I drag myself around, falling and running into things, until my mom goes insane.

After school, Matt comes in and helps me into my chair.

"Well, I was beginning to think you wouldn't come back," I say.

"And miss torturing you? Not a chance." He pulls me backward in my chairs downstairs.

"How's school?" I ask.

He rolls his eyes.

"Any dates? The big dance is next Friday." I touch his nose.

"No, I'm working."

"Oh, *working*," I say, mocking him.

Matt takes me deeper into the orchard.

"Why are you so quiet?" I ask.

"Talon thinks I am cruel. He's not speaking to me. I don't know whether to be happy or worried." Matt picks me up from my chair and flings me over his shoulder.

"Must you throw me about like a ragdoll?" I ask. He kicks my chair away. "Matt, I might need that."

He sets me on the grass. "I get frustrated. He thinks he knows you so well," Matt says.

I edge over to him. "Matt, don't be upset. I was going to save this until we got home and torture you, but since you are so upset, I will show you now. Because you abandoned me. Maybe Talon doesn't know everything." I steady myself and stand up. I take a few steps and then fall, landing on my back.

"Pathetic," Matt says, clearly sulking.

"What I am trying to say is thank you," I say.

"So you are saying that I, Matthew Larkin, was right and that I know you better than Talon? Admit I am the better student than you too."

I freeze. "No, not that," I say, adjusting my necklace.

He grins. "How about I keep you company today?"

I return the grin. "That would be perfect, but no helping or gloating."

"Deal," he says, and we shake on it.

I refuse to let Matt help me up when I fall. When I have convulsing spells, he looks away until I gather my composure. I use my wheelchair as a walker to guide me as I drag myself along. When I need to rest, I sit in my chair, and Matt keeps me company.

Despite my nightmares, I get up on Saturday and Sunday and make myself stumble around. My dad takes all types of scans and x-rays. Jonathon insists on doing my blood work, and my parents make me comply because he is helping. My mom gets my chair ready for school, although I tell her I am not going to need it. Tevan helps me with my clothing. "It is important to keep up appearances," Tevan says as she puts blush on my cheeks. I think I might still look bad by the amount of makeup she puts on me.

Talon picks me up on Monday morning, bright and early. "Well, if it is not my beauty," he says as he looks around for my chair.

"Don't forget this," Mom says as she places a new tracker on me.

I just stare at it. "Why do I need this? It didn't help me."

Talon gets my chair for me, but I tell him, "I won't be needing that." I stand up and pick up my backpack.

"Ready?" Talon asks. He hovers over me as if I will fall. The truth is, it took everything in me not to fall. Mom and Tevan taught me makeup tips to cover up my dark circles because I still can't sleep properly at night, and I'm still pasty. All of my high-powered Tevan clothes reveal healing scars, so I opt for long-sleeved shirts and jeans. I feel I'm in touch with my former self in my old clothing.

"You are doing fantastic," Talon says. "Did you go to therapy?"

I shake my head. "No, it just happened."

He nods. "I feel things haven't been the same with us since the hospital and then Matt," Talon admits.

"I could tell by your face that you didn't know our mom's intentions," I say.

"I would never hurt you. She insists she was and is still concerned," Talon explains.

I don't want to argue with Talon on the matter. I feel he's blind to the truth about his mother. She controls my entire world, and I hate her for it, but I have to pretend all is well. "Okay," I say as Talon holds my hand.

As we leave Axis, I see new faces plastered on the Wall of the Missing. "Stop!" I say suddenly and try to get out of the car.

"Do you recognize someone?" he asks.

"Yes."

There on the wall were some of the detectives who interviewed me about the kidnapping. Also, Rachel's picture was there. I try not to cry.

"It's going to be all right," Talon says and gently pulls me away.

I stay quiet for the remainder of the drive. When we get in front of the school, Talon hugs me.

"No matter what, I'm here," Talon says. The media surround us and begin asking questions. "The lady will not be answering questions today," Talon says as a news reporter practically hits me in the face with a microphone.

"Was your kidnapping a hoax for Candidate Dean to gain votes by recovering one of her own?" the reporter asks.

"No questions," Talon says as he ushers me into school.

"The people demand Rachel Mendel and all the other Lexicon

citizens be returned. They are just as important as a scientist's daughter!" she shouts at the shutting door.

"That was awful," I say, my breath catching in my throat.

"Listen to me. I am used to attacks. Let me handle it," Talon says.

The school day is grueling. I try to walk, but it is so hard to concentrate. I am thankful that I'm wearing my old shoes rather than heels. No one says anything to me; they only stare as if I am a freak. Talon escorts me to and from each class.

At lunch, Tia is attentive. Tiffany and Jason analyze every move I make.

"Was it nomads? I heard some were caught snooping in that very area a week prior," Tiffany says.

I try to focus. "No," I say as I struggle to pick up my food. I think back to my encounter with the nomads who searched for the vans this summer. I wonder why they did that.

"Kaya, will you feel up to the dance?" Tia asks, breaking my train of thought.

"Sure," I say.

Tiffany pulls a face. "Is it true you were found naked in a field?" she asks.

"Yes."

"That was an awful question to ask someone," Tia scolds.

"That's kind of hot," Chris says, and Tia punches him.

"Are you going to dress better?" Tiffany asks.

Tia scowls angrily. "Well, she is going to sit with us."

I zone out while Tia and Tiffany argue.

I watch the conversation between Jason and Talon.

"Is your mom nervous about the elections this week?" Jason asks.

"She couldn't be more confident," Talon says. Jason laughs.

The tension only grows throughout the day as everyone stares and whispers.

By the last class, I look over to Rachel's seat, and I want to lose it.

"Kaya, do you need to be excused?" Mr. Fox asks.

I get up and walk down to the library. Rachel's mother is putting away books.

"Mrs. Mendel," I say.

She stops and looks at me but then quickly looks away. "I heard you were back today."

"I'm sorry. I tried to save her."

She starts crying. "You did all you could, or so a detective told me," she says. "I kept your project."

"May I present it?" I ask.

She nods and then helps me through the door.

As I walk down the hall, flipping through our research, an article falls out. This is Rachel's work that shows security photos of vans abducting people and their pictures later on the wall. Some of the pictures are of people enduring torturous experiments. My body starts shaking involuntarily, and I drop the entire folder, our report included, on the floor. A janitor helps me as I gather Rachel's work into a pile. A loud commotion occurs at the end of the hall. I glance up—it's a fight between two boys—taking my eyes off the papers and the janitor for only a moment, but when I turn back, he's gone, along with all of Rachel's research. I feel as if I'm losing my mind as I search the hall for him.

I take the project and stand outside the classroom door. I walk in and deliver our presentation that questions society in an unforgiving Lexicon.

CHAPTER 10

Talon is a basket case in the days leading up to the election. He picks me up for school because I still am not sleeping and have yet to master fine motor skills.

"Look at these vultures," Talon notes.

"I wonder if they are as aggressive with Jason Johnson's dad," I say.

Talon gives me a look. "How should I know? They probably aren't. His dad is Lexicon's golden boy."

"A mere question, Talon," I say.

"Do you think it was a coincidence she placed me in the same school as Jason Johnson? She has me over a barrel so she can blame me if things go wrong," Talon says, his knuckles turning white as he grips the steering wheel. "Why are you quiet?"

"It just seems some of the things your mom does are for political gain rather than your best interest."

Talon scowls at me. "Can you name one time she has failed me?"

"Where was she in the first grade when you were performing in *Peter Pan* in the lead role? Where was she when you broke your arm at school?"

Talon gets flustered. "Why are you so cruel?" he asks.

"I'm not trying to be cruel. I am merely making a point. You shouldn't be under so much pressure. I'm not the only one who thinks that your mom has questionable motives."

"Who is it? Larkin?"

"No." I say, biting the inside of my cheek.

"I can tell by your face that it is. And it is not like you speak to so many people," Talon says.

"Now who is being cruel?"

"It's just … she has to have a motive for everything," he says, and I agree. "But you should never discuss it with Larkin."

"He's our best friend," I say.

"You still don't have to discuss my mommy issues during your weird therapy with Larkin," Talon snaps, and I roll my eyes.

By Thursday everyone is excited about the dance. I rarely engage in these conversations, so I just observe.

"Chris and I are going to win the costume contest," Tia says. She and Chris kiss.

"Too late. Jason and I have already cleared a space for the trophy," Tiffany says with a smirk.

After everything I have been through, this conversation seems insignificant and small.

As much as I try to be a normal teenager, I've come to realize I'm not. As they talk about costumes, I can barely pay attention. I get distracted when I hear noises from across the cafeteria. The cafeteria seems louder since my kidnapping. When someone drops something or yells, I try not to jump out of my seat. Tia is nice about it, but I can see that the others notice. I catch Tiffany mouthing the word *freak* behind me. Their voices are too much for me to bear at times, so I focus on either Talon or Tia—but now Talon isn't himself.

Talon seems to be living his own personal nightmare. As the elections approach, the news teams turn their attention from me being the lone survivor to Talon Dean, son of Rebecca Dean. When we enter school, he is ambushed with questions. He also has to deal with Jason.

"The big election is this weekend," Jason says. "Is your mom going to retreat behind her giant Axis walls after she loses to my dad and never show her face again?"

Everyone at our table stops to listen.

"Probably," Talon answers casually as he continues eating.

"What? No insults? My dad has it on record from people who worked for your mom that she engages in unethical practices," Jason says.

"What do you mean?" Tia asks.

"Oh, Talon knows," Jason says.

Talon looks up with a smile. "You know what? I have an idea. Since Friday is Halloween and the dance, why don't Kaya and I sneak everyone into the Axis labs to see if there is anything unethical. Think of what it could do for your daddy's campaign if you witnessed anything firsthand."

Jason narrows his eyes at Talon, but Tiffany says, "I thought no one was allowed into Axis."

"For you four, we will make an exception," Talon says, pointing to Tiffany, Jason, Tia, and Chris. "You aren't scared, are you, Jason?"

I pull on him. "What are you doing?" I whisper.

"*My* mom will be at some gala with her goons," he whispers to me. "Security will be minimal. Matt knows the grounds because of his dad. He and I will set up a scene to scare them. Boom—I pay back my mom if it is leaked, and I scare the crap out of that jerk, Jason."

"You are bad," I say.

"No, I'm back," he says, locking his hands behind his head.

"You have a deal, Talon," Jason says.

"How do you know Matt will be on board?" I whisper.

"He can't stand if we are in on something without him. Plus, he will think he has to keep us out of trouble," Talon says.

As soon as we get to Axis, Talon and Matt begin unrolling blueprints from the old school that Matt found on his dad's desk. "These are still under construction because my dad is always talking about the mess," Matt says as he and Talon circle the rooms.

Talon calls his dad and gets the codes.

"Getting codes?" I ask.

"To the doors. I am going to scramble the cameras while I freeze others," he says. "You and Larkin go to the Axis store and buy out anything we can use for our prank. I am going to practice tapping into the store while you are there and freeze a few frames. The set designer will be calling, and I might need one of you to meet him outside the walls for the props I ordered," Talon says excitedly.

"You ordered props from a set designer?" I ask.

Talon ushers us out as he talks on the phone.

"Why would your dad give you codes?" Matt asks.

"Because I am his only son. I never ask for anything, and he hates my mom. Now go," Talon says. Matt and I stare at him. "Really, I promise to discuss it with my shrink during our next session. You know I have been on edge; this will relax me."

Matt and I walk to the Axis store. "Does Talon ever scare you?" he asks.

"No. I think I started this downward spiral by saying some things about his mom."

"Kaya why would you do that? You know they have issues."

"Because she was searching for me when I was missing. The woman hates kids. Plus, I might have mentioned that other people don't like her either."

Matt gives me a look. "Kaya, right before the election? And all while the media monitors Talon's every move?"

"Talon wasn't being himself, and Jason Johnson torments him," I explain.

"And now he's on a path of destruction," Matt says.

"He's happy, though."

"His behavior is not happy healthy," Matt says.

"I know, but he's distracted," I say. When Matt shakes his head in disapproval, I tell him, "You didn't have to help."

Matt quirks his eyebrow. "What if the two of you do something stupid?"

I smile.

"What?" he asks.

"Talon knew you would say that."

"Because the two of you are idiots. One of you gets an idea, and the other one takes it a step farther, never measuring consequences."

I laugh. "It wasn't my idea."

"Yet here you are, going along for the ride," Matt says.

"As are you," I remind him.

Matt gives me an awful look and I trip a bit.

"You are walking well," Matt says.

"Thanks. If you hadn't been so cruel, I'd still be in my room."

"You're welcome. Speaking of people being themselves—your presentation; I was moved," Matt teases.

"It was for Rachel," I say, and Matt smiles.

Once at the store, Matt and I buy everything on Talon's list. When we get back, Talon is excited to announce he has hacked the system and has done everything he set out to do.

"I thought Axis has the world's leading security," I say.

"What can I say? I am brilliant," Talon gloats.

When the sun goes down, and everyone in the labs goes home, Talon breaks us in undetected so we can get ready for tomorrow's prank. Talon sprays fake blood everywhere, and he uses actual equipment—gurneys, lab coats, and everything else he ordered—without being detected. By midnight, Matt and I are so tired we are slouching on the counter.

"We're not done," Talon says as he gets out a fog machine.

"Talon, it will be perfect. You've planned every detail," I say.

"What will I synchronize from the dance and set from my phone?" Talon asks, checking our response.

"Doors, alarms, and cameras," Matt and I say in unison.

"When are we leaving from the dance?" he asks.

"Ten thirty," I respond, but I feel myself falling asleep.

"Who is hiding in your trunk?" he asks.

"Satan," I say. "I mean, Tiffany and Tia."

He nods. "Matt, where will you be?"

"Hiding in the closet so I can scare your 'frenemies,'" Matt says.

"What's in here?" I ask as I try to open a door.

"According to the blueprints, it is a janitor's closet," Matt says as he holds up sketches.

"Why is it locked?" I ask, still trying to open it.

Matt reaches for his phone. "My mom is calling. She doesn't believe I have football practice this late."

"Did you tell her you're with a girl?" Talon teases.

"Yeah, with Kaya," Matt says as he answers his phone.

"Unbelievable," Talon says.

"What did you tell your mom?" I ask.

"She never asks me," Talon says. "Your parents?"

My mom calls, and I tell her I am on my way home. "That I am with you and Matt," I say.

That night I toss and turn, falling out of bed. I see the pictures from Rachel's research and feel needles being driven into my arm. I begin screaming.

"Kaya," my dad says as he turns on my light.

I sit up, trying to catch my breath.

"Your machine is going off," he says.

"I hate this machine, and I hate these nightmares," I say as I throw the oxygen tube.

"They said you wouldn't walk, and look," he says as I try to steady my breathing.

"I am a wobbly mess," I insist.

"Well, once you are able to get more sleep, coordination is sure to follow," he says.

I run my hands through my hair. "I will ever be the same again," I say.

"Explain."

"The kids at school are concerned with dances and maintaining popularity, and I just don't want to feel like a freak. My mind begs me to forgot what happened, but my entire body gets locked in this tug-of-war every night as I try to outrun what happened. I think I am supposed to remember something, but I can't. I feel defeated," I admit.

"You are stressing way too much. How about I take a seat, and you sleep a while."

I nod but tell him, "That's not progress."

"But this chair is comfy. Would you deny an old man who looks through a microscope all day the chance at comfort?"

I crawl under my blankets. "I know what you are doing," I say as I pull my covers up around my chin. "Are you saving the world?" I ask.

"I am running the entire upstairs because Rebecca plans on winning. If she wins, she will rarely be in Axis."

"What goes on underground?" I ask.

"Classified. Jonathan and the Talberts are in that network," my dad says. He looks like he might fall asleep. Even with Dad in the room, I can't sleep. It's as if he's not there, and something is trying to pull me into a dark corner.

The next day Talon picks me up for school. "What is wrong with your eyes?" he asks.

I grab a pair of sunglasses. "I have sleep problems, and thank you for subtly bringing them to light," I snap.

"Do you feel like going to the dance?" Talon asks.

"Yes," I say.

"You will still be the prettiest girl there," he says.

I lean my head back and fall asleep. I wake up in the car, and it is noon. I walk in to find everyone is at lunch.

"There she is," Talon says as he hands me my lunch. I barely have enough time to eat before the bell rings. "You look refreshed," Talon says.

For the rest of the day, I feel like I could run a marathon.

After school, I am met at home by Tevan and Jonathon.

"Did you think I was going to let you go to your first dance without help?" she asks. Jonathon stares at me.

"Why do you bring him everywhere?" I ask.

"Jonathon and I are going to be married one day. He's part of the family, silly," Tevan says as she piles makeup on me. "What are you wearing?"

"Something from the vintage shop," I say.

She gasps. "Kaya, are you in your right mind? I know you have been through a traumatic ordeal, but—"

"Talon and I picked out our clothes before I was kidnapped," I tell her. "So I believe I *was* in my right mind."

She starts to panic. "Mom, why did you let her do this?" Tevan calls out, rushing from the room to find our mother.

"Jonathon, why do you stare at me so strangely?" I ask.

"I saw you the night of the incident, and I am shocked you're here," he says

"Did … you not want me to make it?" I ask.

"I didn't mean it that way."

"Then stop looking at me freakishly!" I snap.

"I'll try. Who helped you to walk?" he asks.

"Matthew Larkin."

Jonathon nods. "The groundskeeper's son."

Just then Tevan and my mom come in, arguing. "Tevan, it's Kaya's dance," Mom snaps. Behind her, Dad is pointedly tapping his foot and checking his watch; they're on their way to the final gala before tomorrow's big election.

"Take pictures," Mom says. She kisses both of us on our cheeks.

I take my dress upstairs. Tevan is upset and shakes her head disapprovingly. Just as I put on my costume and adjust the small white cap, the doorbell rings. Talon waits at the bottom of the stairs. Tevan and Jonathon look us up and down.

"It works," Tevan says, smoothing out my vintage white nurse's dress. "Talon is even holding his hat like a real soldier." Tevan begins taking pictures. "The two of you are so adorable."

"Tevan, I can't even see from the flashes," I complain.

"Do you need your glasses?" Tevan asks.

"No, I haven't needed them since the abduction," I say.

Jonathon seems startled by my comment but says, "You two have fun." He opens the door for us, and I can feel him watching me.

"You look beautiful," Talon says as he opens my car door. "I thought Jonathon was the enemy."

"He just thinks I'm a freak because I survived. I think I'm going to begin a game when he's around, mentioning I have strange side effects from being kidnapped."

Talon laughs. As we drive, Talon seems calm. He smiles, and we chat.

"Congratulations," Talon says as we get to the school gymnasium. "After everything, you made it to your first official Lexicon Public School dance."

"I feel a bit overdressed," I say, as girls run in wearing very little clothing, and boys run by in scary masks, chasing them.

"They aren't classy," he says as I take his arm.

Tia and Chris are dressed as a caveman and cavewoman. "Chris and I had these tailored and shipped. Do you like my outfit? It's actual cheetah." She makes everyone feel it. "Kaya?" she asks.

"I just think it is a shame something had to die for a costume," I comment.

Tiffany and Jason are dressed as a millionaire and a French maid. I have never seen anyone in so little clothing as Tiffany. Jason is wearing a robe that exposes his muscles, and he's chewing on a cigar.

"You guys look amazing," Tia says.

They turn to me. "Who are you and Talon wearing?" Tiffany asks.

"Vintage clothing," I say. "Talon's has blood splatter on his lapel, but I don't think anyone died in them." They all stare at me.

"Lovely," Tiffany says, giving everyone a look.

"Would you like to dance?" Talon asks.

"Thank you," I say with relief.

He laughs. "You looked like you needed saving." He holds me close.

"I don't fit in, and I don't I want to," I say. I watch the others make a scene as they dance.

"That's what I love about you," he says as he spins me. Just then, Halloween confetti begins to fall from the ceiling.

"Oh, there are things you love about me?" I ask, and he nods.

"I have been around so many girls, but you don't even have to try, and you have me," he says.

"So many girls?" I tease.

"I mean, I would do anything. You have such innocence and convictions."

I feel myself blushing. "Stop it."

He smiles. "No wonder Larkin has to keep so busy to keep his mind off of you." He kisses me.

Just then, Talon's alarm goes off.

"Talon, it's time for your prank," I say as he smiles.

"Let's forget about the prank so I can kiss you again," he says as he starts to kiss me once more. Then he looks at Jason, who makes a face. "No, on second thought, I want to crush that jerk."

Talon steps to the side and begins setting up his phone to reprogram security at Axis. It's announced that Tiffany and Jason win the costume contest.

"The first win for my family this weekend," Jason says triumphantly.

We signal Tia and Chris as we make our way out to the parking lot.

"Did Tevan drop your car off?" Talon asks.

"Check," I say.

"What did you tell her?"

"That you were possibly going to meet your mom at the gala," I say.

Tia, Chris, Tiffany, and Jason come out from the dance.

"Look how smug he is," Talon says as he sees Jason.

"Am I going to live to tell the tale?" Jason asks.

Talon pops open the trunks on my car and his.

"You can't be serious," Jason asks.

"Have you ever tried to clear Axis security?" Talon asks. "It's bad enough that Kaya and I left together and are returning separately. Everything is noted. Only we go in, and only we go out. Take it or leave it."

Jason eyeballs the trunk. "Fine," he says.

"Plus, I will need all electronic devices," Talon insists. They all hand him their phones. Jason crawls in the trunk of Talon's car.

"Chris, you're with me," Tia says. She pulls him to her as she edges toward my car.

"Fine," Talon says as Tiffany gets in with Jason.

As I follow Talon back to Axis in my car, I worry about passing security. Security has not done a complete vehicle search in a while. Even though Talon is the son of President Dean of the Thantos Corporation, he is not immune to car searches.

As we near Axis, we notice very little traffic. *Everyone must be at the gala or home*, I think. The air is crisp, as on most fall nights. Only two guards are on duty, and we are quickly ushered through. I follow Talon to the back of the labs, an area that once served as our basketball courts. We park behind some bushes.

"Are you sure about this?" I ask Talon.

He synchronizes his phone with a watch I have never seen him wear. "Let's do it."

We let our guests out of the trunks.

"Oh, my goodness. That was such a rush!" Tia says as she and Chris begin making out.

"Jason was sucking up all the air, and I nearly suffocated," Tiffany gasps.

"There should be one guard on duty, and he should be making his rounds right about now," Talon says.

As if on cue, the guard walks through with a flashlight.

"He won't be back through this section for another couple of hours. Let's go explore, Jason," Talon says, shoving Jason a bit.

"So, this is the golden city," Tiffany notes.

"The homes and quaint streets—it's like going back in time," Tia says as we make our way down.

"I don't see what the big deal is," Tiffany says. She's shivering in her ridiculous costume.

"The air feels cleaner," Tia says as she breathes in.

"It's filtered for perfection. No smog or city pollution here," Talon explains.

Just then, the lights go out all over Axis.

"Oh no, there must be a temporary power outage. That has only happened twice in Axis history," Talon says, slapping his forehead.

"So how are we getting in?" Chris asks.

Talon taps his device. "Three, two, one," Talon says, and the doors open to the labs. "Just as planned." The lights come back on, and the doors close behind us. "Cameras are frozen," Talon says as he checks his phone.

"Are you a criminal mastermind?" Jason asks.

Talon smiles. "Never underestimate a man with a plan." He waves in front of the cameras and laughs.

"Is he always this scary?" Tiffany asks, biting her lip.

"Yes," I answer with a scary smile.

Tia coughs. "Why are the labs full of plastic sheeting and sawdust?"

"Construction," I answer. "These halls were once our schools. They are future labs."

We suddenly hear glass shatter, and our guests become frightened.

"Whatever," Jason says as he pulls a flashlight from his robe. "Talon probably has someone in the back, throwing things to scare us."

"What is the Thantos Corporation?" Tia asks as she huddles next to Chris.

"The most unethical company on the planet," Jason says. "Germ, chemical, and you-name-it warfare disguised by obtaining the Vitae Corporation, which actually did good in the world. Talon's mom has been busted for experimenting on humans. She also has tons of smaller companies that are questionable as well."

Talon clenches his fist as we walk. Hearing Jason insult Talon, I can't help but be proud of the reputation my father built within his company.

Gusts of wind blow through the open windows, making the plastic wave around, frightening our guests. A few birds fly near the ceiling as we near our scene.

For a moment, I begin to panic and have to remind myself it's only a prank. "You wanted to see the labs," I say as I clutch my scarred arm.

The first few remodeled labs are clean and have yet to be used. Tia and Tiffany look through a few cabinets. "Can I look in the cold walk-in area?" Chris asks. I open it.

"Where's Talon?" Tiffany asks.

I look around. "I don't know."

"Oh please," Jason says. "He went to set up some finale." Jason looks through a few vials and then through a case of pictures. "Well, well, well. If it isn't security for everyone at Axis. It seems Talon's mommy cares about everything he does and everyone he associates with. Look—here are you and Talon in Lexicon, at school, and some of just you. Talk about Big Brother."

I look at the pictures. Some are of Matt and me. I stand looking at an entry of a closet, leading to a room that is in the process of becoming the largest security center I have ever seen. Monitors and high-tech screens line a wall that seems to have no end. I also find pictures of my parents and other people from Axis in Lexicon. Every moment is documented outside of Axis. I suddenly wonder if my kidnapping is on file.

There, on the date I was rescued, is a picture of me found in a field. As I look at it, I wonder how I am even alive. I look maimed, like every bone in my body is out of place, and there's blood everywhere.

No wonder Jonathon looked at me like I was a freak. The picture was taken by the Lexicon police, and somehow Axis has copies. I feel that every moment of my life, since Rebecca Dean's entrance into Axis, has been documented, even my near-fatal experience. I hold the picture up to my chest because I wanted to hide.

"Kaya, are you all right?" Tia asks.

I look up and realize she's the only one left in the lab. "I'm fine," I insist.

"Are you sure? You look as if you've seen a ghost."

"Where is everyone?" I ask.

"I don't know. Gone their separate ways."

Just then, we hear screaming from the lab scene. "Oh my!" Tiffany says, running toward us. "Jason was right! They have bodies!"

She screams, and Tia pulls on me in a panic. Matt runs out, covered in blood.

"Nice try, Talon!" Jason shouts.

"Is that Larkin?" Chris asks as he dabs some of Matt's fake blood under his eyes.

"You helped Dean?" Jason asks, and Matt nods.

"Axis for life!" he says.

Chris and Jason laugh and do some handshake.

"Check out the cooler," Chris tells Jason.

"You have to see the lab Larkin put together," Tiffany says as she shows Tia.

I motion for Matt to join me. "This has Talon's calls from the hospital. The conversations are printed, with him giving her details. They even have a picture of me being found in the field," I say, hiding the picture.

"They follow that closely?" Matt asks as he looks at all the pictures. "Here's one of us." "Where's Talon?" I ask as alarms start going off.

"System shutting down," a voice says over an intercom. The doors begin to close.

"Matt, what do we do?" I ask.

Matt pulls me into a closet marked *Hazardous.*

"A closet?" I ask. We begin moving. "What's happening?"

"I don't know," he says.

"It feels like we're in an elevator."

"Thantos is going to kill us," Matt says.

I panic as we move downward at an accelerated speed and then stop.

The door opens. All the doors are opening and closing, and the voice is still speaking over the intercom. I begin pushing buttons.

"Why won't it go back up?" I ask.

"I don't know. My dad is a maintenance guy, not a technician," Matt says.

"System overload," the voice says as a red light flashes.

"Where are we?" I ask. We stare down a long hallway.

"Looks like top security. Look—I'm in; I'm out," Matt says as he steps in and out of rooms. "Aren't you curious? We are probably as good as dead anyway. Talon abandoned us."

"I want to go home!" I cry.

"Has Thantos finally gotten into your head? Think of all the things we can tease Talon about," Matt says he walks away.

I didn't want to follow him, but I didn't want to be alone.

"I've heard my dad talk about the underground," I say. "Jonathon and the Talberts have this level of security. Animal testing."

The animals we pass go crazy from the flashing lights and intercom noise. The next lab is full of samples and has a sterile appearance.

"Look at this," Matt says as he snoops. "This one is marked K. L."

I examine the file. "Why would Thantos want to know about me?" I ask. "Listen to this: 'Day 1: Patient had three broken bones and spinal damage. Bones were reset. Day 2: Patient remains unconscious. Patient struggles to breathe without assistance. Day 3: Subject is not responsive, not expected to make it through the night. Heart stops beating.' *Why?*" I ask, dropping the file on the floor.

"I don't know. Maybe because it was a risk to bring you back to Axis. Rebecca Dean has competitors, and they might have wanted to release a virus on the gated city. Face it; we are Axis property."

I shake my head. "No."

"Are you going to be all right?" Matt asks.

"Keep going," I say.

Matt cautiously walks into the next room. "Look at all these vials. The last room had initials of people. These have illnesses and diseases."

I read the labels. "Smallpox, malaria, influenza B—and look at the size of this room." I can tell that Matt is feeling as nervous as I am. "Jason was right," I say as Matt backs out of the room.

"Maybe Thantos studies diseases to make cures, like your dad Does," Matt says.

"Maybe," I say reluctantly. "Look—some have a cure."

"And then a way to destroy the cure," Matt says.

"Matt, we never saw this," I insist as we leave.

"What about this?" Matt asks.

"Geological," I read aloud. "There is a huge machine leading downward with no end in sight. There's a room marked 'meteorology' with weather labels. There is one marked 'nuclear' with missiles. Is this possible?" I ask as I try to process our discovery. "Why is this door closed?" I say as I tap on it.

"It has a keypad," Matt says.

I type in a code.

"Access denied," a voice says over and over as I type in random codes. Just then another set of lights goes off.

"Do you think security is coming?" I ask as the door opens.

"Kaya," Matt says as I walk in.

"You did it first. I am just following your lead," I say, pulling on Matt.

"I can't believe what we have done," he says. "It's a lab."

We explore and find more vials and test studies. I read one of them: "'Vial A mixed with Vial AZ1 causes subject to have violent seizures and then die.' Look at all of these vials. There are more vials and labels in here than the other two labs combined. Whatever they are doing is causing a lot of rats and animals to meet their demise." I look at a computer screen as Matt examines charts.

"I have never heard of these formulas," Matt says.

"This must be chemical warfare. Jason would love this," I say as I push a few buttons on a giant keyboard. A door lifts. "Another dark and secret room."

"Kaya, I can't," Matt says as I enter.

"Matt, it is just a dark room. Don't be a baby."

He refuses to enter.

"All systems will begin in five minutes," a computerized voice says as the lights begin flashing.

Just then, I see large tubes. The first are empty. Then, toward the back, I see tubes—with humans.

"Kaya, come on!" Matt shouts, but I run to the tubes. The first contains a woman. She has IVs coming out of every vein in her body. Her eyes are closed as she floats in a light blue fluid.

The next is a small girl, probably no older than eight. "No," I say as I touch the glass and begin crying. I have seen her sweet face among the missing persons when her mother lovingly placed her poster on the wall. She has dark brown hair that waves in the blue fluid.

"Sal," I say as I see him in a tube. At first, I don't recognize him. His body looks withered. Each person's body is covered in scars. I look down at my arm to make sure my scar is covered. For a moment, I feel like I too am an experiment from all the information I found on myself filed within Axis.

I begin crying harder and hit Sal's tube. As I do, all the bodies within the tubes come alive as if awakened by my one action. The subjects begin twisting, turning, and convulsing. The movement is so violent that two of the tubes become cracked and begin squirting water.

"Sal," I say, and he places his hand on the glass. Just then the lights go out, and I feel someone pulling me from the room.

"Matt, did you see?" I ask.

He stares at me. "Did I see what?"

"The people in the tubes!" I say.

"No, the lights went out and security systems were about to reboot. I got you out right before the doors locked." When I try to go back in, he tightens his grip on me. "Kaya, we have to leave." He pulls me toward the hallway.

"But the people!" I say.

"Kay, if there are people in tubes, they are gone."

I again try to get back in, but the doors lock back into place. "You have to believe me," I say as the cameras and lights begin to turn back on.

Matt grabs the sides of my face. "I believe you, but we have to leave."

We run toward the closet, and as we get to the elevator, the alarms stop.

"Why are you holding your head?" Matt asks.

"So my brain doesn't explode. That could have been me," I say, trying not to get upset.

"Do you think Thantos kidnapped you?" Matt asks.

I don't want to utter those words because I know I could be in danger. I know I will be unable to trust a single soul. My father, Talon, and everyone within Lexicon and Axis are connected to Thantos somehow. I feel a rising panic.

As the elevator takes us up, it feels like a coffin, suffocating me.

"Kay, we'll figure this out. You need to breathe," Matt says.

I start hitting the walls. "We have to stop this!"

"Kay, calm down," Matt says, but I push him away.

The elevator stops, and we get out to guards all over the reconstruction site and sirens going off on the other side of the building.

"What was that?" Matt asks.

"Talon," I whisper as we sneak out of the building.

"Are you going to tell him about what you saw?" Matt asks.

"No. I can't trust him. I can't trust anyone," I say as we stumble our way to the cars.

"It's about time," Talon says.

"Where did you go?" I ask as I shove him.

"We've got to get our guests out of here. The gala is over, and there were flaws in my plan," Talon explains.

"This is awesome," Tiffany says.

"I can't be around you, Talon," I shout at him. "You are Thantos, and you always will be."

Talon pulls me to the side. "Kaya, I can't have this conversation now." He tosses Matt my keys. "Larkin, you take Chris and Tia."

"Some truths were revealed, Talon. I guess you can't run from who you are," Jason says as Talon pops his trunk.

"Get in the car with Matt and pretend everything is all right," Talon snaps as everyone gets in the trunks.

I get in the car with Matt, but all I can do is shake as I flashback to the faces in the tubes and how they came to life. I wonder if my mind was playing tricks on me. I begin shouting as Matt taps my shoulder.

"Kaya, you were having a bad dream."

"I keep seeing them," I say.

"It is going to be okay, but *you* have to be okay," he says.

I pull away from him. "Where are we going?" I ask.

"Back to Axis. You slept through us dropping off your friends," Matt says.

"Matt, let's leave."

He looks at me strangely. "What do you mean?" he asks.

"Let's you and me run away together. Let's leave Axis and Lexicon, and put it all behind us."

He turns his head slowly and looks at me.

"What?" I ask.

"What is wrong with you?" he asks.

"We don't even know who we can trust. My dad? Jonathon looks at me strangely. Talon and his mom? Let's go," I say.

When we are a block from Axis, I begin taking off my tracker.

"What would we do?" he asks.

"We could escape and move to Sorellis or Magnis. We could be nomads, if you want," I plead as we turn into Axis security.

Matt begins laughing. "I forgot you know ways to get out of the walls of Lexicon."

I nod. "I can find us a way out."

We pull in front of my house.

"What about nomads?" Matt asks.

"We will learn their ways," I say.

"They ride motorcycles and barter," he says.

I make a face. "I hate motorcycles."

He turns off my car, and we just sit quietly. As we do, Thantos security cars begin speeding through the streets.

"We need to get inside," Matt says.

"Matt, they are speeding toward the labs."

Matt pulls me inside my house.

"There you are," Mom says.

"I thought you were at the gala," I say.

She checks me over, and I pull away. "We were, but then this was released." She shows us a video.

It shows a newscaster outside the gala. She turns to the camera and says, "Presidential candidate Rebecca Dean of the Thantos Corporation has some questions to answer on the eve of elections. Video footage was released of her labs, raising questions over possible unethical animal testing or a secret door leading into Axis, where people have seen black vans. You heard me right—black vans, as described by the citizens of Lexicon, as well as Kaya Lewis, John Lewis's daughter, the only surviving kidnapping victim of Lexicon. Coincidence? Viewers want to know." She follows Rebecca Dean as she exits the gala.

Rebecca stops to make a statement. "This is nothing but a final attempt from my opponent to get votes while maintaining his golden-boy image. He's trying to take attention away from photos released last week of him with a mystery woman. Nice try, Richard," Rebecca says.

"Do you deny these images are of your labs?" the newscaster asks.

"Who could tell by the quality?" Rebecca replies.

"I would think you would know your own lab and vans. Would you be willing to invite the public into your labs to put their minds at ease?" she asks.

"First of all, those photos are clearly Photoshopped, and my labs contain highly sensitive materials, backed by thousands of investors worldwide. If one person with the wrong motives happened to angle a camera at a computer screen, it could cost the lives of millions worldwide. My supporters know the Thantos Corporation saved three million lives last year alone. Rebecca Dean is for the people."

The newscaster nods. "There you have it, folks. Rebecca Dean."

My mom turns off the video.

"So, there was a breach?" I ask.

Mom shrugs her shoulders.

"Possibly," my dad says. "We have the safest system worldwide. Talon's dad designed it and upgrades it regularly."

"Were the photos real?" I ask him.

"Beyond my area," he says.

"Are we having a lockdown?" I ask.

"No, but we need to remain indoors. Matt, I'll let your mom know you are here."

Matt and I sit on the couch.

"Do you remember watching movies?" I ask.

"Every weekend," Matt says.

I lean my head on him and start to drift off to sleep. Each time I begin having a nightmare, Matt nudges me a little. "It's okay, Kay," he whispers as I lock my arm around his.

I awaken to Jonathon shining a small light in my face.

"What are you doing?" I snap at him.

"You startled her," Matt says as he pushes Jonathon.

"Your mom said your nightmares were better last night. I can't get over that you no longer need your eyeglass prescription," Jonathan says.

"Get away from me," I say, trying to catch my breath.

"Kaya, calm down," Matt says, grabbing my shoulders and looking me in the eye.

"He's one of them," I whisper.

My dad has heard the commotion and joins us. "Do I need to check you?" he asks.

I almost try to hide.

"What's wrong?" my mom asks. I hear a beeping sound.

"They are going to be checking the logs of everyone entering and exiting Axis for the past few days," Dad says as I cover my ears from the noise.

"Why?" Jonathon asks and quickly flashes a light across my eyes; then he puts it away.

"It was possibly an inside job, or someone finally cracked ol' Dean's code," Dad says.

"She was trying to keep things quiet and didn't even call for a lockdown on the chances it would leak to the media," Mom adds. "She will find who leaked that footage."

"I'd better be getting home," Matt says.

"I'll walk you out," I say. Once outside, I say, "Matt, I'm sorry I lost it."

"Kay, we are going to be under the microscope because of what happened. We were seen going in and out of Axis."

"What did you think of the footage?" I ask. "It was the same animals. I don't know about the vans. Even if someone ran, how would they have had time to go to the top and ground floor to locate all that footage? Not even Talon when he left the group. The footage was taken on a blurry device. The person was moving around like he didn't know his way around."

"It couldn't have been anyone in the group. Even if they split up, Talon had their devices," Matt says.

"I wonder if there is a basement with black vans?"

Matt shrugs his shoulders. "We'll have to see what happens with today's elections. Get some rest," he says as he leaves.

My parents and I stay close to the television all day. Tevan joins us in watching the elections.

"I have been calling Jonathon all day," she says. Jonathon walks in just then from grilling food. I hoped Tevan would break up with him, but to my dismay, she is glad to see him and thinks it's sweet that he came over.

Talon knocks on the door, and my parents invite him in.

"Kaya, may I please speak to you in private?" Talon asks as he places a Rebecca Dean hat on Jonathon. I step outside with Talon.

"I thought your prank was secure," I say as I cross my arms.

"I did too," he insists.

"You left!" I say.

"I had reasons."

"I had horrible nightmares from what I saw," I say through clenched teeth.

"What happened? What did you see?"

"Why did I find a file with a log listing every time your mom called from the hospital and details of my condition from the hospital staff? She was keeping tabs on me because she did this to me, and you were her spy. I trusted you."

"My mom might be a lot of things, but Jason has gotten in your head. If she has a file, it is because you are from Axis, and she keeps up with everyone in detail. Hospitals are easily paid off." Talon tries to place his hand on my arm, but I pull away. "Have you been sleeping well? You haven't seemed well."

I get upset. "Don't treat me like everyone else."

"I'm sorry."

"Are the black vans of Thantos hers, like the news accuses?" I ask.

Talon looks away. "Kaya, she is not the only company that has a black van."

"Those allegations Jason brought up about humans?" I ask.

"That was years ago, and people donate their bodies to science every day."

I begin to walk away. "Unbelievable. She has an entire underground world that would cause her to be executed, and you are accusing me of siding with Jason."

"Even if she does, she has powerful friends and labs on every continent to get her out of such allegations," Talon argues.

"Stay away from me," I snap. I go back inside and close my front door.

By ten o'clock the elections are over, and ballots are counted. Top officials have to go behind doors until two in the morning.

"What has happened?" I ask my dad as we wait.

"I don't know. Some of the sections were close."

A report then comes on the television. The newscaster says, "After deliberation lasting hours, senators have finally made a decision. Richard Johnson is the president of Nambitus. Rebecca Dean has prepared a statement."

The camera pans to Rebecca. "My fellow citizens of Lexicon, I know a decision has been made, and it was a tough one. Remember in the days ahead that we all are unique and contribute to the system, but we must maintain our standing because Lexicon is the city of an entire world within walls. I thank you, Lexicon, for the opportunity, but beware of the choices you make and the consequences that result." Her guards whisk her away as newscasters try to interview her.

Various channels show people celebrating possible freedom on the horizon. We even hear fireworks just outside the walls of Axis.

"Her statement sounded threatening," I say.

"She is just worried about our fragile system and what Johnson intends to do. Should you call Talon?" Tevan asks. I shake my head. We all look at each other with the same feeling in the pits of our stomachs, but we don't say a word. Rebecca Dean has lost, and although Richard Johnson has offered hope of a brighter future, we know Rebecca Dean was not one to lose.

CHAPTER 11

Talon didn't talk to me at school following his mom's loss.

I try to keep everything as it had been so we don't fall under any suspicion after our prank. When my dad gets home from work each night, I listen to his conversations with my mom to see if he has any news on the breach in security.

Our table at lunch is the same, except that Jason gloats over his father's victory. Talon keeps himself covered in girls, so he doesn't seem bothered.

"Does it bother you that you and Talon only broke up days ago, and he's been seen with girls?" Tia asks.

"Not really," I say.

She gives Chris a look.

"Do you date anyone besides Talon?" Tiffany asks.

I shake my head. "No."

"I would be livid," Tiffany says.

"Yeah, I'm dying inside," I deadpan as I continue reading.

"She must be. She's reading," Tiffany says.

"You went off with that Larkin kid. He's lower class, but the two of you seemed cozy, and now that Jason's dad has won, things will be changing," Tiffany says.

I put my book down. "We grew up in Axis, so we are allowed to talk."

Tia and Tiffany look over at Matt's table. "There are so many cute guys at that table," Tiffany says; Jason seems offended.

I can't wait to get home each day and hide. Sometimes Matt sneaks over, but on this day, Talon is there.

"Kaya, I miss you," Talon says.

I glare at him. "You could have fooled me, by all the girls."

He looks down. "Kaya, you don't understand. It's all a ploy. Jason tries to have people assault me."

"How's your mom?" I ask, rolling my eyes.

"She keeps watching tapes of her debates and recent appearances. It's disturbing."

"I trusted you, Talon," I shout at him, causing a scene. He pushes me against a wall. "What are you doing?"

"Pretend," Talon says as he places his arm above me and strokes the side of my face. "There are eyes and ears everywhere. I found that out. Pretend to laugh." He leans over to whisper in my ear as a man goes by on a bicycle. "That man has been following me since the breach. I overheard my mom say she was suspicious of people within Axis. We could be in danger."

"Why did she have logs of you calling her? Why did the hospital tell her of my confidential condition?" I ask.

"I didn't realize the extent to which she was using me. I'm sorry. I know things, and Kaya, I won't let her hurt you. I promise. You just have to trust me until I can get out a message."

The man goes by again on the bike, and Talon grabs me and kisses me.

"That was too convincing," I say, and Talon smiles.

"I am very committed to not raising suspicion," Talon says.

"What is the message?" I ask.

"I won't involve you. You've been through enough. I know you think I have betrayed you, Kaya, but I haven't. I know I don't deserve anything from you, but I need a favor."

"What?" I ask.

"My mother has been asking me questions about the dance, you, and school. She even asked me questions about my dad. I think she is suspicious. She wants to invite you over for dinner. Come over and pretend like everything is wonderful," Talon pleads.

"No. I can't." The thought of being around her truly terrifies me.

"Kaya, if she unscrambles the footage, she will know Matt was there too. He was there first," Talon says.

"Did you set him up?" I ask.

"No, but because of his dad having the blueprints to the building, and Matt being there first, and what she believes about people, we have to play this out. Let's just hope this is my mom having one of her episodes or that she's spiraling down from not winning the election. Either way, we won't give her an excuse to draw attention." Talon says.

"Let me get ready, but after that, I am not ever speaking to you again," I say

He smiles. "Do you know how many times you have said that to me?" Talon asks.

"Too many to count," I say.

When we get to Talon's house, I can't make myself get out of the car. "How should I act?" I ask.

"Be yourself. It will drive her crazy, and she will leave us alone." He walks around to open my door.

"So, I'm annoying?" I ask. We get to the front door. "Your mom had more work done to the house."

Talon rings the bell. "And to herself," Talon says. He sees me frown and asks, "What's wrong?"

"It's just when my dad was president, we all had the same size houses." I stare at all the ridiculous add-ons.

"Mention it." Talon says. We continue to wait.

"You ring the bell at your own house?" I ask.

"We have servants," Talon says. I try not to get frustrated.

A butler answers and takes my jacket. "Do come in."

"Talon, dear, is that you and your girlfriend?" Rebecca asks.

"Yes, Mom," Talon says.

Rebecca offers us a drink of wine.

I look at the bottle. "Water, please," I say.

I know she's watching me. "So how is school, Kaya?" she asks.

I look at Talon. "Good," I answer.

"Are you well?" she asks.

"Yes."

She toasts me. "Your healing has been indeed remarkable," she says as she looks at me, tilting her head.

We awkwardly sit through four courses as Rebecca watches Talon and me. "I have been wanting to have you over for some time, and now with the elections out of the way, I have more time to focus on what matters most, which is Talon." She gets up and hugs him. "I feel that so many times Talon has done things to try to get Mommy's attention. He's either felt pushed away or unloved, but he mustn't worry." She chops up some of his food and feeds it to him.

"Thanks, Mom," Talon says.

"I wish Talon's father would contact me over my lab footage," she says, breaking the silence.

"He always gets back to you, Mom, even though you have had him banned from six countries."

His mom pours more wine and begins laughing. "What do you think of the house?" she asks me.

"The pool is nice," I say.

"That's right. You were raised by John Lewis, sharing the views as my opponent, Richard Johnson." She laughs again. "Tell me how you really feel, John Lewis's daughter."

"The servants are a bit much," I reply.

She laughs yet again. "I like you."

Rebecca stares at me throughout dessert. "Do you still have nightmares?" she asks.

"Mother," Talon says.

"No," I answer as I eat a piece of cake. "How's work?"

"Most days are dead," she says.

Just then, Talon's phone rings, and his mother sighs. "Just when

I was about to have some fun with the two of you. Talon, you tell your father when he calls that if I have to figure out who broke into Mommy's lab, I will cut their hearts out along with his." She gets up and kisses Talon's cheek. "Good night, Kaya. We must do this again." She leaves the room.

As soon as we get outside, Talon gets out his phone. He immediately begins entering codes and numbers.

"What are you doing?" I ask.

"I'm contacting my dad."

When we get to my house, I refuse to get out of the car. Instead, I listen to Talon's conversation with his dad.

"Yes, I debugged the car," Talon says as he reaches into the air vent.

"Are those in all of our cars?" I ask.

Talon nods.

"Houses?" I ask.

He nods again and signals for me to be quiet. "Are you getting the files?" Talon asks his dad

I can hear his father shout at him. "Talon, why would you do this? You know she is the most powerful person on the planet!"

"Just look, Dad," he says.

Now his dad's voice is calmer, but I can still hear him. "Talon, I can't have these. I thought you were going to pull a prank, not hack your mother's entire system. I didn't even think you knew how. I don't know whether to be horrified or proud. My first system was a convenience store."

"Mine was a bank oversees. Mom cut my allowance," Talon says.

"Dammit, Talon, you decoded these as if they were unencrypted!"

"Dad, quit scaring me. I still have a few more to go," Talon says.

"Talon, you should be scared. Did you release information to the media?"

Talon hesitates and then says softly, "She needs to be stopped."

"Talon, you know once she gets started on a mission, your mom knows only to get her desired results, which is revenge. If she can override what you did for just a second or if you missed something, someone could suffer at her hands. I want her to go down for what I'm seeing, but this isn't a game, son."

"Who can I trust?" Talon asks.

"John Lewis. Get out of there as quickly as you can because, believe me, she has a plan, and you are at ground zero." Talon ends their call.

"So, this is what you wouldn't tell me?" I ask.

"Yes. Basically, anything bad that has been done on the planet in the past ten years, my mom has done for the highest bidder. Then she counters the assault. That epic tsunami that had scientists baffled and killed thousands was created in her labs. It was released and sold in secret to the highest bidder over a border dispute. You know that disease mimicking the bubonic plague that was not from a rat infestation, as told by the media. It too was lab-created by the highest bidder over water. Why not help drill with all those tools and find water?" Talon asks, visibly agitated.

We sit in Talon's car for a while. "Here comes your bicycle guy," I say as I grab Talon and kiss him.

"What was that for?" he asks.

"Appearances, and for you not being like your mom."

Talon puts the bug back in his car. As we walk to my front door, I worry about what will happen when we tell my dad.

"Who's in your house?" Talon asks.

"Matt," I say, and he rolls his eyes.

Matt greets us at the door. "What's going on? Are you all right? I heard you were eating dinner at Talon's."

"Hold that thought," Talon says. He uses his phone to do something to all the cameras in the house. "It was awful, like we thought it would be," I tell Matt. Talon gives me a look.

"Get your dad," Talon says.

We walk down to the basement, and I knock on my dad's lab.

"Company," he says as he wipes his hand.

"Mr. Lewis, my dad said I could trust you," Talon says. Then he shows the footage of everything he downloaded from his mother's network. "I just couldn't get footage of her inner labs—the ones that have come up in speculation," Talon says.

"Matt and I didn't get footage, but we saw," I say.

"We hid in a closet when the alarms began and were taken underground," Matt explains.

"She has the machines to create all the files you found," I say.

Talon holds his face in his hands.

"It gets worse. She's experimenting on people," I say.

Talon shakes his head. "She wouldn't. She merely creates diseases and releases them. Jason is not right."

"Talon, I saw them," I say. "She keeps them in a blue fluid. She has some of the missing from Lexicon, Talon. She has Sal."

Talon loses control and pushes some glass beakers from my dad's counter onto the floor. "I don't believe you! Not until I see it for myself."

I back away.

"My dad told me to get out, and I just had to take it a step further. Kaya, you and Matt had to take it a step further and go into the labs."

"The prank was *your* idea," Matt reminds him. "You left us."

Talon begins running his hands through his hair.

"Everyone calm down. I talk to your dad often, and we will reconvene," my dad says.

"My dad said this is it. Good as dead. She knows and has been encircling me like prey, about to pounce," Talon says.

"Listen, I've stopped her before. If we work together, we can do it again. In the meantime, act naturally," my dad says.

Talon gets up from the floor and walks out of the house, never blinking.

I go to bed and toss and turn most of the night. Just when I think I might get a reprieve from all the chaos, the alarms go off.

"Kaya, come on," Mom says.

I'm twisted up on my bed. "Leave me," I insist.

"Kaya, we have to follow protocol." She grabs me.

"Could they not do this on a school night? I am a child in need of sleep."

We make our way into the basement. As we go downstairs, we hear glass breaking.

"Hurry, Kaya," Mom urges me.

"What was that?" I ask. Dogs bark, and lights shine under the door.

"It must be another breach," she says. My dad slides closed the steel basement door after hearing the commotion.

"Are we under attack?" I ask.

"No news; the radio waves are dead." He pulls out one of his inventions and turns it on. We listen as my dad tries to pull up the Axis security channels.

We hear "Suspect cannot be located"—and then the airwaves go dead.

"They must have switched channels. This thing is a dinosaur." Dad hits the side of it.

"Mom?" I say as she holds me.

"It won't be long. Rebecca has top-notch security," she says. My mom tries to play a movie and encourages me to go to sleep.

"Dad, do you think Thantos kidnapped me?" I whisper as I lean my head on his shoulder.

"No, you wouldn't be alive." He pulls the blanket around me.

Our neighbor, Mrs. Riven, knocks on our basement door at 5:50 a.m. "I'm checking in as part of our agreement, as outlined by Mrs. Dean," Mrs. Riven says.

Mom rubs her eyes. "Is everything all right?"

Mrs. Riven looks at our steel door. "Is this standard issue? And I am not at liberty to say, Ms. Lewis."

Mom becomes upset. "We are in the most secure community in the world. We have someone clearly breaking into our home, and you are worried if our door is standard issue?"

"Your family seems fine," Mrs. Riven says as she makes a note and leaves.

We walk upstairs and find glass all over the kitchen from our back door.

"John ..." my mom says as my dad gets a broom. "Kaya, get ready for school," she says.

As I walk up the stairs, I wonder if this was because of Talon's footage or what we saw. Our entire house has been ransacked. "Mom ... Dad," I say.

My dad comes upstairs and looks around. "I don't think anything is missing," he says, "so we pretend that nothing has happened. We go about our day."

When Talon picks me up, he is quiet.

"Are you all right?" I ask.

"Yes, mild breakdown. I am ready to do whatever it takes to stop her," Talon says.

"What happened last night?" I ask.

"It was the highest-level security. My mom has yet to return," Talon says.

"Someone broke into our house." I say. Talon looks worried.

During lunch, it's hard for me to pretend everything is normal. I look over at Matt, and he notices something is wrong with me. I try to look away.

"Matt knows," Talon whispers. "He can watch how you walk in a room and know if you are all right."

"I'm not myself."

"I'll figure out who broke into your house," Talon whispers.

Tiffany and Jason discuss their Thanksgiving tour over Nambitus, and Tia and Chris make out. I want to escape, and for once Talon doesn't try to pull my book away from me.

After school, Matt is waiting on my porch. "I thought you said he has to work for college," Talon says.

"He does," I say, smiling.

"I made the mistake of telling him about what happened because he is a part of this, and he freaked out," Talon says.

"What did he freak out over?" I ask.

"The possibility of an intruder being within Axis. He panics over everything," Talon says as I smile. "I have to look over a few things. Tell Matt to chill."

I nod. I get out of the car. I can tell Matt is upset.

"Are you all right?" he asks.

"I'm fine."

"You didn't tell me," Matt says as I stare at him, fretting.

"How were you when I was kidnapped?" I ask, and he takes a step back.

"I was fine," he insists.

"I remember you reading to me, and when I had nightmares the other night while you were on my couch, you calmed me."

He seems nervous. "I don't know what to say." He stands there.

"You care more than you want to," I say.

"From now on, call me," he says as we sit on my porch.

"Like a friend?" I ask.

He glares at me. "Yes."

"Do you work today, friend?" I ask. He shakes his head. "May I walk you home?" I ask as I throw my backpack down.

"Sure."

When we reach his house, I sniff and ask, "Friend, is your mom making her famous chocolate chip cookies?"

"Stop calling me 'friend,'" he says.

I frown. "We *are* friends for an eternity, then you ditch me, then we're friends again, and now you're taking it away once more. Such a roller coaster of emotions, Matthew."

"Kaya, stop calling me Matthew and 'friend,' and I will invite you in for one chocolate chip cookie."

"Deal." I say as we walk into his house.

Matt's mom is the opposite of my mom. She stays at home and cooks delicious meals. When we were kids, we went to his house for after-school snacks, and she would help us with our homework while my mom finished up at the school. It was perfect until we fought, which was at least once a week. Then our parents would have to intervene because everyone suffered from our misery as we tortured one another.

"Mom, I have company," Matt says as we walk into the kitchen.

"Hi, Mrs. Larkin," I say.

"Kaya, how are you? We have missed you."

I act like I am crying. "I've missed you too, but Matt broke up our friendship."

She gets a look on her face. "Really?" she asks.

I nod. "He said I should be around other people."

"Why would he say that?" she asks.

I make a face at Matt over her shoulder. "Because of all the rules. It took me almost dying for him to be my friend again."

She pulls away and gives Matt a look. Then she looks at my necklace. "That is a beautiful necklace. I have one similar. Where did you get it?" She looks at Matt.

"Matt bought it for me on vacation for my birthday. He knows I love pieces with a mysterious past," I say as I eat a chocolate chip cookie.

"Really?" She and Matt exchange looks.

I want to tell her of the nomad story, but I have to stop myself. She is too busy signaling Matt, so I don't bother explaining myself. "You read about history. Do you know where it might have come from?" I ask.

She laughs. "Kaya, I am not a professor like your mom." She pats my face.

"But you are self-taught. You learn as you please. Surely you must know something of the patterns?" She gets her glasses. "I never take it off. Matt acted so strange when he gave it to me."

She quirks her eyebrow. "Did he, now? Aren't you with that Dean boy?" she asks.

"Mom," Matt says.

"Yes, because Matt won't break the rules and run away with the nomads to be with me," I say.

She laughs. "Well, Mrs. Dean was strict about the rules but was so concerned with your recovery that she encouraged all your friends to visit." Mrs. Larkin ruffles Matt's hair. "You never know—the markings might be nomad."

I get excited. "Tell me about your nomad studies, like when we were kids," I say.

"Those were just stories told by a man we helped after his car broke down on the side of the road, long ago," she says. "To him, there are nomad clans outside the walls of Lexicon all over Nambitus. They live in camps. There were, at the time, three main camps. One was run by a man who fought with his son, and they split into two powerful camps. The son's name was Skall."

I freeze. "Skall, you say?"

She looks at me and nods.

"What if this necklace is of Skall's people?" I ask.

Her brow furrows as she asks, "Why would you say that?"

I shake my head. "It is just an interesting name." She stares at me, and I grab another cookie. I don't want to tell her that the nomads suggested taking me to Skall.

"The third camp was run by a cruel leader named Nato. They trade among people in Lexicon, Sorellis, and Magnis, as well as each other. They have their own laws and customs," she says.

"I hope this necklace is nomad," I say.

"Only you, Kaya," she says.

"Thank you, Ms. Larkin, for the cookies. I miss you." I hug her once more.

"I'll walk you home," Matt says as we leave. "Why did you put on that sad scene for my mom?" Matt asks.

I smile. "Because I owed you."

He shakes his head. "No, I owe you."

"No, you told Mrs. Larrs last year that I copied your homework and cheated after I lost your music player."

As we get to my house, he says, "I had just put together those songs."

"You made it sound as if I violated and abused you," I say.

"You violated and abused my trust. I had just gotten that player. I have had to buy three new ones since."

I reach into my pocket. "I found this one when my room was ransacked," I say.

He smiles. "I knew it! Call me if anything ever happens like that again."

"If I ever find more music?" I ask.

"No, if your house is ransacked. I'll be there, friend."

"Good evening, friend," I say as he leaves.

When I get into my house, I cannot find anyone. My mother is still at work, and my dad is down in his lab. I walk down to the basement. I feel safer when in the basement than in any other room in the house.

As I turn on the television, I hear someone sniffling. I jump up to find Jonathon in the corner of the room.

"What do you want?" I ask, and I grab a chair to defend myself.

"I need your father. And why do you feel the need to defend yourself?" Jonathon asks.

I continue holding the chair behind my head. "You work for Thantos. Your parents betrayed my father. Plus, you still treat me like a science project. Therefore, you are the enemy."

He slides to the floor. "I am not your enemy," he insists.

"That lockdown last night was because something happened to my father," Jonathon says as I look for the cameras. "I froze them, and how do you know about those?" he asks.

"What happened?" I ask.

He wipes his nose. "An accident," he insists.

"Like?"

"Classified," he says.

I roll my eyes. "What if I guess?"

He shrugs his shoulders.

"He poisoned or released a disease upon himself, thus meeting his well-deserved end," I say.

Jonathon gives me a horrified look. "No, and you are unforgiving."

"I know."

"He was attacked," Jonathon says as my eyes grow big.

"Are you trying to play me for information so you might take it to your leader, Rebecca Dean?" I ask.

"My dad is one of her most trusted and was doing trials on something when he was attacked and killed. The thing escaped," Jonathon explains.

"What was the thing, and why would you admit that your dad would do such a thing to another human being?" I ask.

Jonathon runs his hands through his hair. "I don't know. My father would never talk of him. He said he was possessed. Working for her changed him. He even worked for her sister companies, carrying across findings and information. Only three people were that privileged. He was so close," Jonathon insists.

"So close to what?" I ask.

"I don't know. Now he's gone, dead." Jonathon says as my father comes in.

"Jonathon, get it together," my dad says.

"We have to stop her," Jonathon says.

I shake my head. "No, not him," I say.

"Don't stand there judging me. I'm tired after all I have done for you," Jonathon says. My dad pulls on his arm.

"What are you talking about?" I ask.

"Shut up, Jonathon," Dad says.

"Who do you think swapped Tevan's blood for your blood to throw them off?" Jonathon asks.

"Why would anyone need to do that?" I ask.

"Because you should be dead. It intrigued Rebecca. She requested samples, so I switched your blood," Jonathon says.

"Why?" I ask.

"Because you are my family now, and I hate it," Jonathon snaps.

"If I'm alive, then why would they need my blood?" I ask.

He laughs as my dad tries to cover his mouth. "Because you are not the same, and the two of us cannot figure out why. Didn't you have some inkling when they said you would never move, let alone awaken, yet here you are? You don't need glasses any longer. Don't you find that strange? Your secret is hard one to keep," Jonathon says.

I look at my dad. "Is this true?"

Dad nods.

"Am I dying or turning into the thing that killed Jonathon's father?" I ask.

Jonathon sobs, and Dad says, "I have no answers, other than you're alive, just altered. You are still altering."

Jonathon throws his hands up. "So what do you have to say for yourself?" he asks.

"If you think I'm going to thank you, then you are sorely mistaken. I hate you, Jonathon Talbert. I think my sister can do so much better than you. I wish you would give my blood to Thantos, and I will tell them of your confession and how you took my sister's blood in her sleep like a monster, or better yet, like your father."

He becomes enraged. "I am nothing like him!" Jonathan yells.

"I think your father finally got what was coming to him for all the damage he has caused to the innocent in Lexicon," I say. "I won't rest until Rebecca Dean reaches the same fate. I think it is fitting to be destroyed by the monster you inflicted pain upon and created."

"The two of you, stop. We won't make it out of this if we don't work together," Dad says. Jonathon and I swat at each other, but my dad pulls us apart. Tevan comes downstairs and holds Jonathon.

"Kaya, how can you be so cruel? His father just died," Tevan says.

"Kaya, get some rest," Dad says.

I glare at Jonathon, but then walk upstairs and go to bed.

I am plagued by nightmares. I am in the labs, and Thantos finds out my secret. They try to kidnap me to study me. I hear Rebecca while at dinner with Talon saying things are *'dead'* at work ring in my ears. I stand in front of the giant tubes as Sal calls out to me, as well as the others. Matt pulls me from the lab, but I am the only one who can hear them. The vans throw hoods over my head, but I can't overpower them. The thick liquid they inject in my body makes me scream and convulse once more. I stop breathing as we struggle, and then I turn into a monster, as described by Jonathon.

"Kay." I hear someone whisper.

"Matt?" I ask.

"I saw your lamp on from the street. You were violently tossing and turning." He gets a cloth and wipes my face.

"So you climbed my tree and came through my window?" I ask.
"Yes."

"It never ends. Then tonight, Jonathon and I played confession," I say. I tell Matt the story.

"His dad just died, Kay," he says. "Lie down."

I look at him strangely. He rolls his eyes and takes out his music player.

"Didn't I just give this back?" I ask.

"We each get an ear, like in the orchard," he says. Matt lies beside me, and we listen to music until I fall asleep. I wake up the next morning feeling rested, and Matt is gone.

Talon picks me up for school. "How are things?" I ask.

"My mom has a new plan for her life," Talon says with a strange look on his face.

"That's interesting."

"She is leaving to go overseas. I think it's a good idea we are having a meeting tonight," Talon says.

"How are you?" I ask.

He fidgets. "Nervous. Always on edge." When we get to school, I say. "Let's have some fun."

"You mean ditch?" Talon gasps.

"Precisely," I say, and he agrees. Talon speeds away from the school. We soon realize we are being followed, but Talon quickly loses the Thantos guards.

"What do you have in mind? The mall, bookstores, restaurants, or movies?" he asks.

I pull out a pamphlet and scan it. "There is a rally today. Let's go see what the news doesn't tell us."

He laughs. "Always an adventure." We drive using a map that pops up. "These directions are leading us all over the place. This freedom rally better be fun," Talon says. We get to an abandoned lot. "I think your directions were wrong," Talon says as we get out of the car. Then a few people begin walking around the streets.

"Look—a warehouse." I point to it.

We see a side door where people are entering. Talon and I get in line. We are ushered into the warehouse as music plays, and people dance.

"This is fun," I say as I make him dance.

"A little," he says as I spin him. There is artwork, signs, and people wearing shirts demanding changes within Lexicon. After everyone gets settled, speakers begin to take the stage. Stories range from persecution to kidnappings, prejudices, and boycotting businesses that try to change the system. "If my mom knew I was here, she would kill me," Talon whispers, I lean on him.

Then a woman takes the stage. "Lexicon, we have made strides since rioting and demanding Richard Johnson be placed in office after the win of Rebecca Dean. We presented evidence and won, but more change is needed. We have to annihilate the system and dare to dream to rise, or we are doomed to remain." Everyone cheers.

"Your mom *won*?" I say.

Talon shrugs his shoulders. "The people rioted

I look confused. "Why wasn't this on the news?"

Just then police break up the demonstration. People begin scattering and shoving as they are arrested. I grab Talon, and we run through a metal door as people fight.

"That was a rush," he says as we fall in the field near his car and begin laughing.

"If change was accepted, why are people still being arrested, and what evidence was presented?" I ask.

"I don't have any answers," Talon says as he kisses me and then falls on his back. "Can I ask you a question? Do you believe this way because you have feelings for Larkin?"

"I came today in honor of Rachel, and Larkin is okay. Plus, I love a fight," I say.

He laughs. "You always have." Talon hands me a strange-looking drink.

"What is that?" I ask.

"Someone gave it to me at the rally. It's not as fun as what I've had a boarding school, but it gets the job done."

I take a drink. "It's horrible!" I say.

He laughs. "You're adorable."

I take another drink and fall backwards to look at the sky.

"Let's leave," Talon says.

I sit up. "What?"

He places his hand behind my head. "Everything is about to get bad. I know my mom when she doesn't get her way. Those people are nowhere near being free, and neither are we. You and I can run away. I have houses all over the globe," Talon says as he kisses me.

"What about your plans to stop her?" I ask.

"It will never work. She always wins. I can send all the information to your dad, and you and I can walk away. I can have a jet pick us up in twenty minutes. My mom is out of town by now." Talon kisses my neck.

For a moment, all I can think about is running away and not having to worry about Rebecca Dean. Then I think about my family and the footage of Matt from the Halloween prank.

"Talon, we can't do that. We are already involved."

He sighs. "I don't want to be. I want a new mom."

I laugh. "Then you wouldn't have your car, houses all over the globe, and computers to hack systems," I whisper in his ear.

He smiles. "I got that skill from my dad." A black van pulls up. "Busted," he says as he helps me up.

Two men jump out with guns. "Talon Dean?" one asks as Talon smiles.

"Guys, I skipped school. It's not like I robbed a bank. You must be new at this." He raises his hands as a joke.

"Talon," I say in warning as I look at the guards.

The taller guard strides up to Talon and hits him across the face with a gun, knocking him to the ground.

"What are you doing?" I ask, getting in between the guards and Talon.

"Our issue is not with you. We need him," the other says as he shoves me.

"Don't hurt her. Take me," Talon says. They force his hands behind his back.

"I'm just as valuable," I say. "My father is the vice president of Thantos. I'm Kaya Lewis."

They laugh.

"Dammit, Kaya, do you ever know when to shut up?" Talon asks as they push him toward the van. "Have you not learned anything from your previous kidnapping? They don't want you. You should have some inkling it's about to go very badly for me," Talon says as one of the men throws him violently in the van.

"You should listen to your boyfriend," the man says. I kick him in the crotch, and he falls to the ground. The other one laughs. I pounce on Talon's captors, ripping one's shirt. He has a mark on his chest that resembles my necklace. These guards aren't from Lexicon. They are nomads. He slowly gets up and grabs me by my hair. "You have no idea what you have just unleashed," he says as he throws me in the back of the van with Talon.

The windows are blacked out so we can't see where we're going.

"Talon, I'm so sorry." I try to unbind his hands.

"Kaya, are you stupid?" Talon asks as I try to blot the blood from his face. "Push your tracker."

I uncover his eyes. "I can't. I was so moved by the speeches that I threw it in the burn pile at the rally."

Talon bangs his head against the back of the van. "I did too." He starts laughing.

"What's so funny?" I ask.

"Here we are, far away from Axis, and it is near nightfall. Both of us are missing our trackers, and we've been kidnapped by enemies of my mother."

"Don't panic, but I think they might be nomad," I say.

He smiles. "Of course. She's insulted them too."

We drive for what seems like hours.

"Quit trying to pick the lock, peel the blackout on the windows, and fidgeting. My mom never intended for cargo to escape," Talon says as I count turns.

"Shut up," I snap.

"Is this like the van that kidnapped you?" he asks.

"Slightly different," I say as he breathes a sigh of relief. I try to kick out the window, but Talon shakes his head.

"Useless."

"What would you suggest we do to pass the time?" I ask,

Talon smiles. "Kiss me."

I continue counting.

Just then the van stops. "Let me do all the talking. I speak nomad," Talon says.

One of the men grabs me. "No, please. She's in my camp," Talon says.

The man laughs. "She is not, and our fight is not with her." He throws a knife at my feet.

"Where are we?" I ask as I look around.

"The bad part of Lexicon. We trade in packs here, for safety. Have fun," the man says.

Talon shakes his head. "No. Please do not leave her!" Talon shouts.

They shove him back in the van and speed away.

CHAPTER 12

It is dark, and most of the streetlights are busted. The news teams do not report beyond the lower district, nor do the Lexicon police patrol. Judging by my surroundings, I'm past that point. There are no houses, only warehouses.

I can hear music. It sounds like a party in every direction. I grab the knife and begin chasing the van, but I lose it after a block. I become so overwhelmed by my senses that I have to stop and hold my head. I never had this sensation. I smell food cooking, hear a party and fighting, and then I remember what Grandpa told me about my surroundings

I still have the exhaust of the van embedded in my nostrils. I hold on to that smell and begin following the van. I don't know what I'm doing, but I trust my instincts.

As I walk, I don't notice the street party at first, but then the strobe lights and fog finally catch my attention. People begin crowding around me.

"Would you like a scarf?" one asks as I hide the knife.

"If she's not a sight for sore eyes. Check her pockets," another says.

"What is wrong with her face?" a woman asks.

I snap back to reality. I take off running toward an alley. I run, turning back, counting in the direction of the van. A young man comes out from a passageway, interfering with my mission.

"Hello, beautiful," he says as I fall backward.

"I don't want any trouble," I say as I stumble to my feet.

"How cute. You don't want any trouble, as if you are a threat," one says as he steps out of the shadows. The young man is about my age and tall.

"Maybe you can assist me. Did you see a black van in the proximity?" I ask.

"She speaks proper. Almost as if she's a lady in a den of thieves." He sniffs my hair. "I can tell you are far from home," the leader surmises.

"What are you going to do? Ransom me?" I inquire.

"Who knows? We might ransom you or even have a little fun in the process," he says.

I pull out the knife. "I don't believe you will," I say.

They laugh. "A princess with a knife," one says as three attack me.

Before I even know what I am doing, I kick one in the stomach, sending him flying into trash cans. I kick the feet out from under the next one, and as I spin around, I grab the remaining one and hold a knife to his throat. "I don't believe any of us will have fun tonight. The black van?" I ask as silence falls.

"You wouldn't," the leader says.

I press the knife deeper into the boy's throat and blood begins to drip.

"She's serious, Jess," he says. "Call her off."

I tighten my grip.

"They were heading east and stopped at a warehouse eight streets over," a voice shouts.

"Thank you," I say as I let the boy go. As he stumbles forward, several kids make their way into the light and hand me pictures of men, women, and children.

"What is this?" I ask.

"The missing who don't make it to the wall," Jess says.

"Do you live here?" I ask.

"We live everywhere and stay on the move for safety," Jess explains. Some of the children seem no older than six.

"You're not a gang?" I ask.

"You're not what the media portrays. It's survival from Lexicon," a girl says as they back away from me.

"We need you to tell someone. I know who you are," Jess explains.

"I will. Can you help me? A van has my friend."

He rubs his face. "What do you have to offer?"

"I will publicly announce what you have shown me. I give you my word."

He laughs. "That is precious, princess, but I am going to send some of my best soldiers as a distraction for you to retrieve your friend. I have an army to feed."

I dig in my pockets. "Fine—here," I say as I pull out Talon's keys.

"Are these what I think they are?" he asks as I hold up the keys.

"Yes," I say.

"I've heard of these cars, but I have never seen one."

I smile. "Now you will have one. It's about twenty-five blocks away. Click the button, and it's like a map, but you have to help me first," I say as I pull the keys away.

"Army. Lock and load!" Jess shouts as a child militia gets guns.

"Is that a child ninja?" I ask.

"Only the best for my best-paying customer." He places his arm around me, and I slide it off.

The army has small vehicles and rocket-like motorcycles. They hide as we approach Talon's location. Jess's team stakes out the building. "Your friend is definitely in there," he says.

"Nomads have him," I say as Jess makes a face.

As we get to the building, there sits Talon on a stool, badly beaten. He's holding a paper and asking for the return of nomads by name, those kidnapped from the Nambitus desert, and an end to storms.

"Is that Rebecca Dean's son?" Jess asks, squinting his eyes.

"Maybe," I say.

"So that's why an army of nomads hijacked a Thantos van and kidnapped Rebecca Dean's son. If they have pinpointed the evil, maybe we shouldn't get involved or better yet assist in their endeavors," Jess says.

"Talon's not bad," I argue.

"I hate nomads," Jess insists.

"There couldn't be more than ten," I say.

He hits his head against the brick.

"Remember all yours," I say.

He grabs the keys out of my hand. "Get your friend, and get out," he says as he signals. "Attack!" he shouts as the kids begin breaking in through windows. The nomads fight back just as hard. Shots are fired, glass breaks, and lights flicker. I run in and begin untying Talon. I grab a brick and smash it over a nomad's head. One of the kids shoots a nomad as a nomad stabs a kid.

As I pull off Talon's mask, he's horrified. "Are those kids?" he asks. Talon watches the fighting all the way to a van. "Hurry, Kaya. I feel like I am in a scene from *Peter Pan* gone wrong," Talon says as we look for the keys. "Here," Talon says as he flips the visor down, and the keys fall in my lap.

I start the van and step on the gas, running down a nomad.

"Kaya," Talon says as he turns his head, "that kid just killed a nomad."

I speed out of the building.

As we drive, Talon is quiet.

"Do we need to go to the emergency room?" I ask.

"No. I'll heal," Talon insists.

"It's all my fault. If we hadn't skipped school and gone to the rally, you never would have gotten hurt," I say.

"It's not your fault that my mom causes destruction wherever she goes. She has taken so many of their people and has done weather experiments in Nambitus. It is all true, if they even know. She probably took you too." Talon leans over and runs his hands through his hair.

"Talon, listen to me. My dad says if she had taken me, I'd be dead. This is her, not you."

"Kaya, you are the craziest, most beautiful person—going to rallies, kissing in fields, fighting kidnappers, coming back for me. I don't think anyone would have come back for me."

As we get to a safer place in Lexicon, he grabs me and kisses me.

"I will always come back for you, but I need to tell you something," I say. Talon looks at me strangely. "I needed help getting you back," I say as Talon holds my face in his hands.

"Okay."

"I had to make a trade," I say.

"Whatever it was, I'm sure it was worth it. Those child warriors frightened me, and my mother is Rebecca Dean."

I begin driving once more. "I'm glad you feel that way because you were worth it to me, Talon," I say. We pass his car as Jess and his gang drive it away.

"Kaya, why are those children driving my car?" Talon asks as he plasters himself against the van window.

"Talon, calm down," I say.

He punches the dashboard. "She was one of a kind. Custom." He tears up.

"Talon?"

He signals for me to look away. "Everything. My baby." He passes out.

"Talon?" I try to wake him.

I know I can't drive a black van into Axis. It's late, and Talon and I have trashed our trackers. I pull into a gas station and try to call my house and then Tevan and Matt, but no one answers. The only person I can think to call is Jonathon.

He comes immediately.

"I can't wake up Talon, and he didn't want to go to the emergency room," I say as Jonathon puts Talon into his car.

"What happened?" he asks.

"We were kidnapped by nomads," I say.

Jonathon looks horrified. "Your dad and I can fix him, but unfortunately, no one can fix you," Jonathon says as we pull into Axis.

"Thank you for keeping us safe," I say.

He tears up. "You're welcome."

When I get home, my parents are less than thrilled about my and Talon's adventure.

Jonathon and Tevan laugh the entire time my parents yell at me. To make matters worse, my parents make Jonathon out to be a saint for being on Kaya patrol. I have to explain that I am the reason Talon passed out because I traded his car to child warriors.

"Go to bed, Kaya," Mom says.

After a hot shower, I can't sleep. I toss and turn, worried about Talon.

"So, Talon couldn't handle the fact you traded his car for a child militia against a small nomad army?" Matt asks.

"You heard?" I ask.

"I was waiting, and you never showed," Matt says as he hands me the music player.

"I'm worried. I've never seen everyone so upset. He even handled his mom's destruction of humans and weather better than the loss of the car," I say

He smirks. "He loves that car more than anything," Matt says as he lies beside me.

"More than his own life?" I ask. "His mom is Rebecca Dean, Kay. When you have her as a mom, it's the little things."

"He tried to negotiate with the nomads and even tell them I was in his camp, claiming to speak their language," I say.

"What did they say?" Matt asks.

"That I wasn't. They acted like he was stupid. Besides, nomads are cool with me."

Matt rolls his eyes. "Are you like Talon? Do you speak nomad?"

"No, but their fight wasn't with me. They weren't even going to take me. I knew they were nomads because they had a similar symbol on their chests like my necklace. I knew after I got in a fight with one and ripped his shirt."

Matt looks horrified. "Do you wake up in the morning looking for trouble?" Matt asks.

"No, but I hate injustice. In all fairness, they threw me out with a knife. Not like the nomads before." Then I become frightened from the information I have revealed.

"What nomads?" Matt asks.

I shake my head. "I shouldn't have said anything."

"Nomads. You always want to talk of nomads. You have to tell me," Matt insists. "We never have secrets, and then the other day you mention Skall, as if the name is familiar."

"If they ever found out, they could kill my grandparents. They were looking for the vans. They came across my grandpa and me on our camping trip. They were going to kill my grandpa and me to maintain their mission until they saw my necklace. Your necklace saved my life. They even said someone named Skall would like me. I'll wear this until I die."

Matt smiles. "And I'll keep your secret until I die. Go to sleep, Kay," he whispers.

I wake up the next morning, and Matt is gone. I walk downstairs and find everyone crowded around the breakfast table.

"Are you better?" I ask Talon.

"Yes."

I take a seat next to him.

"My mom just landed," Talon says as he looks at his phone.

"Where was your phone yesterday?" I ask.

"In my car, but I have five phones, and those kids you gave my baby to will never get into my phone." He stabs food on his plate.

"I guess we're not over the car," I say.

"Maybe you shouldn't skip school," Jonathon suggests.

"How was I to know nomads were following us?" I ask as I get up from the table. I go outside and I walk around the neighborhood because the thought of seeing my family or Talon makes me want to scream.

"Hey, I'm sorry," Talon says as he grabs my hand.

"I'll try to get your car back," I say, but he shakes his head.

"I don't want to be that person."

I try to wipe my face so he can't see I was crying. Talon hugs me. Just then the earth begins to violently shake.

"What's happening?"

The street splits down the middle.

"Earthquake," Talon says. We fall down on the sidewalk.

"The Riven kids," I say as one begins to slide near the opening.

"Kaya, no," Talon says. He limps after me because he is injured.

Josie Riven falls into the opening in the ground. I go in after her, barely catching her. I hold on with one hand, swinging her until I can fling her back to safety. Beneath me, the ground begins to break, and I can scarcely hold on from the impact.

"Kaya!" Talon pulls me up with his uninjured arm, just as a branch falls from a tree and knocks him unconscious.

I pull him to safety and desperately try to awaken him. I am then tackled by a creature unlike anything I have ever seen. The creature pins me down, and I am unable to move. He stares into my eyes; it's as if I know him. He hisses and snarls. Just when I think he is going to attack me, guards begin firing, wounding his arm. He lets out a sound I have never heard. Before I can blink, he is gone. The guards do not take notice as I help Talon to my house.

When we get inside, I discover Talon and my mom both have suffered injuries. Just then the television makes an alert, calling all the citizens of Lexicon to take notice.

"Attention, citizens of Lexicon! There has been a devastating earthquake. Streets and homes were destroyed within Lexicon. The casualties sustained today are too numerous to count. During the earthquake, an attempt was made on President Richard Johnson's life. He has been taken to Lexicon General. When we have more information, we will have updates on the situation." The television screen goes blank.

"The footage!" I say. Lexicon is in ruins. Cars are piled the street with fallen streetlamps and stoplights. Citizens run around, panicked and bloodied, trying to help trapped people.

Talon huddles on the floor. "It's her. She tried to release the earthquake and assassinate Johnson to take over," he says as he rocks himself.

The Axis alarms go off. "We have to get downstairs." Jonathon insists.

"Because of an earthquake?" I ask.

"No," Jonathon says as he looks at his Thantos alert system. "The earthquake was obviously not meant to be so detrimental to Axis. One should never play with nature. We have bigger problems, and they are headed this way."

I grab my head and fall to the floor. The next thing I remember is waking up in our basement.

"Kaya," Talon says.

"What happened?" I ask.

Jonathon stabs me with a needle.

"No!" I scream as I stumble to my feet. I grab a piece of broken glass from the floor and stab at Jonathon.

"Ouch," he says as I swing at him.

"It's okay," Talon says.

I shove him. "It's not okay. He thinks I am one of those things that escaped and pinned me down during the earthquake. What if I am? If you stick me with needles, I will kill you like that thing killed your father." I begin making my way to the stairs.

Jonathon gets wide-eyed. "Are you speaking of Gravis?" Jonathon asks.

I scratch my face. "I am not him. I need to leave!" I shout as I check the door.

"Put down the glass," my dad says, but as I grip it tighter. He looks at Jonathon.

"Don't," I say.

"Don't what?" Dad asks.

"Don't look at me like that."

"Kaya, we worked out a plan," Dad says.

"My dad made contact," Talon says. "We are going to release all the information we obtained on my mom to the Nambitus Senate. Her plan didn't work entirely because President Johnson is going to pull through. I am going to place your dad as president over the Thantos Corporation once we have her arrested."

I shake my head.

"You and Grandpa were right about the weather," Tevan adds.

"Shut up, and stop the ringing!" I shout as I scratch my head with the glass, cutting my temple, making myself bleed. "Make it stop!"

Everyone stares at me.

"Why is she behaving that way?" my mom asks.

"Maybe the high-pitched frequency debilitates whatever escaped, and it somehow affects Kaya," Jonathan suggests as I cut myself more.

"Kaya, put the glass down," my dad orders me. He takes a step toward me, and Jonathon comes around from the back and injects me with something that causes me to go insane before I calm down. I am in and out of consciousness for a while. I feel my dad and Jonathon take blood samples from me, and I viciously attack them. I have to be placed on machines.

My body pulls and tugs. I hear Matt and Talon talking to me, but I can't respond. I am once again trapped inside my body. I hear a strange voice summon me from a dark abyss. At first the voice is kind but then becomes angered, wanting my obedience. I hear the voice until I go mad. I twist and turn, trying to expel it from my body as we fight for control. I have come so far to once again be pulled under as it tells me of evil deeds and plots. The thing is, when you go insane, you don't remember the things the voices say as you lose control.

As people come near me, I try to hurt them. I attempt to hurt myself to make the madness stop. Dad and Jonathon finally make a decision to send me into total darkness, and they strap me down. They cram a feeding tube in me. I hear Jonathon say that because my body is pulling in so many directions, if I am in a darker state I might be able to rest.

If they only knew that the darkness is what I fear the most. I can't see, but I know someone can see me. I've dreamed about times past, but every time I am on the verge of happiness, I am pulled back into nothingness until I hear the voice. I block it. I run through halls of my subconscious, searching for doors, until, after days, I find a door with a small amount of light under it. I am scared to open it.

As I open it, I am sucked back to the darkness, as if it's mocking me. I fight, running through the halls, knowing that if I can find the light once more, I might escape. Once I do, I open it, and I find humanity. I sit up so fast and take a breath so that the fight might be over.

"Kaya," Matt says as he drops my hand.

"Where am I?" I ask.

"Your dad's lab."

I catch my breath. "What happened?" I ask.

"No one knows," Matt says. He brushes my hair out of my face, and I slap him.

"Are you real?" I ask. I begin pulling out tubes.

"I don't think you should do that," he says.

"I hate them." I say as I shake a bit. "Where is everyone?"

"Making plans to destroy Rebecca Dean," Matt says.

"Why aren't you?" I ask.

"I sit with you. You have assaulted everyone, even in your state. I think you need to make amends," Matt suggests.

"It was dark in there," I say. Matt sits next to me as I clutch my bedding.

"Okay," Matt says. "You used foul language." He laughs.

"Why would that be funny?" I ask.

"Your parents left. I think they were ashamed. Jonathon and Talon were frightened. It was like you were coming out of your body. It was worse than the movies."

"Matt, you have too much fun telling me of my shortcomings, yet you stayed."

"With everyone making plans and the constant stress, I needed the entertainment," Matt insists.

"That's cruel," I say as he laughs.

"I knew you'd make your way out. I'll help you up," Matt says.

I try to walk. It seems everyone looks at me differently. I clean up and go outside for some fresh air. I see the damage caused by the earthquakes is almost repaired.

"Horrible, isn't it?" Mrs. Riven says as she stares at me.

"Yes," I say as workers repair the Axis wall.

"Thank you for saving Josie. I know you sustained injuries," she says. I nod.

Talon arrives and walks past me.

"Talon!" I say.

"Are you yourself?" he asks as he pokes my face.

"Yes." I rub my face.

"After the past few days, everyone is terrified of you. You were evil. You said you wished I had died when I was kidnapped," Talon says.

"I wasn't myself," I say.

"I didn't have my therapist to walk me through," Talon says. "She died in the earthquake. You were so mean. Larkin was the only one who checked on you because he found you amusing."

Jonathon walks up. "It lives," Jonathon says.

I roll my eyes. "I'm a human," I insist.

"That was up for debate at the time," Talon says, and Jonathon laughs.

"For what it's worth, I am sorry," I say.

Talon nods and Jonathon squints his eyes at me.

"We have a meeting tonight," Talon says as they leave.

I turn on the television to find Rebecca Dean on every channel.

"Mom, what's going on?" I ask, pointing to the TV.

"She has been appointed emergency president by the Senate while President Johnson is on the mend. Everyone else important strategically died or was injured by the earthquakes."

I sink down into the couch.

CHAPTER 13

I fall asleep on the couch, and the next thing I remember is my dad shaking me awake to eat something.

"I think we need to take her to the hospital, John," Mom says.

I eat in order to avoid the hospital.

"She'll be fine," Dad insists. "Kaya, after dinner we have a meeting to decide our next step, but I think you need to rest."

I shake my head. "No, I'm all right."

As soon as dinner ends, people begin arriving with covered dishes so as not to make the neighbors suspicious. First Talon, then Jonathan, and then the Larkins, who bring maintenance equipment to maintain appearances. We take our seats downstairs. Talon types in a million numbers to contact his dad.

"What about the cameras?" I whisper to Jonathon.

"They are still broken after the earthquakes, so we may talk freely, but I am not talking to you after your exorcism scene," Jonathon says.

"You, of all people, being a man of science, know I was not in control of my extremities." I argue.

"You cut me and called me things I dare not repeat," Jonathon says.

I try not to laugh. "I'm sorry."

"Apologize all you want, but I know your heart."

My dad loudly clears his throat. "Would the two of you care to share something?" he asks. Everyone stares at Jonathon and me, and we get quiet.

Talon's dad's voice is clear in the room. "I will release documents to the proper national authorities so Rebecca's labs can be shut down worldwide permanently. I will return to an isolated section of Nambitus on the chance Rebecca sends her people after me. Talon and I have designed undetectable communication devices," he explains as Talon passes them out.

"I am also in the process of getting into the camera system and files that I wasn't able to access from the night of our prank," Talon says. "Some of the files were heavily encrypted. We also obtained information from her inner circle that details underground activity and occurrences in Thantos-related companies. We also have two senators who have received evidence and are on our side."

"One of you will have to meet with a person who has come forward with evidence from the labs," Talon's dad explains.

"Why can't it be sent electronically? It sounds risky to meet someone in person," Tevan comments.

"These will be items of evidence, and the person is willing to testify in exchange for protection. Who is going to get the witness and bring me the files?" Talon's dad asks as the room remains quiet.

"I'll do it," Talon offers. "If she is solely behind the black vans and disappearances, we need to stop her from further plans. She is already tearing the city apart with earthquakes, tornadoes in the east, and a tsunami in the south as a distraction from the assassination attempt on President Johnson."

I look at a paper. I missed an entire week of destruction while under sedation in my dad's lab.

"What is she trying to achieve with humans?" Tevan inquires.

"The perfect human bioweapon. Humans are the perfect weapon because they are among the populace," Jonathon explains. He places files he has stolen from the lab on the table for Talon.

"I will have this decoded before tonight," Talon says, and Jonathon reluctantly lifts his hand.

"That brings us to who will lead our expedition through Lexicon and out into the wilds of Nambitus—Mrs. Larkin," Talon says. She nods.

"Mrs. Larkin?" I ask.

"She has studied and knows the social patterns of nomads," my dad explains.

"When will this take place?" I ask.

"Before Tuesday, when President Johnson is released from Lexicon General," Talon explains.

"Should we leave Axis?" I ask.

"No, we have to keep up appearances. The Senate won't allow my mother's crimes to go unpunished. This will be the final time we will meet, so if there are any questions, ask now. Otherwise, I will see you when we have Axis," Talon says.

As everyone goes over maps and strategies, I scan the room. Jonathon is still in deep mourning over the loss of his father, so much that he is willing to steal files and risk everything to ensure no one else dies. I watch as Tevan comforts him. I go upstairs to get some fresh air.

As I sit on the porch, I am joined by Matt. "Why aren't you aiding in the endeavors?" I ask.

"I was told to act naturally to keep up appearances. My dad knows the layout of the grounds; my mom is a nomad expert; and I am just a pretty face," he says.

I laugh. "Everyone sees me differently," I say.

"That's because you are different, and that has never been a bad thing," Matt says as he winks at me.

That night, I don't sleep. I catch myself rolling on the floor. All I can think about is the monster that escaped the labs and how Jonathon cringed when he said his name—Gravis. I dream about him breaking into Axis and destroying the houses, trying to find the culprits that tortured him. Maybe he was in search of Jonathon when he tackled me. The only time I received any rest from my nightmares and wandering thoughts was when Matt slept in my room.

"Why do you come to my rescue?" I ask as Matt quietly opens my window.

"Because you would for me," he says.

I toss him a pillow. "It's not too late to run away," I say.

"We are too brave to run," Matt says, and we fall asleep.

The following days seem like months. Rebecca Dean is too preoccupied with Lexicon affairs to come near Axis. Talon decides to tap her phone while I drive us to school.

"I hate your car," Talon says as he tries to get comfortable.

"Talon, you said you were no longer angry," I remind him as he begins intercepting calls.

"My mom has a device that records calls on the chance she needs to blackmail people," Talon says, as I make a face. "I got it." He begins listening to calls. Talon intercepts and listens to calls on the entire ride to school.

"Ready?" I ask.

Talon nods but then seems to panic. "She gained international backing! They say if she can maintain control of Lexicon, then she has a chance of gaining seats in senates worldwide."

"She's going to kill President Johnson," I say.

"Kaya, I have the senator on the phone. I have to go!" I get out and Talon slides into the driver's seat and speeds away.

Matt quietly walks over. "What is going on? I thought our big plan was tomorrow."

"Talon discovered his mom is going to finish off President Johnson. She has international backing if she succeeds. She is also taking over the world," I explain.

"Of course she is," Matt says as he quietly walks away from me.

Talon doesn't come back for the remainder of the day. After school, I find him in the parking lot.

"Are you all right?" I ask.

Talon shakes his head. "She got to everyone on the Senate. It's

over. Even my witness disappeared, probably dead. I had to do it."
Talon starts shaking.

"Had to do what?"

He shows me video on his phone of people rioting in the streets worldwide. I look across the street and see officers arresting people.

"Go home immediately, students," a voice says over the loud speaker on the outside of the school. Talon quickly pulls me into the car as people begin breaking into other cars in the parking lot. "We have to get back to Axis," Talon insists.

The streets were full of fires and people looting and fighting one another.

"What happened?" I ask.

"I released everything to the media," Talon explains. "President Johnson died strangely today, and the senators that were on my side suddenly weren't. Since it's a state of emergency, she gains Lexicon."

We see people shooting one another.

"Why this?" I ask.

"She has her loyal following. They are calling for an investigation, and my mother is pushing through for a presidency. I thought if the people knew, then they would demand action."

Two women roll out into the street, and he slams on the brakes.

"The protestors," I say as we approach Axis. Blocks away from Axis, people line the street with signs. Some praise Rebecca Dean; others called for her to leave Nambitus.

"How will we get in?" I ask. People begin hitting my car.

"We won't be able to," Talon says. Then we see Matt. He signals to us.

"Follow me. I found the secret entrance," Matt says. We go around to an area covered in trees, away from the crowds.

"This is amazing," I say as the trees flatten, and we get into Axis. We are taken underground to an area with black vans that were on the video.

"Where are the vans?" I ask.

"Talon's mom probably has them in another location," Matt says.

When we get to my house, Jonathon is outside waiting.

"Why, Talon?" Jonathon asks.

"Because she has everyone worldwide backing her," Talon says.

Jonathon sits on the curb.

"Why aren't you at work?" Matt asks.

"Investigations going on as to who stole data and film," Jonathon says as he lights a cigar.

"I didn't know you smoked," I say.

"It was my father's. I am as good as dead," he says.

"Jonathon, I'm sorry," Talon says.

Jonathon stands up. "It was an attempt at a good cause. The media will turn this for her good," he says as he begins walking.

"Jonathon, where are you going?" I ask.

"Home."

I walk inside and turn on the television. Worldwide, Rebecca Dean is up for seats in various countries and is winning. Talon leaked footage in every language and in every country. "Talon doesn't do anything halfway," Matt says.

"The authorities are defending her, causing the people to be divided. She has called in favors. A tornado in Europe. A strange flu wiping out people in Africa. I don't want to see anymore," I say. Footage of Sal pops up, and I turn the television off and slide down onto the couch.

"She needs Lexicon. It's the strongest city on the planet," Dad says as he walks in.

"What if the people don't allow it?" I ask.

"The people of Lexicon pushed until Johnson was in. We shall see." Dad takes off his glasses and rubs his eyes.

Just then the television turns back on. "This just in: We have a special announcement from the potential president of Lexicon, Rebecca Dean," the newscaster announces.

"Citizens of Lexicon, I know footage has been released casting doubt in your minds as to my integrity. I am not your enemy. I am already trying to find the parties responsible for tarnishing my good name. I know I won the Lexicon elections, and I know many of you were unwilling to give me a chance. Stop rioting; stop tearing up the city so many of us love. I have set up stations to aid the wounded. Let us rebuild and become greater as we rise up out of the ashes. Allow me to be your president." A rioter jumps through her barricade and attacks as her guards engage with people on the street. The screen goes blank after gunshots are fired.

"Are you still leaving tomorrow?" I ask Talon when he finishes speaking privately to my dad.

"Yes, to have the original files and the few I have yet to open here is a risk. I promise I'll be careful." Talon says good night, and he and Matt leave.

That night we have a lockdown due to the riots. My parents and I spend the night in the basement.

"Kaya, you are sweating terribly," Mom says as she wipes my face.

I didn't want her to know I had grown accustomed to Matt staying with me at night.

"Are the riots over?" I ask.

"No," Dad says as he scans the outside walls.

"Has Talon's dad landed?" I ask.

"Yes, in old New York," Dad says.

"This is a long shot," I say.

Dad nods. "It is but worth it." He hugs me.

The next morning all I can do is stare at my Thantos tracker.

"Do you feel up to school?" Mom asks as she hands me a tube of concealer.

"Subtle, Mom, and yes," I say. I try to make my face presentable.

It seems strange not riding with Talon. I have to take my mom's car because someone hit my window in the riots. As I leave Axis, people still are fighting and lining the streets. I feel a little better as Matt pulls in behind me as we leave Axis. The traffic is horrible. SWAT teams fight with citizens. I haven't seen extra militia before now.

As I pull into school, I lose Matt in all the traffic. Talon pulls up in a car and shouts to me. I park and walk over to him.

"Get in the car," he says.

"Why?"

"We need to leave."

I look over at Mrs. Larkin. She's looking around.

"I thought you and Mrs. Larkin were going on the mission," I say.

Talon shakes his head. "You don't understand. The riots were so bad during the night that my mom had to call for special forces. I intercepted something she is planning. On the chance she loses Lexicon, she is planning something to humble the people. *Get in the car.*"

"I can't," I say.

"Talon, hurry," Mrs. Larkin urges.

"You have to come with me," Talon says. "Please. I have to get you and the remaining files away from here."

I shake my head. "What's wrong?"

"The night you were kidnapped, in a desperate attempt to track you, I reversed the trackers, causing the system to crash. I blamed myself for Thantos not coming, and then I opened the files. What wasn't corrupted, I destroyed."

"What are you trying to say?" I ask.

Talon reaches out and tries to pull me into the car. Helicopters fly overhead.

"What's going on?" I ask.

"I don't know. I think she's releasing something airborne." Talon gets out his phone.

"What are you doing?" I ask.

"Seeing what she's done," Talon says.

As the screams get closer, Talon places his hand to his face.

"What?" I ask.

225

"I'm taking all of this data and erasing everything from her server. I'll have everything. She'll know it was me. I called in a favor," Talon says.

"What did you do?" I ask.

Talon grabs my face. "Everything. All power will go out, satellites will go down, and people will get hurt, and all because she must be stopped."

The entire city gets quiet. People begin getting out of their cars, stoplights quit working, and no one can get service on any devices.

"It's coming, Kaya. I tried to cease all power, but this is all only temporary. She lost this morning." Talon kisses me.

"Talon this is crazy," I say.

"You make me crazy and sane at the same time. I love you, Kaya. If you won't come with me, get to safety." He hugs me. We hear screaming as the crowd begins to rip one another apart.

"Oh my God!" I say as a woman savagely bites a man on the neck. He falls to the ground. The crowd sniffs the air and jumps on top of him. "They're eating him!" I say.

Talon pulls on me. "Come on!" Talon insists.

"I can't. I have to find Matt."

Talon places his tracker in my hands. "Use it. She'll come. She knows I have everything," Talon says.

"Kaya," Mrs. Larkin says, "find Matt and tell him, no matter what happens, I love him. Take care of him."

"I promise," I say. Talon gets in the car, and they speed away.

In the crowd, some pile on others who have remained normal, ripping the flesh off one another. It's if they are hunting. When they get up, the crowd is covered in blood and body parts. They walk sluggishly, but the more people they pass, the more they acquired in their mob. The ones that get up should not have been able to even stand. They are dragging limbs, and their necks are squirting fluid; their internal organs are hanging from their bodies. The ones not devoured convulse and turn into the mob within a matter of minutes.

Students in the school parking lot panic, and the more they scream, the more the crowd is drawn to them.

"What are you doing, Kaya?" Tia asks as she runs past me.

"Observing," I say calmly.

She cries, "I can't find Chris."

I point to the crowd. "Don't go up to him," I warn her.

She shouts, "Chris, it's me!"

I try to fight her to stay with me. She shoves me and runs to him and the rest of the mob. Chris slightly tilts his head and then bites Tia in the face, ripping into her cheekbone. She screams, attracting a crowd. Another student bites into her arm, and another rips into her abdomen. I look away. The survivors begin to run inside the building. Some even barricade doors, locking the rest of us outside.

As people beg to be let in the doors of the school, they are torn to pieces. I scan the parking lot, looking for Matt's truck. I can't find him anywhere. Within the few minutes of turning into monsters, the creatures become faster and more alert of their surroundings. It is as if they know to signal the others for prey. They have one basic desire and that is to kill, and their desire is never quenched.

The number of survivors dwindles as we try to gain access into the school. The new ones joining the undead army are never ending. Students panic and desperately throw one another to the masses, trying to get to safety. We finally gain entry, and the halls look like something out of a horror movie. There are bloody handprints and students eaten down through the torso. The lights were never turned on, but some are flickering.

"I'm going to be sick," a familiar voice says.

"Tiffany!"

She's covered in blood. "I can't get phone reception," she says as she falls to her knees, holding up her phone. I hear a strange gurgling sound. "What is it?" she whispers.

"I don't know, but it isn't a human," I say. The rest of the students become panicked. "Shut up!" I hiss.

"We're going to die," Tiffany wails.

"There are more of them than us. Do not come in contact with one. We have to get to safety," I say as rummage through my backpack, trying to find a weapon.

I run into a classroom and find a container of scissors. I begin passing them out. "You can't hurt them. They are our classmates," Tiffany argues.

"They are killing people and turning them into monsters. I don't think the process can be reversed once you are dead or become whatever they are," I say.

"This is the closest thing I have ever seen to a video game. I am going to earn points," a kid says.

"Who is he?" Tiffany asks.

"I don't know, but I like him," I say.

He takes two pairs of scissors. "Aim for the eyes," he says. "We have to kill all brain activity, if this is anything like a game. Avoid bites and fluid. My name is Theo, and I sit at your table. You just never talk to me. We need to move."

"Shouldn't we wait for help?" Tiffany asks.

"I think the entire city is as good as dead. Everyone check your phones," Theo says.

Everyone takes out their phones and tries to get service.

"Told you. No one is going to help us. We're on our own. Just like in the movies," he says as Tiffany stands next to him. "Ready?" he asks.

Another guy places his hand on the door. "Wait," he says. "I can't go out there. I just can't."

"Pull yourself together, or we will never make it!" Tiffany snaps.

"Where's Jason?" I ask.

"He's not at school. His dad passed away," she explains.

Just then the masses ram the door. The guy holding the door is knocked on the floor and devoured within seconds.

"We have to find another way out!" Tiffany shouts. The other door is covered in clutter. The students begin throwing books all over the floor as the masses of undead pile through. I recognize so many faces that now are no longer my classmates. I quickly begin helping so we might escape.

We open the door and begin running down the halls. The numbers of undead are now greater than the living. Tiffany shoves past the undead, knocking them down like bowling pins, as Theo stabs them in the eyes with scissors.

"Wow," a kid says as we run toward the south exit. The last hall is quiet and dark.

"I guess the janitors didn't get to this hall," Tiffany says as we peek through a set of doors. We make our way through. "Stay quiet," Tiffany says as she and Theo lead us.

"Why does she always get to be in charge?" a girl asks.

"Politics," I say.

"Shut up—I hear something!" Theo says as we get to the larger of the halls. Tiffany latches onto his arm.

"Typical for her to go for the alpha male," the girl says. Tiffany glares at her.

"I think we are about to have company," Theo says as he draws back his scissors.

I quickly run over to the fire emergency box and take off my jacket. I wrap up my hand and punch through the glass. It has an ax in it.

"It's only a few. We can take them," Theo says as he and Tiffany engage in battle. I grab the ax. "Nice. Let me have that," Theo says.

"Finders keepers," I say as an undead student walks around the corner. I take his head off.

"That was a hundred points," Theo says as we look at him. The halls begin to get quiet once more.

"This is eerie," someone says.

"I still don't have cell service. Why isn't anyone coming for us?" another asks.

I look at my tracker. I wonder if I push it if Axis would come. Just as I am about to push my tracker, we almost collide with another set of students.

"You scared us to death," Emily says as I put my ax down.

"Emily," I say as she holds up a pencil for protection.

"I never thought I'd be happy to see you, Kaya," she says as we hug.

"Have you seen Matt?" I ask.

Emily shakes her head. "No, he was with the football team."

"Where are they?" I ask.

"They were getting letters for their jackets," Emily says.

"And?" I ask.

"I heard screams," she says. "I'm sure he's all right, Kaya." Emily places her hand on my shoulder.

For a moment, I feel as if time is standing still, and I am anchored to the earth, unable to move.

"Guys, we have to move if we are going to get out of here. If you have keys, get them ready," Theo says.

"What your friend doesn't realize is that it's a war zone out there. Good luck getting out. That's where we came from." Emily slumps against the wall. We all look at each other.

"We can't stay here," Tiffany insists.

I ready my ax. Theo opens the door, and the earth begins shaking.

"Earthquake!" he shouts as he slides under a desk. The earthquake lasts longer than the first that Rebecca Dean set off, and it causes places within the building to crumble.

"Kaya, help!" I hear Emily shout as everyone begins to run around in all the chaos, and undead students flood from every exit and entrance.

"Emily, where are you?" I ask. I cough and wave my hand from the debris that continues to fall, making it hard to see.

"Kaya, I'm here!" she shouts.

I run to a row of lockers that have fallen over. Under that row of lockers is Emily.

"Emily, hold on," I say as I lift them.

"How did you …" she asks as she shakes her head. "I can't move," she cries.

I pull her out from the debris. As I remove Emily, blood goes everywhere, and the undead smell it and begin to go crazy.

"I can't feel my legs. It still feels like something is cutting into me," she cries, and she coughs up blood.

"I think my moving you made it worse," I say, trying not to panic.

"Kaya, I'm not going to make it," she says, grabbing my hand. "Don't leave me. I'm scared."

I sit beside her. "Does it hurt?" I ask. She shakes her head. "Hey, remember that time you invited me to your slumber party, and I blew up your miniature bake oven?" I ask.

She smiles. "You never could cook."

"I know, and you are good at everything," I say.

She closes her eyes.

"Kaya, get away from her. She is either food now, or she will turn into one of those monsters," Tiffany says as she drags me. "We need your ax."

The doors begin to fall off the school. I run back to Emily, and she is no longer breathing.

"She's gone," I say, feeling dazed. Just then, a few football players get in by breaking through the doors that are merely hanging by the hinges.

"Why would you break the door?" Theo snaps. "Have you seen what's out there?"

The other student snaps as he breaks the rest of the door just to show Theo.

"Matthew!" I say as I look through the team as Theo argues, and some begin securing the door with a cabinet. "Where is Matthew Larkin?" I ask as people fight the undead. "Matt!" I shout.

He gets through the door. I run up to him, and all I can do is throw my arms around him as he does the same to me. "I thought I had lost you," I say and begin crying. I check him over.

Just then the undead throw themselves up against the cabinets, trying to get through.

"We're not going to hold them back for long," someone says as Theo gets ready.

"They are not going to make it that way. We just came from out there," Matt says. He pulls me into a janitor's closet and closes the door.

"What do we do?" I ask. We hear crashing and fighting.

"Stay quiet. I saw the entire team almost devoured in front of my eyes," Matt says.

I nod. "Emily didn't make it. I always told her, 'I hope you die, Emily.' I didn't mean it."

Matt hugs me. "Rebecca Dean did this, all because of being exposed and not getting her way," Matt says as we slump down against the wall.

"So many are dying," I say. I lean my head on his shoulder. "What do you think the rest of Lexicon is like?" As I glance at Matt's arm, I see his tracker. "Did you think about pushing it?" I ask.

"Should we?" he asks.

"I have Talon's to ensure they'll come for us. Now or never," I say. We push both trackers. "Do you think they'll come?" I ask.

"Our enemies and yet our saviors," Matt says.

Just then the trackers light up. "What does that mean?" Matt asks.

"I don't know. I wasn't rescued from the lab. You said I was found naked in a field."

"Do you think my mom and Talon made it out?" Matt asks.

"I do," I say.

"How do you know?"

Someone hits the door as the fighting continues.

"I don't know what to do!" I cry.

Matt shakes his head. "We can't open the door, Kay," Matt insists as he blocks it. "You said they made it."

"Talon wanted me to go with them," I say.

"You should have, if you knew this was happening."

"I didn't want to."

"Kay ..."

"I had homework, and I have seen how your mom drives," I say.

Matt laughs. "She is a scary driver. Talon deserves that."

We hear gunshots.

"What is that?" I ask.

"I think it might be Thantos," Matt says.

Next we hear the dragging of feet and gurgling and then a few last gunshots.

"They are in here," a muffled voice says. Someone taps on the door. I look at Matt. I toss him my ax and cautiously open the door.

"We received a distress signal," a guard dressed in all black says.

As Matt and I walk out, we see five more guards dressed head to toe in black, with boots, shields, and helmets. They have guns, batons, knives, and other items I cannot identify as they escort Matt and me back to Axis. As we round the hall, there are piles of undead from the battle.

"Hey, those are our friends. Tiffany, Theo, come with us!" I shout as they try to get away. They are the only ones left and barely can get through the undead.

"Sorry, but we were specifically told to bring those only from Axis and no one else," the guard insists.

"They need help!" I say.

"Orders, miss," the guard says.

"I won't go. You can't just leave them. Rebecca Dean is responsible for this disaster!"

Another guard grabs me and throws me over his shoulder, and another drags Matt by his arm as we exit the building. I watch as Tiffany and Theo fight off the masses. Matt slides them the ax, but as we near the van, it seems they are losing the battle.

"I can't believe you would leave innocent people!" I say. We pass a school bus that has hit a fire hydrant. The kids inside run up to the windows, and I can see that all have turned into undead monsters.

"They didn't have a chance," I say. I struggle to get off the guard's shoulder.

One small child practically flies out of the bus window, and he shoots her in midair. "Stop making a scene," he snaps. Papers and books blow all over the schoolyard as the guards shoot undead students of all ages. The guard finally sets me down. I look at the devastation. Parents drive up on the school lawn, looking for children, and are quickly attacked, turned, or devoured.

"Make it stop. I know she didn't mean for it to go this far," I say. I push through the guards. They shoot one of the parents. I fall to my knees, and they drag me.

"Don't hurt her!" Matt snaps. A guard punches Matt and drags him. The commotion causes the undead to turn their attention toward us. The guards encircle us with their shields out, until one of the undead students drops down and bites through a guard's boot, breaking the human barrier. Another guards panics and takes off running, shooting the undead around him.

"Jeremy." The main guard shouts as he shoots the guard running and the one bitten in the head, splattering blood on Matt's jacket and across my jeans. The guards open the doors to the van and throw us in. Two get in front, and the remaining two get in the back with Matt and me.

"Hurry!" the main guard says, as masses of undead pile up against the front windows. The two up front begin shooting, trying to clear a path on the streets.

This isn't a typical Thantos van. We can see what's going on. I wish it had been like the previous Thantos vans with dark windows because the devastation is difficult to view. Smoke rises from the business sector of Lexicon. Debris is piled in the streets from the earthquake. Cars are running off the road, and the undead masses cover the streets. Buildings have fallen and lie in ruins all over the sidewalk and streets.

Worse are the citizens of Lexicon. The ones who have the disease walk around bumping into one another until they are fully aware of their surroundings; then they became vicious predators. If people are alive or in need of assistance, the undead pile on them, ripping them apart. Entrails snag on objects, and they can't be alive in an earthly manner, but they continue. They rip apart the living as soon as they catch the scent. They have no regard for humanity because in the process, they lose it, along with their dignity. Some lose clothing. Their faces tell signs of their kills as blood drips from their chins and smears across their faces, like animals in the wild.

"Matt, how is Lexicon going to recover?" I ask.

"Maybe she has an antidote," Matt says.

"We can't get through," one of the guards says. We pause and back up.

Just then, we hear a message over loud speakers throughout Lexicon: "We are under attack. Please remain where you are until help arrives. I repeat: We are under attack."

"A little too late," I say.

I huddle next to Matt. Sensing I'm uneasy the guard next to me introduces himself.

"I'm Todd. Across is John, up front you have Henry, and Jake leading us."

This introduction did not put me at ease after seeing Jake shoot members of his own team after becoming bitten and the other for running.

Monsters break through the side window and grab Todd. The undead violently pull him out of the window, cutting him on the glass. He is pulled so hard glass flies imbedding in my arm. There is no way to get a clear shot. Henry shoots some of the undead from the side of the van, but they are pulling so hard on Todd's gear and body that they strangle him somehow in the process. Blood pours from his mouth. I turn my head as he falls back into the van, covered in bite marks. Todd then begins convulsing and rolling.

"What's happening?" John asks.

"Shoot him!" Matt yells as he tries to take his gun.

"This man needs medical attention," John insists. The now

infected Todd lifts up and bites John's face. He then reaches up front and bites Henry in the shoulder. Jake, while driving pulls out a hand gun and shoots Henry in the head before he has a chance to turn as he continues to shoot undead that crowd our path. He begins driving at an alarming speed.

"Help!" I shout. I try to use my foot to get Todd's gun as we struggle. John begins convulsing. Matt rolls near him grabbing a gun shooting him in the face. Jake swerves in traffic, trying to avoid all the debris and undead. I hold on to a bar and kick Todd in the head. I cause the back doors to fly open. He flies out, but other undead try to get in. Matt begins shooting as Jake once again takes off.

When we get to Axis, it's covered in people begging to gain entry. They are holding up children as they fight off undead. "Can they come in?" I ask. When Jake remains silent, I shout, "Dammit, people lost everything today!"

Jake drives to the side of Axis. "President Dean has a plan," he says as we drive into the parking garage. As we step out of the van, none other than Rebecca Dean herself—with her entourage of body guards—awaits us.

"Miss Lewis. Where is Talon?" she asks as she takes his tracker from me.

"I don't know. He said he had an errand."

"Interesting," she says. "Did he happen to say where he was going?"

"No, he asked if I would take notes in case he didn't make it back to class. Is he all right?"

She glares at me. "I don't know." She signals for her guards. "If you see him, please tell him I am looking for him."

Matt and I are left all alone. We quietly walk out into the Axis daylight, and it is as if nothing has happened. Axis is unscathed by the day's earthquake and attacks.

"Do you think she knows?" Matt whispers.

"Possibly."

I hear the cries on the outside. Matt and I walk our separate ways.

CHAPTER 14

I get to my house, and my parents start crying. I think I am in shock over the ordeal. All I can do is stare. "Tevan?" I ask.

"She was down at Jonathon's when everything happened," my dad says as they check me over.

"Were you at work?" I ask my mom.

"No, I hadn't left yet."

"What happened?" my dad asks. "How bad is it?"

"She released a virus that makes people eat each other. If you get bitten, you turn into one of the undead, and they kept coming."

Jonathon runs in just then, followed by Tevan.

"She did the unthinkable!" Jonathon shouts, clearly panicking.

"We know," Dad says.

Just when I think I can catch my breath, Mr. and Mrs. Watson drive up, looking for Emily. They rush from their car, and Mrs. Watson says, "We heard there was an accident, but the kids made it back from school. Where's Emily?"

"Kaya, did you see Emily?" Mom asks.

"She was with me at school, but during the earthquake she got pinned under a row of lockers that toppled over," I say quietly.

Her mom begins shaking her head. *"No!"* she shouts, as Mr. Watson grabs her.

"I tried," I say. "I sat with her until ..." I can't finish.

Her mom falls to her knees. "Not my baby."

Dad helps get her into the car.

"I'm so sorry," I say, crying as my mom holds me.

"Kaya, do you need to go inside?" Mom asks.

I stand watching the Watsons leave. I pull away as Jonathon goes through his notepad.

"There was never a cure, John," Jonathon says, sliding down to the ground.

"Never," my dad says. He takes off his glasses and rubs his eyes.

"Wait a minute—there was some type of new research going on in other labs. If I can get in using Talon's codes ..." Jonathon opens his computer, and his face goes blank. "All my files to Thantos ..." Jonathon says as he stares at us. "They're gone. Talon has all the hard copies. He took everything. How?"

"Years of our work," Dad says. "Even things on my personal devices are gone." He looks at Jonathon. "Someone shut down all of Lexicon's power. All diseases and cures, without maintaining a certain temperature, are rendered useless."

"So it will take longer to find a cure for this nightmare?" Tevan asks.

"Yes," Dad says.

"We can't lose hope," Mom says. "Who would wipe out everything?"

"I don't know," Dad answers.

Judging by their present state of shock, I thought it was best not to tell them what Talon had done.

"Is it this bad everywhere?" Mom asks. "Maybe other places could help."

"The last footage I had before my server was wiped stated the virus was in Japan, Australia, and Europe," Dad says.

"She lost Lexicon and her backers, and this was her final attempt to prove her worth—or wrath," Jonathon says.

"What do we do?" I ask.

"There's not much we *can* do," Jonathon says as he punches the wall. "We can hope Talon made it and gets his data to the right people."

"Anything else?" I ask.

"Keep a low profile," Dad says. "It's bad in here but obviously worse out there."

We all get quiet.

"Will there be more earthquakes?" I ask.

Jonathon nods slowly. "She can't stop them since the last one damaged her machines," Jonathon admits.

"Mom, every inch of Lexicon was hit by this," I say. "What about Grandma and Grandpa? And Stevie?"

Mom looks away. "There's no way of knowing until we get communication back." I try not to get upset. "Grandpa was and is so proud of his girls. He taught you well. We have to think good thoughts."

I hug her. Tevan and the rest of the family join our hug. When Jonathon joins us, I freeze.

"Kaya!" Tevan snaps.

"Get some rest," Mom insists.

When I get upstairs Matt is waiting for me. "I heard they were going to start letting people in, and the virus is now morphing or something," Matt says.

"What do you mean?"

"With some people, it stays dominant in their bodies after exposure, and they just turn with no warning."

"How do we know we aren't infected?" I ask.

"We don't. I just figured my dad has been through enough today. He has been staring at that transmitter, hoping my mom makes contact. I don't want to turn in front of him," Matt says.

I make a face. "So you thought you'd come over and infect me?"

He shrugs his shoulders. "I don't know."

I try not to laugh. "Where are you going to bite me?"

"Shut up, Kaya." Matt snaps suddenly. "I thought I'd babysit you because of your nightmares."

"Okay." I turn off my lamp and get into bed. "Matt," I whisper in the darkness, "Talon was the one who shut down the power, but I know he had good reasons."

"That jerk," Matt says.

"Matt, he was so passionate about it."

"He might be your boyfriend, but I hate him."

"Don't be cruel."

Matt was silent for a moment. When Matt did this, he knew he was getting to me and loved it. "The media and everyone else calls him your boyfriend. Talon loves to talk about his girlfriend. Kaya. I want to hear you say it. Call him your boyfriend."

I sit up and turn on the light. "You know I don't believe in labels."

"You care about him. Call Talon your boyfriend," Matt demands.

"I don't want to, and I don't have to." I snap. "I saw you around Emily all the time. Were you and she an item?"

Matt shakes his head. "No. Friends."

"What about the tons of cheerleaders and Matt fans?" I ask.

"Stalker," he says, and I turn red.

"You're a stalker if you have memorized my mannerisms around Talon to know my truest feelings," I say. "I hate you."

"Not as much as I hate you at this moment," he says.

We both get quiet.

"Leave," I say.

He shakes his head. "No."

I point to my window. The truth is, I'm terrified for him to leave.

Matt grabs a blanket and pillow and slams down in the chair next to my bed. I switch off the light and toss and turn until I think I am going to scream.

"Kaya, stop," Matt finally says after several hours.

I pull him to lie beside me and put my arm across him.

"What is this?" Matt asks as he moves my arm.

"I beat all the stuffing out of my pillow during a nightmare," I say.

"So I'm your new pillow?" he whispers. He looks at my room in disgust. "I might have nightmares as well." Then he rolls over to face me. "I had to kill that guard—or thing—today. I don't know if I am a murderer. What if I get arrested? I keep seeing the guard's face."

"I don't think you can come back. You did what you had to do to save us," I say.

"I didn't know a mob could break bullet-proof glass so easily," Matt says. He looks over my head and pulls a sock from the top of my pillow.

"Me either."

"Have you ever thought about cleaning your room?" Matt says.

"No," I say.

"Do you think Talon and my mom are safe at this very moment?"

"Without a doubt."

Matt breathes a sigh of relief.

The next day I wake up to find Matt still asleep in my room. I can't help but ruffle his hair.

"Did I turn?" he asks.

"Yes."

He feels his face. "Shut up, Kaya." He pulls his arms from around me.

"Why didn't Talon offer to be on nightmare patrol when everyone thought I was evil?" I ask.

Matt tries not to laugh. "You spit on him and Jonathon."

I duck my head. "Oh. At least make me feel better and lie. What did I say to you?"

Matt turns red. "Remember when I went through that weird phase of wearing pink? I didn't know you thought less of me as a man." Matt says. "When you were horrible to Jonathon and Talon, it was everything I wanted to say, so I stayed. You were just Kaya but took it even farther than usual. I would tell you to shut up when it got out of hand."

I smile. "Did I listen?"

"Yes, you still spit, though," he says. "I figured I taught you how to spit, so I deserved it."

I laugh a bit.

"Do you practice spitting? I wonder because your aim was impeccable," Matt says.

My face flushes. "No. I don't want to talk about it." Matt points to his eye. "Stop it. I don't want to fight today."

We hear someone in the hall and then a knock on my door. Matt quickly rolls off my bed. I signal that I will go downstairs so he can sneak out.

"Were you talking to yourself?" Mom asks as I walk downstairs.

"I was dreaming."

I take a seat next to Tevan at the table.

"We have cameras again," Jonathan says. He sits next to Tevan, grabs a pancake, and flips open his Thantos device. It shows outside the Axis walls; the scene is chaotic as police cars and ambulances try to organize rioting people. The cameras pan up briefly to Rebecca Dean on the top of the Axis walls as she tries to address the masses. In the streets, citizens beg her to create a cure or reverse the madness.

A man struggles with his small daughter, who has been infected. He has her on a stick with a collar-like device. She goes mad, trying to attack everyone within reach. "I can forgive you for whatever the media claims you have done," he calls to Rebecca. "Please. Fix her." He sobs as he struggles to control the child.

As Rebecca tries to console the noninfected who are begging to enter Axis, the infected attack and have to be taken down.

"Have the camera networks and communications been repaired worldwide?" Tevan asks as the picture gets fuzzy.

"No, this is just the Axis cameras," Jonathon says.

"Citizens of Lexicon, if you can hear me, we have safe havens set up every ten to fifteen blocks that contain medical supplies, food, and security. Do not come to Axis, for we do not have the room for everyone," Rebecca announces.

Some of the people become enraged. "You don't want us in your precious city because the virus wasn't released within your walls!" a woman accuses her.

"We need not blame during these tragic times. My team of scientists are doing all they can to find a cure," Rebecca says.

"In the meantime, what are we to do?" the woman asks.

"Go home, and do not go out unless necessary. We are doing everything we can to get the virus under control," Rebecca says.

Her guards shoot the man's little girl, the child he brought, pleading for a cure. The man falls to his knees by his lifeless child.

"There's no cure," the woman says.

"She's a monster!" a woman shouts from the crowd.

Just then gunfire is released on the crowd. As the guns begin to fire, the undead break through the barriers, attacking the living.

"Help them!" Jonathon says as he shakes his phone.

Rebecca pulls her hand back, signaling that the Axis guards should not aid the people on the street.

Jonathon loses reception, but the last thing he sees is Rebecca losing guards as the streets go wild. The undead have broken through the barricades because the gunshots attracted more activity.

As Jonathon tries to get reception, the television turns on for an announcement.

"Citizens of Axis," a voice says, "we will be having a meeting at noon so that we may work together during these troubling times. Together, we can rebuild and make Lexicon into Axis." The screen goes blank.

"We have an hour. What do you think she wants?" Mom asks.

Dad signals for us to get ready. "I don't know," he says. "but we'll get through it together."

When we get to the meeting at the former town hall, the area is sectioned according to class status. Matt sits in his section and makes a face as he follows his dad. As soon as everyone is seated, Rebecca Dean comes out on stage with bodyguards.

"Good afternoon, Axis. The events in Lexicon were tragic. We must prepare. Here in Axis, we are self-sufficient and prepared for anything. Since regaining power, I have had my teams searching for answers to this mystery disease."

Mrs. Watson begins laughing loudly. Emily's father tries to quiet her.

"Is there a problem?" Rebecca asks.

"There's not a problem," Mrs. Watson says, "other than the fact that you are the reason our daughter is dead."

Mr. Watson holds up his hands to indicate there won't be any trouble, and he pleads with his wife to be quiet.

Mrs. Watson ignores him. "The woman didn't get her way, and she has led us all to our demise."

Rebecca quirks her eyebrow. "Detain her," she says. Her guards take Mrs. Watson away.

"Fight her! Stop her!" she shouts as they drag her out. Then they stick something in her neck, and she passes out.

"Now that we've taken out the trash, would anyone else like to say something?" Rebecca asks. The room falls silent. "Good. I see we have people who feel I am to blame for these outbreaks. Why would I release an outbreak in Lexicon when my goal is to make it like Axis through trying to win the Nambitus elections? I have competitors who would like to take Lexicon. In fact, we could have traitors among us now. Until we locate the problem, Axis has to be the model of the rebuild—the gold standard of what the entire world should look like once we annihilate what's out there."

Jonathon raises his hand. Everyone in the room freezes, waiting for him to be detained.

"How are we going to annihilate the diseased?" Jonathon asks.

Rebecca smiles. "I like how you think, Jonathon, much like your father. We are going to wait it out. I have set up a study, and according to my trajectory, this couldn't last more than six months without a sufficient food source."

Everyone breathes a sigh of relief.

"Excuse me, why don't we use weapons of mass destruction or

one of your weather devices you are rumored to have to annihilate the undead?" Mr. Watson asks.

"First off, the idea of such devices is preposterous, and with the earthquakes, my labs sustained irreparable damage. This was an act of terrorism committed worldwide. Until we find cures, we will continue order within society, as well as our duties, as ordered previously. Everyone will work and socialize within their divisions. We will progress and overcome the obstacles outside these walls and prevail in being a model for the world."

Everyone remains quiet, except for Mr. Watson, who asks, "Why do you need so much control?"

"Remember there are people who would kill to be in your place. Good day," Rebecca Dean says as she exits the stage.

I try not to make eye contact with Matt.

"I'll take scientist. You take professor," Tevan says. I shrug my shoulders as a guard approaches me.

"Miss, President Dean would like a word," the guard says.

"Kaya, do you want one of us to come?" Mom asks, but they block her.

"I'm fine," I say.

I follow the guards to a hallway, where I am told sit. Within a few minutes, Matt exits.

"Are you all right?" I ask.

He ducks his head. He is followed soon after by Rebecca Dean, who ushers me into her office.

"Ah, Miss Lewis," she says, extending her hand. I reluctantly shake it. "I'll get right to it," she says as she signals for me to take a seat. "Where's Talon?"

"Where is Talon?" I repeat.

She purses her lips and breathes heavily. "Do not play games with me. I know what he and his father have done. I know I haven't always been Mother of the Year. I'd like to find Talon to make it up to him." Her tone seems sincere, but I watch her. "You are not going to talk? Fine. I know what you and Talon are guilty of." She removes some photos from her desk drawer, and my heart begins racing. They shows Talon and me at the freedom rally—kissing, dancing, and participating. "*This* is punishable," she says.

"It was during Johnson's presidency, if you will check the dates," I say.

She tosses the pictures. "You got to him."

I shake my head. "No, *you* did."

"Where is he?" she asks again.

"I don't know, but I can tell you about our last conversation."

She nods. "Any detail."

"He begged me to go with him. He kissed me passionately. Then the outbreak happened."

"In what vicinity?" she asks as she gets out a map.

"We were at school, and then he left."

She slams the map down. "Which direction?"

"He didn't say, and I ran toward the school before I could see."

"Well, thank you, Miss Lewis." She pushes a button, and a guard enters.

"How long until the virus is contained?" I ask.

She slams her hands on her desk and glares at me. "It will *never* be contained as long as Talon has my data!" The guard pulls me by my arm. "The only way is if we get him back," she says.

As the guard escorts me out, I tell her, "He's not going to come back. He told me good-bye."

"I had a feeling you'd say that." She picks up a phone. "Just a quick question, Miss Lewis—you said Talon begged you to go with him, and by these pictures, the two of you are in love. Why didn't you leave with him?"

"I had to try to save friends and family. Talon didn't have anyone to save, other than me."

She quirks her eyebrow at me. "Speaking of friends, remember you can no longer talk to your friend Mr. Larkin. That is a social crime and punishable for both parties."

The guard shuts the door behind me.

I slowly walk home. Guards line the streets as people begin their new jobs.

When Mom sees me, she grabs me.

"What are we doing?" I ask.

"Setting up the school," Mom says. Matt walks by and looks away.

"Why are guards everywhere?" I ask.

"To maintain order and prevent the outside from getting in. Do as we are told," Mom says as she hands me books.

"Where are Tevan and Dad?" I ask, and the guards listen.

"In the labs, along with Jonathon," she answers.

At five p.m., a whistle blows. "What is that?" I ask.

"Other shifts within Axis begin. Since we are at the school, we will be done for the day," Mom explains as the guards signal us to leave.

"What are they doing?" I ask.

"We have a curfew now. We have until seven. Let's get some dinner." She steers me toward the exit.

The walk home is devastating. People huddle together in fear as guards with guns stand at posts.

At dinner, I go over the details of my conversation with President Dean.

"I can't believe you taunted her," Tevan says as I pick at my food.

"Talon would have wanted me to," I insist.

"Kaya, this isn't a game," Jonathon says.

"No, it's far worse. We are prisoners. Maybe Mrs. Watson was right," I say.

Jonathon grabs my wrist. "There are eyes and ears everywhere," he hisses. "You need to shut up." A whistle blows. "Curfew. I have to go." He kisses Tevan.

As Jonathon leaves, I smile.

"I haven't seen you smile in so long," Tevan says.

"I thought I was going to hate this new world order, but Jonathon's having to leave for curfew is the exception," I say.

Tevan frowns. "I'm going to bed. I have to learn how to be a scientist." She kisses Mom and Dad.

"Good night," I say. I turn in for the night.

I lie in bed but can't sleep. I picture my entire life laid out in front of me and everyone too terrified within Axis to talk about the world ending, just outside our front door. I begin tossing and turning, clearly panicking.

"Kaya," Matt says as I try to find my lamp. "No lights. Someone might see." He takes a seat next to me on my bed.

"I feel suffocated by all of this," I say. "What did President Dean say to you?"

"She asked me about Talon, wording her questions a million different ways, as if I would change my story," Matt says as I lean my head on his shoulder. "I can't come over anymore. I don't want to risk getting you in trouble."

"I taunted her," I confess.

"She asked about my mom," Matt says.

I start to place my hand on his but stop. "I'm sorry," I say.

"I told her my mom went into Lexicon for shopping, just like we rehearsed," Matt says. "But I feel like this was all for nothing. We failed, and look at our lives. We have monsters outside the door and a crazy lady dictating our every move." Matt kicks something.

I have never seen him so upset; he was always rational. "Matt, you can't give up. Your mom wouldn't want you to."

He slips to the floor. "I don't even know if she's alive," Matt says.

"Matt, this whole thing was worth it because it was a plan to stop evil. We didn't sit around and accept our fate. My parents, your parents—they want the world better for us. We can't let them down when things get tough. We can't give up. We can do this."

Matt ducks his head. "Why is it that you always have the right pep talk?"

"Because I know you better than you know yourself."

He wipes his face. "Thanks, Kaya."

As Matt leaves, I want to scream. He is the only person who

has kept me sane in the midst of all the madness, and now I am forbidden to communicate with him once again. I lie awake until the sun comes up over the Axis wall. The whistle blows for a shift change. I lie still because I don't have to be up for a while. Just then, I hear an explosion—and then three others. I have been through several earthquakes, but this is different. The earth shakes as before, but the sound causes a ringing echo in my ears. I look out the window, but all I can see is smoke and debris.

"Mom!" I shout, trying to make my way downstairs. I slam against the walls and hold my head, hoping for a reprieve from the ringing. "Dad!" I hear crashing outside, and I hear the Axis emergency sirens go off. I walk outside, trying to find my family, but instead I see holes blown through the Axis walls. I watch as people fight to get in. Guards and militia shoot the living and undead invaders. I see smoke rising from three different areas.

"Kaya, we have to get to safety," Mrs. Riven says as she pulls me toward her.

"What happened?" I ask.

"Protestors blasted through the gates. You can come with my family." She tugs on me again.

"I have to find my family," I say.

Undead begin running into Axis. Mrs. Riven shoots them, but more are attracted by the noise and come toward her and her children. As she gets to her front door, she shoves her children in, and the undead overtake her.

"Kaya!" Mom shouts.

The Axis alarms sound. Just then, a woman protestor grabs my mom. "We deserve to be here too!" the woman says. The Axis guards and militia agencies shoot the invaders.

"Leave her alone!" I shout at the woman. An undead man comes toward us, and Mom desperately pulls us toward our house. Just as the undead man is about to bite my mom, I grab the woman protestor and swing her into the undead man. He begins ripping her throat out. It doesn't take long before her lifeless body falls to the ground, and a few more undead ascend upon her, tearing into her stomach.

As I drag Mom to the house, the woman begins to twitch.

"She's not dead!" Mom says. She tries to break free. "She needs help."

I get us inside the house and then into the basement. Mom seems in a state of shock.

"She was dead the second I threw her to him," I say.

Mom pulls away from me. "We should have pulled her into the basement with us. We had enough room."

I latch the doors. Gunfire continues. Mom continues wailing, and then someone does our secret family knock. I unlock the door for Tevan, Jonathan, and Dad. They proceed to have a family meeting.

"Kaya, everyone is worried," Tevan insists as she sits beside me.

"I didn't want to lose Mom. Mrs. Riven was devoured while getting her kids inside their house. We can't stop it. We never could." I throw a packet of food that has fallen from the shelf, and I tear up when Tevan hugs me.

"She is human," Jonathan says.

"Shut up, Jonathon," Tevan says.

CHAPTER 15

We are in our basement for three days. It's hard being trapped with Jonathon. He and my dad want to do lengthy lab work and have philosophical debates on the origins of the virus and how it was strategically placed within Lexicon and then spread. They decide to examine my blood and evaluate me, as if it's a fun way to pass the time. Jonathon seems to be the son my father never had. I don't mind my father drawing blood samples, but Jonathon never seems to warn me and jabs needles into me as if I am an experiment. I have to stop myself from attacking him.

As they work, Tevan and I shoot weapons. We watch movies until I think we are all going to go crazy.

"I don't know why you are so antsy, Kaya," Mom says.

"She's worried about Talon and Matt," Tevan says dramatically.

"Are you sure the Larkins didn't answer when you tried to check in?" I ask Dad. "Has Talon checked in?"

Dad shakes his head and continues to look through a microscope.

"Why don't you do some schoolwork?" Mom suggests.

I roll my eyes. "Why should I worry any longer about furthering my education when the entire world is apocalyptic?"

Mom tosses me a book. "Kaya, read."

On the fourth day, we hear a sound. "What does that mean?" I ask.

Dad checks the signal waves. "That we may go outside."

I run to the door.

"Kaya, let me go first," Dad insists. As we get to the top, we see that even our house has suffered devastation. The windows have been replaced, but the floor has muddy footprints throughout.

I point to the walls. "Look—gooey ooze. It is from the undead. They were here."

Tevan holds tightly to Jonathon, but Mom says, "Nothing some cleaning and paint can't hide."

We walk outside and see places being rebuilt along the wall are. The damage is catastrophic. Entire sections are missing, and electrical fencing has replaced the fallen walls that were blasted by protestors. Undead are piled upon the fencing, causing sparks in sections. Guards stand at posts as people rebuild. The guards shoot the undead through the fence. I see Matt hauling huge blocks.

My first instinct is to run up to him, but I can't. He sees me and a look of relief flashes over his face.

"Back to work," I hear the guard shout. One of the men piling the rocks for rebuilding slips and falls into the undead on the other side, which causes a frenzy. He is quickly devoured. We all turn away as his family watches in agony. "Get to your posts," the guard says over a megaphone.

Mom pulls me toward the school.

"We will be in the labs. Kaya, listen to your mom," Dad commands.

I try to look at the undead crowding the electrical fencing.

"Kaya, look at me," Dad says. "It is all going to be all right."

"How?" I ask.

"Jonathon and I are working. We can fix this if we wait a bit longer. Matt is playing his part. Talon did his. Kaya, please." Dad lets go of my arms. I go with my mom and try not to look at Matt and the other workers.

As the days go by, I find myself slipping into a hole, and I cannot crawl my way out of it. I help my mom with students at the school, but when one asks me a question, I cannot form words. Rebecca Dean allows a new wave of top people from Lexicon within Axis, but within the first few days, some of them turn, due to the original virus strand that was lying dominant. They awaken and attack citizens who haven't been exposed. People become leery of each other and only leave their homes if desperate for supplies or for work shifts. There is little interaction between anyone. If someone sneezes or becomes ill, everyone else stays away from the entire household. If the guards hear about illnesses, the entire home is quarantined, or they disappear altogether.

Once in quarantine, more families are likely to gain exposure to the illness. It seems there is a complete breakdown of civilization within the Axis walls. I often wonder what life is like beyond the Axis walls. Dad is able to grab a few swabs from the infected before we are made to go in our basements when the new people are ushered into screening. Axis tries to locate those who were carriers and discover how it lies dominant and then attacks or mutates without warning in the new citizens. They are unable to solve the mystery.

A muffled voice calls my name over the transmitter. I drop my papers on the floor.

"Talon!" I run to the transmitter.

"Yes," he says.

I begin crying. "Did you make it to safety?" I ask.

"Yes, we did. We're fine. How is it for you?"

I look at everyone. "Tolerable," I say.

"I am trying to tap into the Axis cameras," Talon says.

"She knows, Talon," I say.

"I knew it wouldn't take her long," Talon says.

"Was Nambitus bad?" I ask.

"No, unscathed, but it won't take long for it to spread. According to the nomads, Sorellis and Magnis were hit," Talon reports.

"Talon, no matter what happens, promise me you'll stay away."

"Kaya ..."

"Talon, *promise* me."

"I will. I bet you wish you would have come with me," Talon says. The connection begins to cut out.

"We all live with our regrets," I say.

"As soon as I can get forces, I will be back to get you all. We will contain this or break the sequence of the strain."

"Was the data useful for what she released?" I ask.

"Not so far." Talon sounds defeated.

On hearing this, Jonathon throws a file, and my dad runs his hands through his hair.

"Be safe. I love you, Kaya," Talon says as he cuts out.

"You didn't go," Tevan says.

"And leave all this?" I say.

Mom hugs me. Then she asks Dad, "So have you figured out why some people are changing at different rates upon being exposed to the virus?"

He shakes his head. "No, it remains dominant in some, and then it mutates." He pushes his microscope away. "We think in some areas it was released airborne, and in some it was released through the infected to ensure a successful infestation."

"When things went too far, we think she tried to clean up some of the toxins and purify the air," Tevan proudly explains. "However, some of the pollutants were still left in areas of the city, leaving a weaker strand of the virus airborne. It's there, but it takes longer to weaken the system."

I was proud of Tevan and how hard she was working. I wanted to tell Matt that his mom was all right. I hadn't talked to him in what seemed like ages.

"Kaya, I am going to the market," Mom says. I pick up a few papers off the lawn. "Stay near the house," she insists.

I nod. I know if Matt is anywhere it's in our orchard. I sneak to the side of my house and wait for the man on the bicycle to pass. I walk to the orchard and find Matt in the trees, which are now blooming. When I call to him, he keeps his back toward me.

"Kaya, you shouldn't be here."

"Matt, I wanted you to know that your mom is all right. I ... just have a feeling," I say, in case we are being watched.

"Thank you," he whispers.

I slowly back away and make my way back home, where I quietly sit on my porch.

I want to cry, but I can't seem to form tears. I watch as workers build the walls of Axis thicker and taller. Rather than creating the safe haven I knew as a child and the protection I should feel from the infected world, I feel like a prisoner. With each brick placed on top of the next, I feel the outside world slipping away. I watch the undead desperately hissing and groaning and trying to get through the electrical fencing. I wish I could be outside where they were. I trust the outside world more than what is happening within Axis.

Mom returns and asks me for help with the bags. "You can tell we are in the midst of a crisis. Food is scarce," she says. She tosses me my favorite granola bars, but I walk to my room without eating.

That night, I again toss and turn, hearing the undead sounds and all the horrors of Lexicon that have haunted me. It's if they are right outside my window, and I'm unable to shut them out. What's worse, I dream of horrors yet to come, almost a foretelling of darker days.

"Kaya, wake up." Matt runs his hand across my face. "I couldn't talk earlier. I had a feeling we were being watched." He hugs me.

"I've missed you," I say.

"I let my dad know about my mom," he says.

"I hated seeing you build the other day," I say.

He places his arm around me, something he never has done. "We lost over twenty people in one day. They tell us there are more people outside the walls wanting to take our places."

My mouth drops open, and I'm sure he can see the worry in my eyes. "Promise me you'll be careful." I hold onto him.

"I promise," he whispers in my ear. "The protestors have stopped coming around since there are so many undead outside of Axis. I think it's getting worse out there."

255

"I know."

Matt and I sit for a long time.

"Get some sleep," Matt says, but I shake my head.

"I have no one to talk to," I say.

"Now that Talon and I are gone," Matt says.

I give him a look. "Talking to you has always been different," I say. "Remember that time that we didn't talk for a week when we were kids? I was thinking about that the other day."

Matt shakes his head. "Kaya, you promised to never bring that up."

I smile. "Matt, you are the strongest swimmer I know. To pretend to drown and then to actually get tangled in the moss … I had to swim back up, get a knife, cut you loose, drag you to the surface, and perform CPR. Then you grab me and kiss me as I tried to save your life. I still don't know if it was genius or the most horrific act you have ever committed."

Matt turns red. "I apologized repeatedly," he says.

"It changed everything. I couldn't look at you the same. Before that, we had this bubble that only the two of us existed in, and you changed it. Why did you do it?"

"I don't know. Everyone else had girlfriends, and there you were, a girl. I just wanted to see what kissing was all about."

I just stare at him. "Oh, but it wasn't a kiss. I wasn't a willing participant. In fact, I was traumatized and angered."

He rolls his eyes. "Always so dramatic. That counted as a first kiss."

I smile. "What did you think about the kissing thing afterwards?" I ask.

He shrugs his shoulders. "I don't know. You slobbered so much during CPR."

"I thought you were dying, my best friend," I remind him.

"We still can talk, and no one has a clue as to what we are talking or arguing about. I love how it drives your boyfriend crazy," Matt says with a smirk.

"But we've never gone back to the bubble where it was just the two of us. We became Matt the boy and Kaya the girl. It got weird."

He rolls his eyes once again. "You made it weird, and you got girly."

"Now every time I place my hand on you or hug you, things feel weird, and I think to myself, is Matt thinking like he did on that day he got creepy?"

He shakes his head. "It does not change things. You just see me differently. Maybe you shouldn't be friends with me. It's forbidden. Maybe that day was your sign, and that's why you feel so strange."

"If it's so wrong, then why do you come around?" I ask.

"I don't know. I ask myself the same question."

We both get quiet, and then I tell him, "Matt, I want you around."

"I know," he says. "I'd better go."

"All right. Remember your promise. Be careful." I say.

He hugs me. "I will," he says, and he sneaks out of my window.

The days seem to go by at a slow rate. Everyone within Axis seems like robots going to posts. When we are home, my mom tries to keep things upbeat.

"There was an accident at the wall today," Jonathon says.

I freeze. "Was anyone hurt?" I ask.

"A few, but they were transplants. We treated them, and they're good as new," Jonathon says.

I breathe a sigh of relief.

"Kaya, are you sleeping well?" Tevan asks. She tries to push my hair out of my face, and I slap at her.

"I manage."

"You seemed to be doing so well, but I hear you tossing and turning. You fight and practically tear through the wall. I, in turn, have trouble sleeping," Tevan says. Jonathon pats her shoulder.

"I'll try to keep you in mind, next time I am fighting for my life in my nightmares, that I am bothering you," I say.

Tevan bristles. "I'm worried, and there are circles under your eyes," she says.

"I know. I can't help it, and I'm sorry my appearance devastates the family," I say.

Jonathon gets a pen and his tablet.

"Don't," I snap at him.

"I wasn't," Jonathon insists as he tucks his tablet away.

"I think I am going to turn in early and place some of Tevan's magic cucumbers over my eyes," I say.

Tevan beams. "Good for you!"

She doesn't realize I'm being sarcastic.

I don't mean to, but I violently toss and turn all night. I awaken to find Tevan in my room with my hands around her neck.

"Kaya," Tevan pleads. I release my hands and drop her as my parents run in the room.

"Tevan, your face!" Mom says.

I sit up and look around. "What happened?" I ask.

"I was checking on Kaya," Tevan says as she cries on Dad's shoulder.

"Dad, I didn't mean to hurt her," I say.

"Kaya, I've never seen someone picked up with such force," he says.

I cross my arms. "Say you believe me. I was having a nightmare," I explain.

When Tevan turns around, I see her right eye is bulging and bloodshot.

"Everyone back to bed," Dad says. "We will discuss it in the morning."

I can't go back to sleep. I want Tevan to forgive me, but more than anything, I want to be normal again.

The next day, I wait for everyone to leave for their shifts. As I sit, the transmitter goes off, and I hear Talon call my name.

I grab it and hold it close to me. "I'm here," I say.

"I can't talk long, but I want you to know I tapped into Lexicon, and it is bad," Talon says.

"Is help coming?" I ask."

Kaya, she did this worldwide. According to my cameras, this is it," Talon explains. "My dad has people and is taking in survivors, but it will take time."

"I miss you," I tell him.

"I miss you," he says, "and I'm watching."

I laugh. "It feels good talking to someone I'm allowed to speak to," I say.

"You know my mom is a stickler for the rules," Talon says.

"What can I do?" I ask.

"Stay safe."

The transmitter gets fuzzy. For the longest time, I sit there holding the transmitter in my hand.

Just then I hear an alarm go off. I run outside and see everyone running toward their houses and shelter.

"What is happening?" I ask, but everyone ignores me.

Then one woman answers, "The electrical fencing fell down, and the monsters are coming in!"

"Matthew," I whisper and run toward the fences. When I get to the fences, undead are piling in.

"Stupid girl. Why are you running toward the chaos?" a man says as he pulls me toward safety.

"Let go of me!" I say, I shove him, and he falls.

He lands on the ground and looks at me. "How did you do that?" he asks, shaking his head. He gets up and begins running.

"Matthew!" I shout. I see his group fighting the undead. Guards shoot the undead from towers, but several others succumb to the attacks. I grab a guard's gun and begin shooting the undead. Matt's dad and several others work to secure the electric fencing.

"Matt!" I say, running to him and hugging him.

"Drop the gun," a guard says, "and hands in the air. Come with us." He places handcuffs on Matt and me and escorts us to Rebecca Dean's office.

"Miss Lewis and Mr. Larkin, do come in and take a seat," Rebecca says. She studies me for a moment. "It seems we are quite the rebel, Miss Lewis." She plays a video that shows me shoving a man and then taking the guard's gun. "We broke some laws. I knew you would make a mistake, and finally you have." She laughs.

"I saved seven people," I say.

She pulls out a small book. "You took the law into your own hands and confiscated a guard's gun, which is punishable by death," she says.

I quirk my eyebrow. "That would be a terrible disappointment for Talon," I say.

She takes a breath. "It would, and that brings us to you, Mr. Larkin. You talked to Miss Lewis, who is clearly above your station. You embraced her. That is punishable however I deem fit." Rebecca turns back to me. "We are at an impasse. I am willing to let this go if you tell me where Talon is. I am almost positive he has tapped into my system. I can't do anything about it because he is his father's son, so I will let this minor misdemeanor go if you pledge loyalty to me and sacrifice Talon's location. I will even let you have Mr. Larkin. Think of how that would drive Talon insane, since he left you here to rot."

Matt gives me a look that doesn't go undetected.

"Oh, so Mr. Larkin is in this too. The plot thickens," she says. "I *will* get my data back. It is only a matter of time. All the important people are underground worldwide. We are just taking out the trash. Cleaning up the earth, so to speak." She pulls me and Matt out into a hallway. "Is my stage ready? I hope Talon is watching Mommy."

The guard nods. Rebecca walks out to address all of Lexicon.

"Hello, Lexicon and Axis. I am here to address you this evening about the rules being followed within our new world order. Earlier today, there was an undead breach. While we were gaining control, a citizen within Axis had the agenda of a hostile takeover." An image flashes on the screen behind her of me with a gun.

"Wait! She's lying!" I say. People gasp and begin to boo me.

"It gets worse," Rebecca says. "She had an ally." She shows a picture of Matt and me, hugging. "I believe this young lady was coerced, but we must maintain order. Due to her station, she will know now the danger and work that goes into keeping us safe. Her punishment will be to assist in rebuilding the wall. This now brings me to the young man. Having original people clustered here in Axis has caused a division within the people of Lexicon. I want citizens to know all safe havens are equal to that of Axis with regard to security. I am a compassionate person and do not believe this young man, although of a lower station, is a delinquent, but he and this young lady must be separated. This brings me to my other safe havens, set up within five different areas of the city. We need to be placed safely in various areas to ensure the human race survives. One attack could annihilate us all. These new areas will be just as adequate as Axis, if not better." Rebecca indicates points on the map, and the crowd applauds her.

"Wait! She can't take you,." I say to Matt.

"Citizens will pass a rigorous health inspection and be allowed in these Axis-like areas. They will be self-sufficient with protection, and delinquents such as these will build walls, ensuring your safety," Rebecca says. The people cheer. "And finally, as my staff member work around the clock to find a cure for this epidemic, we need preservation, unification, and a mind-set free of chaos, so it is with a sad heart that I will take the best and brightest minds underground, so that they might work on finding you, the people, a cure. Rest assured that you will be safe, as I am leaving my best guards to maintain order and protection." The cheers grow louder. "I love you, Lexicon!" she says. She walks back, shoving Matt and me out as people begin throwing things.

"I wonder how Talon will like his love in the most dangerous area of Axis, building a wall, doing manual labor. Too bad you have been of no use," she whispers. "Transports leave at first light," Rebecca says to Matt.

A guard drags us down the hall. He throws us into a cell with such force that both Matt and I hit the wall. He slams the door and locks.

"What were you thinking?" Matt says.

I remain on the floor. "That I couldn't lose my best friend."

Matt sits next to me. "Did you have to be stupid and break every law in Axis?" Matt asks.

"How about a thank-you for saving your life?" I say.

"What if I don't care if I become one of those things?" Matt says.

"Why would you say something so stupid?" I ask.

"Because this is it, Kay," Matt says.

I clench my hands into tight fists. "I can't believe that of all people I could get arrested with, it's you. I don't even want to wear your necklace anymore," I say.

"I'm surprised you didn't get arrested with Talon," Matt says.

I look at him through narrowed eyes. "What is that supposed to mean?" I ask.

"Kaya and Talon. Talon and Kaya," Matt says through clenched teeth. "The way Talon flaunted you, as if you were arm candy, sickened me."

I smile a bit. "Did you want me to be your arm candy?" I ask.

"No, I can't stand you."

I cross my arms and then quickly uncross them because Matt knows when I cross my arms I am about to explode.

"Kaya, why didn't you leave with Talon?" Matt asks.

"Because I was worried about you. I had to save Matt, like I always do, and look where it got me—wrapped in moss at the bottom of a lake and now in jail."

"Shut up," Matt snaps.

"Exactly." I sneer at Matt because he is now mad.

We don't speak again until they bring us food. I hear his dad and my parents plead for our return.

"My dad sounds desperate.," Matt says.

I sit next to him. "My parents made me sound like I am not myself because of my accident. Everyone in my family is going underground," I say.

"At least they defended our friendship when they heard us fighting," Matt says.

I laugh. "They're used to it. Emily always said I would get arrested," I say.

"She did talk about it quite a bit," Matt agrees.

"Look, I couldn't go with Talon because I wanted to make sure you were safe," I say, hoping it sinks in this time.

"I wouldn't have left you either," he says. I start to get teary-eyed. "Don't let them see you like this. We can't let them win," Matt says as he wipes my face.

"But my heart is breaking, and it's all my fault." I say.

Matt shakes his head. "You were doing the right thing. You can't let them change you, Kaya. You saved people."

"Do you wish we would have run away and become nomads?" I ask as he holds my face in his hands. "Kiss me."

Matt shakes his head. "Kaya, a jail cell scene?" He gives me a disapproving look. "Have you been reading Tevan's books again?"

"I haven't been able to get to the library," I say.

Matt rolls his eyes. "Kaya, get some rest."

I lean my head on his shoulder.

The next morning, the guard greets us by pulling Matt and me to our feet. "Rise and shine," he says, taking off our handcuffs. "President Dean said these won't be necessary."

"I'm not ready," I say.

The guard takes us to a giant clearing.

"Is this being televised for Lexicon?" I ask. The guard nods. "Matt, promise me you'll take care of yourself," I say. I watch as my parents and Tevan wave in the scientist line-up. They hug me. My dad is in tears.

"Kaya, please do as you are told so we can make arrangements," Dad whispers.

"I didn't try to escape or attack anyone," I say.

"We know," Tevan says.

"I love you so much, Kaya. I'm not going," Mom insists.

"Excuse me," a guard says as he whispers in President Dean's ear.

"Julie, do we have a problem?" Rebecca asks my mom, who shakes her head.

"No, I have no right to go underground," Mom says. "I am a professor, and I should be above."

Rebecca tilts her head. "I didn't recall it being up for debate. You know Kaya could face an even harsher punishment if certain parties refuse to cooperate."

"Mom, I'll be fine. I love you," I tell her, and she hugs me again.

"Listen to your daughter," Rebecca says.

Dad tugs at Mom's arm. I feel empty as my entire family descends underground.

"Now, for our people going to their new homes, we did this in a lottery fashion to be fair," Rebecca says.

Family members begin telling one another good-bye. Five different buses are ready to take people to the new locations. I watch as Mrs. Watson gets on Matt's designated bus. Her husband is trying not to cry. New people begin lining up at the Axis gates. "This will stop the rioting. It will be safer," Matt assures me. His dad comes up to tell him good-bye.

As his dad walks away, Matt begins to get on the bus but then pauses. "Kaya, bubble," he says.

"What?"

"I want the bubble back," Matt says.

"All right," I say, trying to block out everyone else.

"You mean everything to me," he says. "I've loved you my whole life, even though I wasn't supposed to."

"Matt, you do not have to be cruel about my reading Tevan's books," I say. When I look at him, he's smiling.

"I know," he says. "I stole a few and read them as well. They weren't so bad." He suddenly grabs me and kisses me.

"What was that?" I ask, placing my hand on his face.

"I'm coming back for you, and I'm going to marry you, by your customs," he whispers as he places his forehead against mine.

I smile. "Those are big ambitions for an arrested teenager. And what do you mean my 'customs'?" I ask, laughing.

"You'll see. I wish I would have run away with you." The guards begin to yell for people to board the buses, so Matt says simply, "Good-bye, Kaya Lewis." He waves and boards the bus. I watch as the buses exit Axis into Lexicon. The undead pile on them, and dust flies everywhere. The gates close. I stand watching until a guard yells at me to begin working on the wall.

The guards get the machinery and tools. Criminals such as I get to haul blocks and move items in the danger zone. Within hours, we get conformation that the buses made it to their destinations, and only two remain. If we stop working to listen too intently, we are threatened with whips.

"Why is the ground shaking?" a woman asks as a man begins to rub his arms violently.

"It's an earthquake!" a guard shouts, and he begins to seek shelter.

At first, I don't know what to do. Everyone is going crazy. A guard falls from the top of the wall. The man who was rubbing his arms next to me grabs the gun and begins shooting everyone. A woman grabs me and pulls me to the ground.

"What is he doing?" I ask as we hide in the grass.

"He's not here for being a good member of Lexicon society," she says. Then she extends her hand to me, saying, "Diane."

I shake her hand and then cover my ears from the sounds of the earthquake and gunshots. "What are you in for, Diane?" I ask.

"Giving an elderly patient medicine. I'm a nurse," Diane says.

"I'm Kaya," I say as blocks begin to fall off the top of the Axis wall.

"I know. I saw your television debut," she says. "Great, here come the exes." She gets up as the undead begin to pile in. The man with the itchy arm takes an interest in them and begins shooting the undead.

"Why did you call the undead *exes*?" I ask.

"Oh, because they look like every ex-husband I've ever had. They all drag around aimlessly, sucking the life out of everyone they come in contact with."

I look at her in shock. "How many times have you been married?"

"Depends. Four or five."

I stare at her. I don't know whether to be afraid or humored by Diane. We get to the community building and close the door.

"I needed a break," she says. "I'm kind of glad arm-guy lost it. I was afraid he was a loose cannon. Nurses know."

"How long is your punishment?" I ask.

"Indefinitely. I don't know. That witch Rebecca Dean never said. There was no trial. I was just guilty."

Gunshots continue to be fired outside.

"I'm sorry," I say.

"I was guilty, but how is giving medicine to those in need a crime? She has a top lab; she should make more medicine." Diane smokes as she rants, and I continue to stare at her.

Just then, we hear a chime. "What does that mean? That's the first time I've heard a chime," I say.

She pulls a knife from her boot, and I take a step back. "You are a wall worker now, and I'm sorry, kid, but you are going to see some things. Take this, and carry it. Stab those things, and do not get bit. We only have two more sections, and then we can do rigorous manual labor rather than dangerous manual labor," Diane explains.

I try to find a place to hide my knife.

"The chime means we are somewhat safe," she says. "There might be a few undead roaming through Axis. The whistle is for the snotty people to come out because they are safe, but it's better in here than on the streets of Lexicon. It's horrifying." She throws her cigarette on the floor of the meeting hall. The chime sounds again. "We'd better go. If it sounds more than three times, and they have to look for us, it gets ugly." She shows me a scar.

We walk out. The guards are still clearing out undead. We drag their bodies into piles and repair the fence. We then begin hauling rocks and blocks for the wall. The Nambitus heat is stifling, and several people pass out. By nightfall, I am exhausted. We eat around a campfire and are fed stew.

"Get some rest," a guard says as he walks us to our houses.

All the people are new and are sent to the new additions, which are single-room units. They seem to notice when the guards walk me toward the older homes.

When I get home, my house has never been so empty. My mom hasn't cooked an awful meal. Tevan is not at the table wearing something beautiful. My dad and Jonathon haven't made a discovery. It is dark and quiet. I walk up to my room, curl up on the floor, and try to sleep. I toss and turn, haunted not only by my nightmares but the past as well.

When the whistle blows at five, I have to join the other workers. I watch as they crowd around monitors. "What's going on?" I ask Diane.

"Yesterday some of the buses lost contact due to the earthquakes and didn't make it to their destinations. Some of us had family and friends on those buses," Diane says. The people push through reading the names of the lost. I look as Mr. Watson begins crying.

"Wait—Matt was on that bus," I say. I push my way closer to the monitors and read, *Lost: Matthew Larkin.* The words hit me as if one of the bricks from the top of the wall has fallen on my head. "He's gone," I whisper as others push past me. Some are relieved; some begin crying. "Gone," I say, trying my best to keep it together.

I look at Mr. Larkin. He keeps his composure, clenching his hat as he walks to the orchard. I want so badly to hug him and cry.

"Hurry up," the guard says. I try to make my legs move. I am forced back to reality as one of the guards hits the woman next to me with a whip. She falls to her knees, crying over her daughter, who was on the bus with Matt. I remember seeing them say good-bye. She was wearing red lipstick. I try to help her up, but the guards hit me too, slicing open my cheek.

"You barely missed her eye!" Diane shouts, and a guard hits her.

"I'm fine," I say. I get up and begin hauling rocks.

As we work, Diane watches me. "Do you want me to take a look at that after work?" she asks, pointing to my cheek.

"No, I'm fine," I insist.

"Did you have someone on the buses?" she asks.

"No." I pick up two rocks. Everyone seems to be watching me.

"Slow down; those are heavy," a man says. He tries to take one, but I push him away and continue my task. Toward the end of the day, Diane makes me sit down. She tries to clean me up, but then stops and takes a closer look at me. "How is it that your cheek is nearly healed?" she asks.

I quickly grab my things without responding, but she and the others stare at me.

Over the next few weeks, I am numb to the concept of time. People talk to me and ask me questions, but I am unable to answer them. I work more than anyone yet I eat very little. People get hurt, die, and fall into the undead. I can't even form an emotion. I just work.

As I gather my gear at the end of this day, Diane asks, "Why are you so distant?" I try to leave, but she keeps talking. "You are the strangest person I have ever met. You work through breaks, you rarely speak or eat, and you look like a skeleton. Are we going to be having your memorial soon?" she asks.

"Maybe I don't deserve to live. I welcome death," I answer.

"Kaya, it was a joke, not something I want to plan. You need to rest." She says as I try to move past her, but she stops me. "Would you please let me get by?" I say.

"Look, I know you are different from the rest of us, and I can't imagine what you have been through, but this path you're on is not good. Let me look at you." She starts to open a kit, and I push past her.

Diane doesn't know, but I have tried to rest. The night remains my enemy. When President Dean took everyone away from me, she created a monster. I don't sleep, and when I do, I lose my senses. I wake up in strange places all over Axis. I have no memory of leaving my house or making it to destinations. I don't know what I am doing when I leave my house after-hours. I sometimes wake up near the fence, listening to the gurgles of the undead, which at times are more of a comfort than the chatter of the living.

When I am awake, I yearn to be among the living, but when they talk to me, I want to run away—the thought of forming words leaves me desperate to be by myself. The daylight leaves me haunted by memories, and the sunset brings nightmares of how I lose control once I close my eyes.

I awaken to the whistle. I get up wherever I am, and I go to my shift.

I begin to avoid Diane, as she keeps up with everyone within camp and their ailments, and she feels obligated to care for me too. I want to be left alone. No one can save me. As the days progress, I spend my breaks near the fences, watching the undead. They have become more frightful. The ones that are recently changed still have humanlike qualities. The ones that were converted during the first few days are emaciated. Their skin hangs on their faces, yet they march. They smell worse than anything I have ever smelled. They pile against the electric fences, zapping themselves until fires break out. They can smell the meals of fresh human flesh that wait inside. One rips her cheek open on the barbed wire, leaving rotted remnants of what was once her face hanging on the fence.

One morning I awake covered in blood. When I get to my shift, I learn a guard has been killed. I hide my hands. Diane tries to look me over, but I fight her. We are questioned, as most of us look like the broken wretches we've become. The cameras were down so there is no way of knowing who killed the guard. Everyone enjoys the break, but all I can do is hit the back of my head against the wall, wondering if I caused his end, judging by the bloodstains on my clothes.

Diane quickly wraps me up, as a few guards have become curious about my behavior. Diane cleans my hands and rips the bloodstains from my shirt. The cries and wailing make me turn my head. Diane pulls me away to clean my face as his family is notified.

"Kaya, do you know anything about the guard?" Diane asks. I am unresponsive. "Oh, Kaya," she says as she furiously scrubs blood off of me. "We have to be better than them."

All I can do is sit; I'm unable to speak. I am trapped inside myself, struggling with being my own prisoner—as if being an Axis prisoner wasn't bad enough. As prisoners, we are the immediate suspects and are severely punished with extra shifts for the guard's death. It sickens me for the older prisoners. When one of them tires or gives out, we all are punished. Eight people die as a result.

On the chance I might be the murderer, I begin to raise my hand when asked once more about the guard. Diane pulls my hand down. "Kaya, they are going to punish us no matter what. There is no way you could have killed him in such a manner."

The punishment intensifies. I worry each night that I killed the guard and have caused the deaths of the eight prisoners because of my mental state—after all, I did unknowingly strangle Tevan, my own sister. I don't know if I killed him. I have no recollection. I debate and argue with myself as to where I was. People stay away from me as if I'm the arm-guy about to snap. I am unable to talk or sleep. I go home and lie on the floor. I can't remember bathing. I just curl up into a ball. Rebecca Dean has broken me.

I have become a crazy killer in the dead of night and can't remember it. What if I kill again? Maybe I disobeyed intentionally so I would be punished; then I would know I was indeed still alive. I feel bad when I see the looks of horror on the other prisoners' faces whenever I'm struck or have to do extra work, but I don't want to go home.

Whenever Diane pulls me aside, offering to check my injuries or stitch me, I refuse.

"What is wrong with you, kid?" she asks, wiping my face as blood drips down.

"I guess I am just a glutton for punishment," I admit.

She stares at me. "She speaks! You have the highest pain tolerance I have ever seen and the worst stubborn streak." She says as I pull away. "I don't want to be here," I say.

"News flash—no one does, but it is better in here than out there." She turns my face toward the undead. "You have a family that loves you. They are fighting for you. Act like you give a damn about something, rather than causing your own demise. I know you lost someone. We all have, and it hurts." She snaps as I look at her and get angry. "Are you finished?" I ask as she

She shakes her head, seemingly in pity. "Yes."

As I leave, all I can see is the workers as they tirelessly slave away; even children are working, rebuilding the once-great Axis walls. Their faces make me realize I need to do something. I finally have had enough.

I grab the guard's whip and roll it on my arm until I get to his face. The prisoners cheer. I punch him with so much force that he flies back. I am just as shocked as he is. Another guard runs at me with a gun, but I take his gun and throw it. Three guards run at me with Tasers. The crowd cheers once again.

I wake up in President Dean's office. "Good morning," she says, as I quickly rise to my feet. "It seems you are incapable of doing anything you are told. Your family, Talon, and now Mr. Larkin are not here to keep you in line. Left to your own devices, it seems you are even worse." Rebecca files her nails. "I've been reading up on you, and you are quite the troubled child." She laughs.

"You are a fascist dictator who experiments on people to create monsters, thus ending the world," I say.

She laughs again. "Confession: the only reason I keep you around is because Talon is obsessed with keeping tabs on you to the point he needs to know your every move. He has almost made a few mistakes. One more, and Mommy will do a reversal and pinpoint his location. It seems love makes you sloppy in your work." She signals for me to sit.

When I refuse, her guards shove me in a chair. As they do, my shirt sleeve tears a bit, revealing my scar.

"My goodness, you smell," She says as she waves her hand in front of her nose. "I want to give you kudos. When I told you to make a scene with the Larkin boy to make my son crazy, I didn't think you would be so cruel." She plays video of me telling Matt good-bye. I look away, feeling guilty at the thought of Talon seeing the footage. "Too bad about the earthquake and our losing him," she says as she stares at me. I look away. "He will be remembered. You, he, and Talon have been through so much together.

"The Larkin boy was around you quite a bit, was he not?" She stops filing her nails and notices my scar. "Have you been injured while working?" she asks as I nod. "I must have been."

She pulls at my hand and looks at my scar. "This is an old wound," she says. "Could it have occurred when you were kidnapped?" she asks as

I shake my head. "I fell from a tree as a kid."

She lifts my arm and examines it further with her glasses. "How peculiar." She takes a step back to look at me. "You know one of the guards was killed on a night shift, and your attack just now was brutal, to say the least."

"Are you accusing me, a mere girl, of such savagery?" I ask.

"We thought it was an undead monster and almost locked down the facility. Strangely, a couple of camera lines were severed, so we were unable to retrieve any footage of value. We do have this." She plays a scene of a blur running, making noises, killing a guard and then another at the gate.

"I thought only one was killed," I say. I almost want to cover my ears as the men scream.

"He had no family," she says as she watches my reaction.

"What was the person's motive?" I ask.

She shrugs. "Revenge, escape, who knows? Possibly insanity. You seem a fright, and I think you have served out your sentence. If you are getting injuries such as these, it is time to be reunited with your family. We need to do all that we can to protect you, especially with you being a scientist's and professor's daughter." I cover my arm as she stares at me. "I will make the arrangements. You can get ready, pack, and meet me back here tomorrow morning. And Kaya, take a shower. Your family would be ashamed at your hygiene." She pushes a button summoning a guard.

The guard escorts me out and shuts the door. I walk home and begin packing. I was excited at the thought of being with my family, but the thought of being underground in Rebecca Dean's inescapable clutches makes me feel suffocated. I have nightmares about the tubes. I see Sal and the rest of the people. They call out to me. I see their bodies covered in scars, but I cannot understand what they are telling me as they twist and turn, nearly peeling out of their own skin.

I wake up sweating, unable to breathe, every few hours. A few times I wake up outside. I run my hands through my hair. I need Matt here. He was in the labs with me that night. They never came to life. My scar was different. Why am I losing my mind? I feel as if I can't breathe. I claw and clutch at my neck.

I walk to Matt's window and see Mr. Larkin crying in his son's room. *He can't be gone.* I walk to the orchard and think of when Matt just dumped me there, trying to make me walk. I hear the hissing of the undead, and I begin to cry. "Don't let anyone see you cry. Matt said that," I say aloud as I walk back to my house.

When I get home, I sit at an empty table, as I do every night. I am haunted by the past. I sometimes pretend my family is there, and I engage in conversation. Then I am struck by a horrifying darkness, and I realize I am alone. The lights are all out, and alas, I am the only one here. Matt is dead, and Talon might as well be a million miles away. I go down to my dad's lab. I look go through all of his secret files, trying to find answers to why Rebecca questioned me about my kidnapping. My dad insisted on doing lab work on me every week following the kidnapping. He and Jonathon pored over my files and even spent extra time when we were last quarantined on my reports.

Maybe I am a monster, and Rebecca is on to something. I find the files and see that my samples never stabilized. I was undergoing a constant change. I know my dad had mentioned it after Jonathon's confession.

I walk upstairs, looking at the dark circles under my eyes, and I punch the mirror and fall to the floor. I grab a lighter and burn my lab results. Why has Rebecca Dean asked me questions about the labs and Matt? It's my fault he was sent away. If only I had stayed away and not touched him, the guards would have saved them that day. I was a fool for intervening. I caused his death.

Why does she have to torture me? Blood spills from my hand where I punched the mirror. I lie on the floor, singing.

"Kaya," someone says.

"Leave me alone," I snap at the voices.

"Kaya," Talon says once more from the transmitter.

I run to pick it up. "What?" I ask.

"Kaya, my mom knows there is something different about you," Talon says. "Kaya, you need to leave."

"Where will I go?" I ask.

"Kaya, she will take you to a lab. Something happened with Matt. Every time I try to tap into the system, she kicks me out within seconds."

"Did he make it?" I ask.

Talon hesitates for a moment and then says, "I'm sorry, Kaya."

"Oh my God!" I wail, sobbing.

"Kaya, you saw what happens in the labs. You do not want to end up down there. If she takes you, I cannot help you." Talon pleads.

"What do I do?" I ask.

"I can create a diversion to get you out," Talon says.

"Okay," I agree.

"Go to your dad's weapons. My mom doesn't know about his guns. The room was left off all the blueprints. Get as many as you can carry. Pack food, clothes, and training items, like your grandpa would have you get." Talon says as I write it down, shaking. "All right." I run my hands through my hair, getting blood everywhere.

"Kaya, you can do this. You will need to get in your car and leave when the time is right," Talon says. "Do you understand me?"

"Yes," I assure him as I look into the broken mirror.

I frantically begin packing my car with every item from our survival room. I pack bows, arrows, and guns. I grab the maps my grandpa created, charting all the cameras within Lexicon. I strap on knives with sheaths. I pack food and medical supplies. I fill my back seat with camping equipment. I catch myself rocking because I am so panic-stricken. I go up to my room and take my music player that Matt and I fought over. The final item I pack is the transmitter Talon built so he can contact me. I fall asleep, waiting for Talon's signal. I do not know how long I am asleep, but I wake up in my front yard, under the tree on the side of my house, with my hands shaking and one burned. I make my way into the garage and then into the car, where I sit, gripping the steering wheel, awaiting Talon's signal.

What if Rebecca sends someone after me because I don't show up? I don't even know the time. Just then I hear the emergency signal. I open the garage door and see the giant gates open, and undead pouring into Axis. I watch as the guards struggle to close them manually. Talon has overridden the system. I get in my car and drive out onto the Axis streets.

I watch as undead attack the wall workers. I have to do something. I stop my car, grab a gun, and begin shooting them.

"Thanks, kid," Diane says as she drags one of the workers to safety. I watch as the power shuts down, and the undead break through the small piece of fencing that remains within the area under construction.

Talon, I think as I try to drive out. Just as I am about to get through, the guards override the system, and the gate closes. Rebecca Dean comes out. "I knew he would have a plan. Where is the communication device he uses to contact you?" she asks. Two guards walk toward me as others still fight with the undead. I look at her, and then I look at the gate.

"Death awaits you out there. You're a fool if you think about leaving."

"Let me out, and no one else will have to get hurt," I say. I stand outside my car door, holding a rifle. I watch as she signals guards but then has them back away. "Admit what you did to all of Lexicon," I demand as I point the rifle at her.

"I did nothing!" she snaps.

I shake my head and shoot a bullet over the top of her head. "Admit it," I say.

"Do you want me to say this was all my doing? I merely returned the missing of Lexicon, like the people asked." She smiles as her guards begin closing in on all sides.

I know Rebecca Dean has a breaker box next to her, in which she can manually override the system. I shoot it, and it begins to smoke. The bullet ricochets, hitting her in the arm. The gun is so powerful it nearly makes her fall from her balcony. The undead begin to make their way toward her balcony when they smell blood. As she hangs off, an undead woman grabs her, and her guards scramble to her aid.

"Get her!" she shouts as her guards pull her to safety.

Just then two explosions go off, one on each side of me, causing me to fall to my knees and leaving a ringing in my ears. Undead pile in as guards attempt to retrieve me.

"Kaya, you need to get in your car and leave!" I hear Talon say from the transmitter.

"Leave," I say, trying to get up. I wipe blood from my nose and get in my car. I quickly shut my car door and press on the gas. I break through the Axis gates, leaving the safety of my entire world for the infected, undead streets of Lexicon that I no longer recognize.

Undead fill the once-great city. Skyscrapers and landmarks lay in ruin. I do not have a definite plan. I just know even if it costs me my life, I have to come up with a plan to stop Rebecca Dean and end the Thantos Corporation.

Printed in the United States
By Bookmasters